Snow White
in His Glass Coffin

By

Iphigenia Strangeworth

A HellBound Books LLC Publication

Copyright © 2024 Iphigenia Strangeworth
All Rights Reserved
Cover and art design by Kevin Enhart for
HellBound Books Publishing LLC

www.hellboundbooks.com

No part of this publication can be reproduced, stored in a retrieval system, or transmitted by any form or by any means, mechanical, digital, electronic, photocopying or recording, except for inclusion in a review, without permission in writing from the individual contributors and the publisher
All contents in this novel are works of fiction. Names, characters, places and incidents are imaginary. Any resemblance to actual persons, places or occurrences are coincidental only.

www.hellboundbooks.com

Printed in the United States of America

Acknowledgements

Thank you, thank you, thank you to the entire team at HellBound, particularly James Longmore and Theresa Scott-Matthews, for publishing my bizarre little story and for your kind, encouraging comments!

I owe a massive debt of gratitude to my first reader, Seraphim, who once told me my writing is "about as covert as a wet sock to the face". In the spirit of continued anti-covertness, Seraphim, you are not only the best beta reader anyone could ask for, but a hilarious commentator, a stunningly brilliant writer, and a wonderful, wonderful friend.

To Grams: thank you for reading my book. I know horror isn't exactly your cup of tea, so your praise of my story and willingness to read it all the way through means the world to me. You are my favorite person in the universe, and there are not enough words in any language to tell you much I love you.

Thank you to my parents for keeping me alive long enough for me to write horror stories that make you wish you hadn't.

Thank you to Aunt Kathy, my favorite good witch! You are the most eloquent and supportive person I know, and I am so, so, *so* lucky that you and Grams found each other; you add a little magic to our lives.

Thank you to Zoe, who took the time to read the first draft of this story while juggling a sort of extended job interview and moving homes; your feedback was insightful and invaluable, and I'm still so grateful that you took the time to offer it during such a busy time in your life.

Thank you to my best friend since high school, Abby. It feels like we were sitting in geography class just yesterday, watching our teacher borderline fight that one kid, and I'm so thrilled that we've stayed friends over the years since then.

Thank you to Brie, the raccoon to my possum, for helping me hone my writing skills, supporting my dreams, and giving me a second chance. Your friendship has helped me through many hard times, and I'm grateful beyond words to have you in my life.

Thank you to Maeve, my oldest friend. When we were kids, we wanted to open a bakery together, you were already an incredible artist, and I was writing ghost stories instead of doing homework. We didn't end up following through on that bakery idea, but you're now making a career out of your art and getting more talented by the day. Thank you for being my friend, and for designing my best tattoos!

Thank you to Pepper, Xando and Zi, not only for your enthusiasm when I told y'all my book was being published, but for your wonderfully weird brand of chaotic good vibes and friendship. Thank you to Piera for absolutely radiating positivity; when I tell people about my housemates, I always say you're one of the kindest people I've ever met. Thank you to Keelan for being your hilarious, witty self; I, too, hope we're reincarnated together in a Monster High universe one day!

To everyone else I live with, thank you for being so welcoming! I was once told by a fortune teller that I feel like I don't fit in anywhere I go, and because of the incredible people that make up my community, that is no longer true. I love you all.

Thank you to Sean, my fellow night owl and late-night kitchen buddy. From bizarre fetishes to the deep, cavernous holes in our souls, there's nothing I don't love talking about with you at 1AM.

Thank you to the rest of my family, both blood-related and chosen. I'm so incredibly grateful for your support, and I hope I've made y'all proud.

I began writing this book while I worked a summer job near Corpus Christi, so thank you to the staff there, who were always incredibly kind to me- Kevin, Tammy, Kathy, Sandra, Ty, Peggy and Robert.

And finally, thank you to Debbie, my elementary school social skills teacher. You were one of very few adults in my life who took the time to understand me, and I will never forget how you encouraged me to write down my daydreams. Without you, I would never have discovered my passion for writing, and this book would not exist.

Thank you, everyone, for being in my life.

ONE

Jonathan was lying on his front in the bed of our daddy's broken-down pickup truck, methodically tearing a leaf into tiny pieces, the bruises on his girlish, pretty face indistinguishable from the forest's shadows dancing over us. Rainwater collected in the truck bed was soaking into my jeans, and he must have been freezing in nothing but his bloodstained underwear; still we sat there, listening to the wind and watching the leaves fall. I was six years old, a decade younger than my brother, and a perfect miniature version of him in almost every way.

When she was sober enough to notice us, Mama whined that Jonathan was trying to steal me away from her, taking over her job, taking her sweet baby girl and trying to make me look like a boy, trying to make me love him more. *She'll starve to death if I don't do anything* was his constant refrain, a defense that only pissed her off more. For my part, I adored my brother, followed on his heels like a puppy and took everything he said as gospel, never listening to anyone else for a moment.

Our daddy's truck broke down for good a year before he left. He shot the radio when it finally gave in, enlisted Jonathan to push it behind the house, and whipped Jonathan with his belt when he couldn't do it. I was almost four years old, and I remember it in flashes, Jonathan wailing as our daddy bent him over the kitchen table, the sharp cracking of leather, blood dripping to the floor and Mama watching numbly, taking a long, slow drink of moonshine.

After he left, the old truck became our fortress. There was enough junk scattered behind the trailer that Mama never noticed us playing in the truck, and she wouldn't really have cared if she knew. As long as Jonathan was around when Mama's boyfriends showed up, she didn't give a damn what the hell we did, so we spent hours out there, locked out the whole world and built a kingdom within the truck's metal confines.

That day, a Sunday, we were skipping church as usual. Mama was in bed with a hangover, and unless Granny came over to personally drag our asses into town, we were not going to church. Jonathan had taken a firm anti-church stance ever since Mama started dating the preacher.

"Aren't you cold?" I finally asked.

"No," Jonathan said shortly, eyes glazed over. Mama's cop boyfriend had shown up unexpectedly early, and Jonathan found me outside the minute he was gone without bothering to get dressed, just wandered out the back door with that awful dead look in his big blue eyes, fresh blood soaking into his gray briefs, and curled up next to me without a word. He held me like a doll, sometimes, and I accepted it without question, let him curl around me and cry into my hair for as long as he needed.

"I'm cold." That made him look up from the leaves, finally, and he cleared his throat before speaking.

"Get the blanket out from the cab, then. I wanna stay here a while longer."

"I *want to* stay," I corrected prissily, mocking his unceasing need to correct my grammar. Jonathan devoured books the way most people drank water and was determined to speak properly, bound and determined to sound high class. "Talk right!"

"Be quiet," he muttered, but for a split second, his lips quirked into a smile. I took my little victories where I could, and making my brother smile even for a moment was always cause for celebration. I would happily freeze for him, so I reached through the tarp he'd lashed over the broken back window, pulled a thick blanket through, and wrapped it around both of us. Jonathan hesitated before rolling onto his side to hold me, whimpering softly into my hair, the same jet-black as his. Skin white as snow, lips red as blood, and hair black as ebony, Jonathan looked like an androgynous, maybe-male Snow White, and I was a little copy of him, identical to the few childhood photos Mama had kept. Like a pair of vampires, Mama sneered every time she saw us together.

I fell asleep with my head on Jonathan's bare bony chest, his rabbit-fast heartbeat pounding in my ear, and woke up hours later on the bathroom floor. The truck bed had become more comfortable than our mattress, a filthy old thing tossed on the floor of what could only generously be called our bedroom; there was nothing of ours in there, just boxes on boxes of family heirlooms Mama couldn't part with, bullshit accumulated when her mother died and she sold the sprawling house, never considered moving in. Our clothes were in a box a few feet from our bed, Jonathan's ever-shifting library books stacked neatly next to it, and that was all.

In the summer I slept outside every night, snuggled in a nest of blankets Jonathan arranged for me. The truck bed was safer, cleaner and more comfortable- because Mama never really knew when her boyfriends would show up, no one ever went through the boxes of ancient heirlooms, and Jonathan wet the bed almost every night, our room reeked of dust, mold, blood, sweat, semen, and urine. The only effort made to counteract any of this was a plastic trash bag over our mattress.

When the nights got too cold to sleep outside, Jonathan insisted I come back to our room, told me I'd freeze to death if I stayed in the truck bed another night, and if that failed, cried that I hated him and wanted him to be alone. *You think I'm disgusting; you don't love me! Why don't you love me anymore?*

If I disobeyed Mama, she hurled the nearest heavy object at my head, slapped me so hard I fell down, pulled me over her knee, yanked my hair out, beat me bloody with a wooden spoon, but when Jonathan wanted something, he only had to cry. At six, I thought his tears were always genuine; later, I realized he'd faked it more than once, but he was in real distress so often I never could work out the difference. Jonathan cried more than anyone else I knew, and every time Mama noticed she called him queer, sissy, crybaby, faggot, pussy, bitch, whatever she could think of in the moment.

When I finally stirred awake, I registered the cold vinyl flooring underneath me before I heard the shower running. I yawned, blinked slowly, and rubbed at my eyes, settled my gaze on my brother's blurred silhouette behind Mama's moldy floral shower curtain.

"Jonathan?"

"What?"

"How long was I asleep?"

"Maybe an hour." He sounded present, overly alert, his usual barely calm self. "I needed to shower."

"Yeah, I know."

"Didn't want to be alone."

"I know that, too." Only during school days and summer nights were we separated- generally, we'd shower together, but Jonathan never woke me from naps. "Are you still bleeding?"

"A little. It's fine, though."

"Okay."

I sat still until he was done, occasionally drumming my fingers against my knees, and didn't bother to avert my eyes when Jonathan stepped out of the shower. Bruises blossomed across his concave stomach, encircled his frail wrists and ankles, set the thin raised scars littering his chest and thighs into sharp relief. Jonathan was short, dangerously skinny, *petite* as Mama's boyfriends said, and I hoped I'd be bigger than him when I grew up.

I knew deep within myself that I was tougher than Mama's boyfriends, knew I could shoot them all through the heart given half a chance, but if I was bigger and stronger than them, I wouldn't even need a gun. My greatest desire was to protect Jonathan, to eviscerate Mama and her boyfriends and all the bullies at his school, to burn the world down and take my brother somewhere safe, no one but the two of us in a perfect paradise for all eternity.

"It's getting too cold for you to be sleeping outside," Jonathan said, holding my hand as I hopped out of the truck bed.

"I ain't cold."

"I'm *not* cold, Chastity, talk right."

"'Talk right,'" I mimicked in a nasal voice, dodging when he reached to smack me upside the head. "Fine, I'm not cold. I want a few more weeks."

"Maybe a few more *days*. It's September."

"I like it out here."

"What's wrong with sleeping inside?"

"It's…" I looked up at Jonathan, took in the way his lip trembled and his baby blue eyes welled with tears.

"What? Is there something wrong with me? You don't want to be near me?"

"No! No, I can sleep inside." My brother nodded, sniffled, and rubbed his eyes, and I felt so guilty I held my arms out to be picked up. He obliged at once, smiled weakly when I patted his soft cheek with a sticky hand and carried me inside.

"Are you excited for first grade?"

"No. I wanna stay home, why can't I?"

"Want to stay home, talk right. There's nobody to watch you all day, and the law says you have to go to school."

"You watch me."

"No, I have to go to school, too."

"Then I'll go to your school!"

"I bet you're smarter than everybody there," Jonathan said, grinning, "but you're too little. I'll take you to class and pick you up in the afternoon, just like last year, okay?"

"I hated it last year."

"It'll be better this year."

"No, it won't. I got all-" Jonathan raised his eyebrows, and I rolled my eyes pointedly, "-I *have* all the same kids in my class. They're all fucking cunts."

"Well, one day they'll turn out like Mama, and you'll be a famous ballerina." I'd been obsessed with ballet for months at that point, and furiously jealous of Lily Faith Albrecht, whose parents paid for her to take dance lessons in town.

"What's that mean?" We both jumped at the sound of Mama's voice, and Jonathan shrank in on himself, slumping his shoulders, lowering his head, holding his arms behind his back, becoming as small and submissive as possible in a desperate, futile escape attempt.

"Chastity wants to be a ballerina," he said meekly to the floor.

"Before that. The fuck you said *before* that? Turn out like me, fuck's that mean?"

"Nothing."

"Nothin'?" She crossed the tiny, cramped living room before we could run and backhanded Jonathan as hard as she could, sending him sprawling to the floor, already sobbing. "There you fuckin' go again, goddamn. D'you want somethin' to cry about, Jonathan? 'Cause I can damn well give your ungrateful ass somethin' to cry about."

"No, ma'am. I'm sorry, Mama, I'm sorry, I'm so sorry, I didn't mean anything by it, I didn't mean-!"

"Crybaby fuckin' faggot," Mama spat, kicking him hard in the chest for good measure before storming off without a backward glance. I sat on the floor and let Jonathan rest his head in my lap, stroked his greasy hair and wished Mama had thought to buy shampoo when she went to Winn-Dixie last week. He sobbed into my stomach for another ten minutes, and all the while I heard Mama clattering around the kitchen, cussing at the stove that rarely worked, the empty pantry, the long-age broken fridge no one had ever cleaned out.

Finally, Jonathan got to his feet, pulled me to mine, and mumbled, "You ready for school, sweetie?"

"Yeah."

I could never predict Jonathan's moods, but I was never afraid of him. I was afraid *for* him, afraid he'd go into hysterics, and I'd have to calm him down, afraid he'd go into one of his even worse near-catatonic states, afraid he'd try to kill himself again, sure, but never for a second did I think he'd hurt me. Mama, on the other hand, was always the same: if she wasn't angry, she was passed out. Mama's wrath was as inevitable and unavoidable as bad weather; we'd long since learned to just put up with it.

My brother was dead silent for the entirety of our walk. We lived five miles outside of town and two miles from the bus stop, and as much as I loved seeing the leaves turn, the beginnings of the autumn foliage, I couldn't help but worry about how miserable our walk to school would be come winter.

"Are we going to the library after school?" I asked, hoping to brighten Jonathan's mood, but he just shook his head. He started limping again halfway to the bus stop, and I wondered just how rough Mama's cop boyfriend had been if he was still hurting a full day later.

Adabelle was, and still is, a town of about 200 people. The nearest school was two towns over, and almost no one raised in Adabelle had a car, so everyone except Lily Faith Albrecht took the bus together every day. Officer Albrecht, Mama's cop boyfriend and Lily Faith's daddy, had a shiny new pick-up truck, and last year he'd given her and her friends a ride in it. I was not invited, on the grounds that I was dirty and smelled bad, both of which were true. Still, I hated her for saying it, threw mud on the stupid new truck when he parked it outside our trailer.

Jonathan gripped my hand too tightly as we boarded the school bus, quickly sitting in the first seat and pulling me onto his lap. He made a pained little gasping noise as he sat down, and I rested my head against his chest, squeezed his hands reassuringly. He held himself stiffly the whole ride, clinging to me with his eyes fixed firmly on the window, breathing unsteadily in my ear.

"I wish we didn't have to go to school," I whined when the bus finally arrived, barely loud enough to be heard over the clamor of forty kids throwing on worn-out backpacks, shoving their friends playfully, and hurrying to get off the ancient bus that always smelled faintly of mildew.

"If you do good in school, you can go to college," Jonathan mumbled vaguely, obviously not really listening. "Then you'll never have to set foot in Adabelle again." My brother was top of his class in everything, which, as he often bitterly pointed out, was a pretty unimpressive accomplishment in Briar County, Georgia.

"I hate school. Why'd I want *more* school?"

"Talk right," Jonathan said softly, taking my hand to lead me off the bus. "Don't worry, okay, honey? You're gonna love first grade."

"I am *not!*"

"Well, try it, please? It'll make me happy if you try it," Jonathan pleaded, looking down at me with wide, sad puppy eyes. I was, overall, a terrifyingly well-behaved child, fear of Mama's wrath keeping me perfectly in line, and I never wanted to make my fragile brother cry, so I considered arguing further but then scowled, nodded, and heaved an overly dramatic sigh.

"Fine," I huffed, dragging it out into at least three syllables. Jonathan grinned and ruffled my short, uneven hair- he always cut it with rusty sewing scissors in our backyard, hacking it into a purposefully unattractive rat's nest. When Mama asked, he claimed it had to be short so I wouldn't get lice, but I knew why he really did it. Jonathan fretted over how similar we looked, worried that Mama's boyfriends would think I was cute, would want me to take his place since I was younger and a girl, so he dressed me in his worn-out hand-me-downs, gave me unflattering haircuts, and only let me bathe once a week, determined to make me as unappealing as possible.

"You'll have fun, sweetheart. I promise."

Just as I'd expected, there were no new faces in my first-grade classroom. Everyone else wore their Sunday clothes for the first day of school, but I was dressed the same as always, faded jeans with holes worn in the knees, a too-big flannel shirt, sneakers held together with duct tape. I slunk to a table in the rear corner of the room and slouched as far as I could in my chair, scowling at the back of Lily Faith Albrecht's blonde head.

Our teacher was new, a homely, overweight young woman with wide-set brown eyes and crooked, gapped teeth.

She wasn't from Adabelle. I watched with detached annoyance as she wrote *Ms. Heron* in neat handwriting, tuned out everything she said until she reached my name during roll call.

"Chastity Caldwell?"

"Here," I said, too quietly, raising my hand so she'd see me. Jonathan and I both spoke in whispers, all our lives, always trying to disappear.

"Lovely to meet you," Ms. Heron said, smiling sweetly. "You have *such* a beautiful name!" I wondered how my brother's first day of school was going.

"No *way* am I workin' with *her*," Lily Faith sneered, exaggeratedly waving a hand in front of her nose and backing away from me. "Can't Missy be my partner?"

"No, dear. The point of this activity is to get to know someone *new*," Ms. Heron cooed. She had an obnoxiously high-pitched voice. "Missy is your best friend, isn't she?"

"I don't *wanna* get to know Chastity," Lily Faith whined. "I knows her good 'nuff already. And she stinks."

"We use our nice words in this classroom, dear."

"She *does!*"

Everyone else had turned to look at us, giggling into their hands. Lily Faith was already popular, a cherubic little blonde adored by all, spoiled by her parents, and worshipped by her peers, and I was the dirty white trash girl living in the woods with my crazy, crybaby brother. I would have been bullied anyway, but if Lily Faith Albrecht disapproved of someone, everybody else followed suit.

"I want you to get to know each other," Ms. Heron said firmly. "We are *all* going to pair up and learn something about our new friends, okay? And after that, we're going to share what we learned with the class, is that crystal clear? Anyone who doesn't want to participate is welcome to visit the office and talk to the principal instead."

No one argued, so Ms. Heron returned to her desk and sat to watch us, leaving me alone with Lily Faith among a rising tide of voices, everyone around us reluctantly beginning to chat.

"Well," Lily Faith sniffed, side-eyeing me, "I'm Lily Faith, and you're Chastity. So now we've got to know each other."

"You do ballet," I blurted out. It was a stupid thing to say, but it got her attention, and she tilted her head curiously to the side.

"Yeah. How'd you know that?"

"I remember from last year, you said so then."

"I ain't never told you 'bout that."

"I overheard you tell your friends." A disgusted look crossed Lily Faith's angel face, and she scooted further away from me.

"You was spyin' on us?"

"No! No, I just… I just heard…"

"Fuckin' creep," she spat.

Jonathan met me outside the elementary school entrance just as he had last year, rubbing his thumb over a newly split lip.

"You're hurt," I said, unhelpfully.

"Oh- yeah. Bonnie punched me in the hall. Hurry up, we need to get home before the landlord shows up." Jonathan was distracted, jumpy, and clutching my hand like a lifeline as we walked across the parking lot, cringing away when a group of significantly bigger boys ran past, yelling and shoving at each other. He was trembling by the time we sat down.

"Bonnie's gonna be in jail one day," I said gently. "He's just a big idiot, that's all. You're better than him."

"I'm tired," Jonathan whispered, tightening his grip on me.

I hated all Mama's boyfriends, but the landlord was the worst one of all. He never failed to remind us how grateful we should be to him, how much we owed him, how kind he was to let us stay in the trailer essentially for free. Jonathan said he was worse than the cop but not as bad as the preacher. I was always supposed to hide in the old truck when Mama's boyfriends came over, but there were times I couldn't resist sneaking to our closed bedroom door, overwhelmed by morbid curiosity. It made me sick, but I kept doing it, time and time again.

I was drifting to sleep under our daddy's truck, in the dark little cave hidden by tall grass, when the front door slammed shut. I jumped, nearly hit my head on the bottom of the truck and listened to the landlord's car start, ran around the side of the house to watch him drive away. Our trailer- or his trailer, as he liked to say, the trailer he owned and let us live in- was hidden in the woods, down a long, overgrown driveway.

I constantly imagined my life as a fairytale, and in my fantasies the trailer was an old cottage made of rotting gingerbread, Mama was a witch hoarding little white crystals, Jonathan was Snow White, and I was a brave knight in shining armor, I was going to rescue us both one day. I'd never eaten gingerbread, but I knew it smelled spicy-sweet, so I pictured a sickeningly sweet stench, sugar heavily entwined with decay, an oversized gingerbread house sagging in on itself, gumdrops and candy canes melting down the soft walls.

I slipped through the screen door, the only thing separating our house from the wilderness since Daddy ripped the back door off its hinges, and deftly navigated through the maze of boxes, trash bags and random junk that made up our living room, ran as fast as my twig-like legs could carry me and found our bedroom door cracked open, knocked cautiously, quietly. Mama hated repetitive noises. "Jonathan?"

Receiving no answer, I gently pushed the door open further and stepped inside, gagging at the overpowering stench. I was pretty sure something was rotting in one of the boxes lining the walls; our room smelled better than Mama's, at the very least. I'd only been in there once, and that was more than enough. Jonathan made every effort to keep our room clean, but since Mama flew into a rage if we touched the boxes, that just meant washing our sheets when he wet the bed- except we didn't have laundry detergent and weren't allowed to use the bar soap for anything but bathing, so really he just scrubbed them in the washtub out back and hung them to dry.

"Jonathan," I repeated, approaching our bed nervously. He was curled on his side, fresh blood dotting our sheets and smearing the inside of his thighs, and didn't react at all. "Jonathan!"

"Oh, Chastity," he mumbled, blinking slowly. "Hi."

"You're hurt."

"It's fine. It doesn't hurt."

"You're bleeding."

"It's fine." Jonathan uncurled himself slightly, reached out hopefully, and I laid down, letting him hug me. He was shivering, his breath unsteady, and I worried that he was going to freak out, so I wrapped my little arms around him as best I could.

"Maybe they'd be nicer if they knew it was hurting you," I suggested. Jonathan just laughed quietly, and I tensed up, worried he'd have a hysterical laughing fit like he did a few weeks ago, but then he clutched me tighter and relaxed, so slightly it was almost imperceptible.

"I don't think so."

"Well, I'm gonna make them all sorry," I vowed. I must have sounded ridiculous, but I really, truly meant it. I genuinely thought I could help him.

"I know you are, sweetie. I know you are."

I was always eager to help Jonathan cook, but Mama hadn't bought much food at the store last week. There had been dried pasta and canned tomatoes originally, made into what even Jonathan couldn't convince me was spaghetti, and after that it was just open-faced peanut butter sandwiches.

"We're out of bread," Jonathan announced, reaching further into the cabinet as if there might be more food hidden back there.

"Do we have rice?"

"She didn't buy any." He took the jar of peanut butter and grabbed a spoon, shrugging apologetically. "It's fine."

"You keep saying that, but-"

"Because everything is *fine*," Jonathan said desperately, and I nodded at once.

"Everything is fine."

There was only one chair at our kitchen table, an old diner chair, so I sat on the table and ate in silence, watching Jonathan to see when he'd get a spoon for himself. "Aren't you hungry?" I finally asked.

"You need to eat. Mama's not going back to the store until Wednesday at least."

"So, you're not gonna eat until then?" I spoke with all the sarcasm a six-year-old can muster, fixing Jonathan with my most unimpressed look, and he avoided my gaze, dragged his toe through the dirt on our floor. "I won't eat if you don't."

"No, Chastity, you have to eat."

"So do you, dumbfuck." After a second, my brother nodded weakly and went to get a spoon. Neither of us ate much before he put the lid back on, mumbling that we had to make it last. "Doesn't she usually buy more food?"

"The preacher didn't come by last week." Jonathan licked his lips nervously, tried to smile. "I'm sure he'll be by this week, it's fine. And- and if I do a really good job, sometimes he pays extra, so she might spend that on food, maybe. If we don't piss her off."

"I'll behave," I promised.

The preacher eventually stopped by, and while he did pay extra, he also yelled so loud I could hear from the truck, *sinner sodomite bastard whore*, left my brother trembling on the floor, begging me not to hurt him when I stroked his hair and tried to convince him to get up and take a shower.

"I hate him," I said, trying to wash Jonathan's hair with a bar of soap, since Mama *still* hadn't bought shampoo. My brother's legs were too shaky to support him, so he was sitting on the shower floor while I stood above him, instructing him to move his arm or tilt his head back, watched his blood mix with the water and vanish down the drain. It was very important to me that I get our hair clean; Lily Faith had pointed out how greasy and limp my hair was yesterday, and I imagined the high school kids said similar things to Jonathan.

"He pays for our food," Jonathan reminded me, twisting his bony hands together. "He's a nice man who pays for our food." I could tell he had gone away into himself and was just parroting Mama, so I didn't comment.

"Well, *I* don't like him," I huffed.

"I need- I need to shave," Jonathan said suddenly. "I need to shave."

"You can wait-"

"No, no, I need to shave, they won't like me if I don't, Mama says so, I need to shave, I need to-"

"Okay," I said quickly, handing him the razor. "Just be careful." I watched him shave his legs, which really didn't need it, but Mama insisted he shave his entire body every other day. It was important to her boyfriends that Jonathan look like a child and a girl. I set about washing my hair while he worked on that, absentmindedly wondering what kind of shampoo Lily Faith used, since her hair always smelled like strawberries. It had to be one of the fancy kinds with pretty packaging- Mama didn't take us to the store very often, but when she did, I liked to look at everything we couldn't afford and fantasize about having nice things one day.

One day, I told myself, Jonathan and I would live in a lighthouse, a pink lighthouse that smelled like roses, and it would be just the two of us, no one else, with floral shampoo and real spaghetti sauce and two chairs at the kitchen table. We'd have a clean shower curtain, too, I thought, wrinkling my nose up at the mold creeping up to cover long-faded daisy patterns.

When I turned to wash the soap out of Jonathan's hair, I noticed his legs were covered in little cuts, but I didn't say anything, just let him run the dull razor aggressively over his chest. He was mumbling something about looking pretty for Mama's boyfriends, so I patted his shoulder, softly reassured him, "You're very pretty, Jonathan."

TWO

Priscilla Forge joined my class two weeks into the school year. She wore a Queen t-shirt under neon yellow overalls, and everyone stared blatantly when Ms. Heron called her to the front of the room.

"Priscilla here is from *Tennessee*," she said, widening her eyes dramatically, and we all leaned forward, shocked that someone would ever move *to* Briar County. "Tell us where exactly you're from, dear."

"Gatlinburg," Priscilla said proudly. "We moved here 'cause my daddy's starting a church in Adabelle."

"Gatlinburg is a big old city," Ms. Heron informed us.

"Dolly Parton's from Tennessee," Priscilla added quickly.

"Yes, she certainly is. Well, why don't you have a seat? You can sit next to Chastity." Every head in the room turned to face me, hiding in the back, and for a second, I wondered why in the world Ms. Heron wanted a new student so far away, then realized I was the only student without a "desk buddy", as Ms. Heron called it. Someone giggled, someone muttered *poor Priscilla,* and Priscilla herself just took in my grubby appearance, nodded slightly, and stomped over to join me.

She was wearing mud-splattered pink cowboy boots, and I pushed my chair back to look under the table at them. Priscilla smiled, threw her leg onto my lap, and eagerly whispered, "See, they're pink! Mama bought 'em before we moved. Pink's my favorite color, what's yours?"

"Uh- pink," I lied, overwhelmed by the unfamiliar sensation of another child treating me with kindness, of someone actually seeming to like me. I was worried she'd be put off by the way I smelled, my choppy haircut, my dirty, ragged clothes, but instead she grinned and grabbed my hand.

"Perfect! My big sister hates pink, she says it's for sissies. I haven't even been here more than a week, y'know. Where d'you live?"

"Adabelle. Like you."

"Oh, we're gonna be best friends!"

Priscilla sat with me at lunch, in a dark corner near the cafeteria exit, and frowned when she noticed me staring at her paper bag lunch. "What's wrong?"

"Nothing," I said quickly.

"You gonna get some food?"

"No. I, um- I can't afford to eat at school. You need to pay for the school lunch."

"Oh. I always brought mine last year. Well, here, we'll just share."

"Thank you," I stammered, accepting the orange she handed me. "Th-thank you so much."

"Aw, don't even mention it! It's good to share, Jesus said so. D'you go to church?"

"No."

"Well, y'oughta come to my daddy's church! We're Episcopalian, and we don't have a building yet, it's just our house, so you can come over on Sunday and then we'll play after."

"What's Epis- Episc- Ep-"

"Episcopalian! It's like being Catholic, but also being hippies. My mama was a hippie. What d'your parents do?"

"Uh…" I fidgeted with the orange, bit into it with the peel still on to avoid the question. "My brother goes to high school."

"So does my big sister! Her name's Apple, 'cause Mama was still a hippie when she had her, so I call her Apple Pie and she hates it."

"My brother's name is Jonathan."

"That's my uncle's name. Chastity's such a pretty name, I've never heard it before."

"Priscilla's really pretty, too."

"Aww, thanks! I'm named after my grandmother, but she's dead."

"I don't think I'm named after anyone."

"I bet my sister and your brother are gonna be best friends, too," Priscilla declared.

"Jonathan! This is my brother, Jonathan," I explained to Priscilla, hurrying over to him. We'd been joined at the hip since lunch, and I'd already promised to go to her father's church on Sunday. "And this is Priscilla, she's my best friend."

"Your best friend?" Jonathan looked bewildered and took a second to register Priscilla's hand before shaking it awkwardly.

"It's nice to meet you! Did you meet my big sister? She's sixteen, too, isn't that *crazy?* It's like we're sisters, right?"

"Right," I giggled.

"But you don't have a sister. You have me," Jonathan quickly interjected. "We need to get on the bus, Chastity."

"I wish I could ride the bus," Priscilla pouted.

"You're not missing anything," I assured her. Before I could say anything else, a teen girl's shrill voice rang out across the parking lot.

"*Priscilla!* What are you *doing?*" I looked over to see a tall, pretty girl stomping towards us, dressed immaculately in skinny jeans and a red tank top that complemented her auburn hair. She did not look like the sort of person who approved of neon yellow overalls.

"Oh- this is my best friend, Chastity, and her big brother J-"

"I *met* her brother," the pretty girl snapped, grabbing Priscilla by the arm. "I don't want you talking to these hillbillies. God, Priscilla, didn't you notice how bad she stinks?"

"Don't take the Lord's name-"

"Shut up!"

"This is Apple Pie," Priscilla chirped, seeming cheerfully oblivious to her sister's hostility.

"I told you not to call me that!"

"Hey, do y'all want a ride home? There's room if Apple Pie sits up front-"

"They are *not* getting in our car, they fucking *reek.*"

"That's a bad word! And yes, they *are* gettin' in our car, on Sunday, 'cause they live too far to walk, and I invited Chastity to church, so *there!*"

"We need to leave," Jonathan whimpered, trembling like a leaf. "Need to go home now. Chastity, let's go, please? Can we go?" I looked up to see that there were already tears streaming down his face, so I nodded quickly.

"Hey, um, Priscilla, we gotta get on the bus, but I'll see you tomorrow," I mumbled. She yanked her hand away from Apple and hugged me quickly, grinning.

"I'll see you then! *And* on Sunday!"

Jonathan was quiet as we boarded the bus and sat in our usual spot, but he hugged me tighter than usual the whole way home, petting my hair compulsively. I felt a little like a cat, and started imagining what it would be like if I really was one, if I could go anywhere I wanted. There were feral cats near the library, tough little creatures that hissed and scratched if you got too close, and I thought I was sort of like that, too.

A little over a year ago, one of Mama's ex-boyfriends, a farmer, tried to talk to me after he left our bedroom. Mama was passed out drunk on the couch and Jonathan was catatonic on the mattress, leaving me alone in our dim living room, all natural light blocked out by boxes stacked to the ceiling, trying to catch a spider I'd seen crawl across Mama's face and disappear. I had Jonathan's pocketknife tucked into the waistband of my jeans; I'd confiscated it after I walked in on him trying to cut his wrists.

"What's your name?" I jumped at the farmer's voice, narrowed my eyes at him as I stepped closer to the couch and pulled my knife out, clenching both sweaty little fists around it.

"Get out," I ordered, and he laughed, stepped closer.

"I just wanna be friends, sweetheart. You're a cute little thing, you know that?" I swung the knife wildly before he could come closer and, miraculously, managed to cut his arm, just bad enough to make him swear and jump back. I ran outside while he was distracted, crawled under the truck to hide, and stayed there for hours, until Jonathan came to find me. The farmer didn't come back; Mama beat Jonathan half to death when he stopped showing up, convinced he'd done something to piss him off.

I was jolted out of my memories when the bus shuddered to a stop and Jonathan picked me up to carry me off, apparently unwilling to let go of me even for a second. "You can put me down," I offered, arms around his neck.

"No."

"You don't have to be jealous of Priscilla, okay?"

"I'm not."

"Okay. But if you *were,* just so you know, I still love you most." I kissed his cheek, and my brother smiled faintly.

I was terrified Apple would turn Priscilla against me, but the next day found her just as perky as ever. She hugged me before she sat down, and I took in her outfit- another Queen t-shirt, a violently pink tutu, and the cowboy boots again. "You look nice."

"Ooh, thanks! My daddy *loves* Queen. Did you know Freddie Mercury died a few years ago?"

"Who's that?"

"The best singer ever," Priscilla proclaimed emphatically. "He was the lead singer of Queen."

"Oh, that's a band?"

"What did you think it was?"

"Just a cool shirt."

"You're silly," Priscilla giggled. "But yeah, he died. It was really sad."

"Was he old?"

"No, he was sick."

"That *is* sad."

I could hardly sit still that Sunday morning and ended up bouncing around the end of our driveway as we waited for Priscilla's mother to pick us up, literally running back and forth to work my energy out. Jonathan watched me, his piercing blue eyes following my every move, looking completely miserable.

"You know we don't *have* to go," he reminded me for the millionth time. "Nobody except your *friend* wants us there." Jonathan spat out *friend* like it was a dirty word, his jealousy pathetically obvious.

"Priscilla said her parents want to meet me."

"They won't like us once they do," Jonathan whined. "I want to stay home, Chastity, can't we stay home? We should just stay here and play in the truck."

"We can play after church," I said firmly.

"I hate church."

"It's nothing like Granny's church." Granny was our paternal grandmother, a sweet old lady who hated both our parents in equal measure but doted on Jonathan and I, and always claimed to have no idea where our daddy had run off to. She'd stopped coming around after Mama broke a beer bottle over her head, but she sometimes tried to pick us up after school, practically begged us to come stay with her. The few times she'd taken us to her Southern Baptist church, I recalled a lot of yelling about Hell. That was before Mama started dating the preacher; Jonathan outright refused to go afterward.

"I don't *want* to go," he complained again, but I ignored him, sat down, and started digging in the hard packed dirt until Jonathan reluctantly joined me.

Priscilla's mother drove up in a white sedan just a few minutes later, and I jumped to my feet, threw the back door open. Jonathan hovered uncomfortably behind me, didn't move until Priscilla yelled, "You can sit up front!" I watched him get in, glanced at Mrs. Forge and saw her wrinkle up her nose involuntarily, then forcibly relax her face.

"It's so nice to meet both of you," she said politely, giving me a genuine smile in the rearview mirror. "Chastity and Jon, right?"

"Jonathan," I corrected. "He goes by his full name."

"Oh, that's so fun! Well, you can call me Beatrice, or Birdie for short. Priscilla's told us all about you, Chastity, she says you're a big reader?"

"I like fairytales."

"That's great!" Beatrice rolled down the windows, still smiling pleasantly. "I like fairytales, too. My favorite is Rumpelstiltskin, what's yours?"

"Snow White."

"My favorite is Rapunzel," Priscilla chimed in.

"What about you, Jonathan, do you read a lot?" Beatrice asked, glancing at my brother, who'd curled into a ball in his seat. He didn't answer, or even give an indication he'd heard.

"He reads all the time," I said. "Sorry, he's just really shy."

"Oh, it's okay. I know exactly how that can be," Beatrice chirped.

Priscilla's family lived in what I thought was a mansion, but, looking back, was just a one-story, two-bedroom house. There were five cars parked out front, and Priscilla proudly told me that was the congregation.

"We're planting a church," Beatrice said brightly. "Hopefully, there'll be an actual, y'know, *church* in the near future, but this is just fine for now. Come on inside." Jonathan held my hand so tight it hurt as we walked inside, and stepped back when a tall, jovial man hurried up to us.

"Chastity and Jon, I believe?"

"Jonathan."

"Ah, my bad! Well, it's wonderful to meet y'all either way- I'm William. Thanks so much for coming to join us, we're so thrilled you and Priscilla have hit it off so fast! Are you hungry?"

"Yes," I said immediately. We'd been eating plain rice for two days, and I was getting so hungry I'd started peeling the dead skin off my lips to chew on.

"Let's get y'all some food before the service starts, okay?" Father William exchanged a concerned glance with Beatrice, but at the time, I didn't think anything of it. "Do you like scrambled eggs?"

"Yes."

I devoured my eggs with alarming speed and aggression while Jonathan sat in silence, staring at his plate uncomprehendingly. Several random people wandered in and out of the kitchen to chat with Beatrice and Father William, which thankfully kept their attention off of us, but once I'd finished in a few seconds flat and Jonathan was still just sitting there, Beatrice reached out to tentatively pat his shoulder.

"Aren't you hungry, sweetheart?" she asked, cautious and gentle. Jonathan shook his head.

"Maybe you can eat after church," Father William suggested hopefully.

Episcopal church turned out to be pretty boring, but much more pleasant than Southern Baptist church. Father William's sermon was about the boundless mercy of God, and every Bible verse he read focused on love- a far cry from the preacher's hateful ranting about the Old Testament and sinners damned for eternity. I stood up and sat down at the appropriate times, but for the most part I tuned out and looked around at everyone else in the tiny congregation.

It was primarily older people; Apple, Priscilla, Jonathan, and I were the only attendees under 40. Apple glared at us every time her father wasn't looking, made a point of sitting as far away as possible. When the service ended, she stomped off to the room she shared with Priscilla immediately, never saying a word to either of us.

"Wasn't that awesome?" Priscilla exclaimed as her parents folded up the chairs they'd set out. "We can play in the backyard now, if you want. Apple Pie said we're not allowed in our room while she's in it."

"Sure, if Jonathan can come."

"Oh- I mean, I thought he'd play with Apple, 'cause they're the same age."

"Uh…" I glanced up at my brother, trembling with his arms wrapped around himself. "I don't know if that's a good idea."

"Well, sure. I guess he can come if he wants."

"Jonathan, we're gonna play outside," I said gently, tugging on his sleeve. He followed us like a sleepwalker and sat down on the grass, idly pulling up daisies to make a bracelet.

"Let's play funeral," Priscilla said, eyes gleaming. "I'm gonna be a mortician when I grow up, y'know."

"I'm gonna be a famous ballerina."

"That's *so* cool! Okay, lie down, I'm embalming you."

We played Priscilla's morbid game, which mostly consisted of me lying still while she mimed everything she thought went into embalming, for about ten minutes, at which point Jonathan wandered over with a lost, dejected expression.

"What are you doing?" he asked quietly.

"I'm embalming her," Priscilla chirped.

"What?"

"Here, lie down, I'll embalm you, too."

"Okay," Jonathan said meekly.

"What are y'all up to out here?" Beatrice called, poking her head out the back door. Jonathan was still lying on the ground, pretending to be a corpse, while Priscilla and I held a fake funeral for him.

"Playing funeral," Priscilla chirped. "Jonathan is dead."

"*What?*"

"He's playing dead," I corrected quickly. Jonathan remained motionless, staring dazedly at the sky.

"Oh, sweetie, don't make them play that," Beatrice said, frowning.

"I like it," I told her.

"Well, I'm… glad. And I hate to be the bearer of bad news, but I think it's time for Chastity and Jonathan to go home now."

"But, Mama-"

"They can come back next week," Beatrice soothed. I eventually got Jonathan to stand up, and we all followed Beatrice back into the house, Priscilla grumbling under her breath that we hadn't had enough time to play. Before we got in the car, Beatrice hesitated. "Do either of you want to take a shower before you go home? You could borrow some clothes afterward, and we can wash those for you."

"Huh?" I blinked at her, wondering if I'd heard right. I was pretty sure people didn't usually invite you to use their shower. "We can shower at home."

"Oh. Well, y'know, I just thought maybe…"

"Do you think we smell bad?"

"No! No, Chastity, not at all! I just thought I'd offer, since y'all were playing in the grass." Beatrice laughed nervously, ran a hand through her hair, and I nodded, scowling.

"We're fine, but thanks anyway."

"I'm not going back next week," Jonathan informed me as we walked back down our driveway. Beatrice had asked to come see our house, but I frantically declined, told her I was tired and wanted to take a nap straight away.

"Why not? Didn't you have fun?"

"No. I told you I hate church," he snapped. "And Priscilla's a creepy little kid. Who the hell wants to be a mortician?"

"Don't be mean! She's my best friend."

"*I'm* your best friend," Jonathan whined, and I just sighed heavily.

"Can't I have two best friends?"

"No!"

"Okay, then you're my best best friend and she's my best friend, are you happy now?"

"No, you've only known her a week! I'm your best friend, I'm your brother, you can't just run off with some-!"

"*Jonathan!*" He flinched back when I yelled, and I gestured for him to kneel down so I could wipe the tears from his face. "I can have a new friend and still love you! I want to have playdates with Priscilla *and* play with you."

"I don't want you to."

"Please? It'll make me really, really happy." I fixed him with a pleading look, mirroring his own puppy dog eyes, and Jonathan looked away guiltily.

"Just on Sundays," he finally muttered.

"I promise."

"Where y'all been?" Mama demanded when we walked inside. Jonathan tensed up next to me, and I patted his hand soothingly. "That old cunt took y'all to church again?"

"We went to church," I said cautiously.

"How's the preacher?" she sneered, meeting Jonathan's gaze. He stiffened up, and when I looked at his face, I saw his eyes had glazed over, his lip was trembling like he'd burst into tears at any moment.

"Preacher's fine," I snarled, wanting to shove her in the oven like the witch she was, in her rotting gingerbread house falling in on itself, rescue Snow White and run far away, outrun everybody else in the world- except I wanted Priscilla to come with us, too. Priscilla was like a fairy, bright and sparkly and of another, better world, and I wanted her to spirit us away to safety. "Jonathan's tired, we're going to lie down."

"Lie down in your bed, I don't want him sleepin' on my couch- he'll ruin it. Worse'n a fuckin' dog, least you can housebreak a *dog.*" Jonathan sobbed, and I hurried him out the back door, kicking an old beer can on the porch. Mama *knew* how insecure he was about his bedwetting problem, she knew damn well and yet she never failed to remind him, shame him as often as possible for something he couldn't control, something that was, I believed, her fault, hers, and her boyfriends.

We curled up in the truck bed, me resting my head on Jonathan's chest as usual, and watched the leaves dance in the breeze above us. "Have you talked to Apple in school? Maybe y'all could be friends, too."

"She hates me," Jonathan said at once. "And she's a shallow bitch anyway."

"I think she's pretty."

"Not *that* pretty."

"Well, maybe she'll get nicer."

"I'm not holding my breath."

THREE

As the year stretched on and I kept going to church with Priscilla every Sunday, Beatrice and Father William started asking more and more questions about my home life, questions that seemed, at the time, totally innocuous.

"Do you get enough to eat at home?" Beatrice asked, setting a plate of real spaghetti in front of me. She insisted I eat breakfast and lunch with them every Sunday, had started sending Priscilla to school with an extra lunch for me, and sent food home with me after church.

"Yeah," I said, immediately on the defensive. Jonathan went into hysterics if he thought he wasn't taking good enough care of me, and even if he wasn't around, I was determined to stick up for him. "Mama goes to Winn-Dixie every week, and Jonathan cooks. He's really good at it."

"I'm sure he is," Beatrice said quickly. "You just seem so skinny."

"Well, we've got enough food." She always gave us food anyway, things she called "staples", which Jonathan hid at the back of the pantry in hopes Mama wouldn't notice. It was a valiant effort, but it only lasted a couple weeks- even Mama couldn't miss something so obvious for long.

"What the *hell* is this?" she demanded, storming into our bedroom with a loaf of bread clenched in her fist. "I ain't bought this shit."

"It's just bread," I told her, eyes downcast.

"The hell it's just bread, I ain't fuckin' bought it! You stole this shit, Jonathan?"

"No!" I cried, wishing I was big enough to push my brother behind me, act as a shield against Mama's anger. "Priscilla's mama gave it to us!"

"*Priscilla?*"

"My best friend. Her daddy's a priest, I go to their church on Sundays."

"Priests cain't have kids."

"They're not Catholic, they're Episcopalian."

"What the fuck is Episcopoalian?"

"It's *like* Cath-"

"Shut up. Just shut the hell up," Mama groaned. "You think I cain't provide for you, then? Is that it? Someone else's mama gotta give y'all food 'cause I ain't *good enough?!*" Her voice abruptly rose into a shrill scream, and Jonathan yelped, covered his ears with his hands.

"No, no, I don't think that, I don't-"

"You is an ungrateful, spoiled little brat," Mama snarled, stalking forward and pulling me forward by the hair. Jonathan and I cried out in unison, and he stumbled to his feet to shove at her ineffectively before she backhanded him, grabbed my shoulders, and shook me violently. "I had better *never* see no one else's damn food in this house again, y'hear me? D'you fuckin' *hear me?!*"

"Yes, ma'am," I gasped, unable to catch my breath. Jonathan picked me up the second she released me, bouncing me on his hip and hushing me like a baby, swaying slowly until I was still. The next Sunday, I told Beatrice I couldn't take food home anymore, and she reluctantly stopped offering it.

"Do both your parents live with you?" Father William asked, carefully joining Priscilla and I where we were sat playing with Barbies on the rug.

"No, my daddy ran off somewhere."

"So, your mama takes care of you and Jonathan?"

"Yes, sir."

"Does she make sure you bathe and go to bed on time?"

"No, that's Jonathan's job."

"Really? And how old is your brother, again?"

"Sixteen."

"You're both so small for your age," Father William said quietly, a sad expression flitting across his face.

"Is your house warm in the winter?" Beatrice asked, throwing an armload of quilts into the backseat of her car as November slipped away.

"Yeah."

"Well, we just thought you might like these anyway. They're super warm, super cozy!"

I struggled under the weight of the blankets when I got out of the car, and Beatrice quickly called for me to get back in. "I can drive up closer to your house," she offered, and I shook my head frantically.

"I'll just take them one at a time," I told her, dropping most of the blankets to the ground.

"Don't be silly, dear, it's no trouble at all-"

"Our house is ugly; I don't want you to see it."

"I used to live in a pretty ugly house. Please, can I just drive up to it?"

I hesitated for a long time, then shook my head firmly. "Mama would be really mad. She's embarrassed of, um, of how bad it looks."

"Alright," Beatrice finally said. "Y'know, Chastity, if you ever want to spend the night at our house, you're more than welcome. And so is Jonathan, of course."

"Thanks."

Most of the quilts were added to my stash in the truck; we only kept one, to replace our old blanket that reeked of urine and mold. Jonathan kept trying to wash it and hung it to dry near the vent, but it was never completely dry by the end of the day. He'd once asked Mama if she could buy him pull-ups, so he didn't have to wash the sheets so often, but she just slapped him and told him to stop being a baby. The subject was never raised again. Our new blanket was very nice for about a week.

"You're invited!" Priscilla sing-songed, pushing a colorful Christmas card across our table. Inside, written in painstakingly neat print, was the message, *Chastity and Jonathan- please join us for Christmas dinner, December 24th. Lots of love, Beatrice, William, Apple and Priscilla.* Priscilla's signature was scrawled in pink crayon at the bottom, and Apple's was written in the same hand as Father William's.

"Oh, that's so nice," I breathed, turning the card over nervously.

"It was my idea," Priscilla said, beaming. "And y'all can both spend the night, too."

"Jonathan won't want to, but I will. I'd love that."

"Perfect! Perfect, perfect, perfect!"

"No way in hell," Jonathan said as soon as he read the invitation. "We're not going to spend Christmas with a bunch of... of crazy religious fanatics."

"They're nothing like the preacher, you know that." Jonathan shuddered at the mention of Mama's boyfriend, and I quickly changed the subject, trying not to think about how he'd been so torn up he couldn't walk for hours after the preacher's last visit. "Besides, they'll have lots of food."

"I told you we don't need their hand-outs."

"They're just being nice."

"We're not going."

"I already told Priscilla yes, so you can stay if you want, but *I'm* going."

"But we always do holidays together," Jonathan said, his eyes welling up immediately.

"And we'll be together for Christmas if you come to dinner with me." Jonathan sniffled, wiped at his eyes, and fidgeted with his shirt for a long, long moment before finally nodding.

I'd never been to a real Christmas dinner before. We barely celebrated holidays; Mama never knew what day it was, and Jonathan worried about doing anything that might draw attention to ourselves, so he just lit a candle at the kitchen table and insisted it was a Christmas tradition. It was clear that the Forge family had *actual* traditions as soon as we set foot in their house; it had been decorated for the past few weeks, but now there were presents wrapped under the tree, a silvery tablecloth laid with fine china, and we were greeted by Father William handing us Christmas sweaters.

"They all match," he said, grinning. "Here, go try them on."

"Not in my room!" Apple yelled when she saw where he was trying to usher us. She always complained that her room smelled bad after Priscilla and I played in there, insisted I made a huge mess and threw toys everywhere, even though I was obsessive about cleaning up.

"Apple, sweetie, it's fine," Beatrice said, a stern note in her voice.

"I don't want him in my room! It's bad enough she gets to-"

"*Apple.* You're being rude to our guests," Beatrice snapped. Next to me, Jonathan was shaking, clutching the sweater so hard his already pale knuckles were turning white.

"We'll just put them on over our clothes," I said quickly, tossing my sweater over my head.

"Are you sure? I don't want y'all overheating."

"I'm sure. Jonathan, sweater." I tugged on my brother's sleeve, and he slowly put the sweater on as instructed, Apple glaring at him the whole time. "Thank you for inviting us."

"It's our pleasure," Beatrice and Father William said in unison.

I tried to act normal at dinner, all too aware that they already thought I was some kind of starving feral child, but I couldn't stop myself from eating ravenously. I'd quickly gotten used to Priscilla bringing me lunch during the week, so the winter break had me feeling hungrier than usual. Her parents watched me with sad, knowing expressions, and Apple sat at the far end of the table, obviously revolted.

"So normally we'd do a Christmas Eve service, but everybody had plans with their families tonight," Priscilla said brightly, eating her mashed potatoes at a far more reasonable pace. "We're doing church tomorrow morning, though."

"Have y'all ever been to a Christmas service before? Your family is Southern Baptist, right?" Beatrice asked.

"Granny is. Mama's not religious."

"Oh, that's too bad. Maybe she'd like our little church-you ought to bring her around sometime," Father William said. Jonathan laughed under his breath, and I giggled, too, but then he kept laughing, until he was practically in hysterics, doubled over with his arms around his stomach. Everyone fell silent, watching my brother collapse into a fit of unhinged laughter, and I ineffectively rubbed his back, trying to calm him down. Finally, Jonathan fell silent, still shaking, and just stared at his lap, breathing raggedly.

"Uh- Mama's *really* not religious," I muttered awkwardly.

"She knows the preacher, though," Jonathan whispered, blue eyes wild.

Much to my relief, everyone moved on fairly quickly, and even Apple started participating in her family's conversation, albeit with much eye-rolling and exaggerated sighing. By the time dinner ended, I felt full for the first time in my memory and copied Priscilla when she yawned.

"I'm sleepy," she announced. "When are we goin' to bed?"

"After Mama takes those two home," Apple said immediately.

"I *told* you they're spendin' the night," Priscilla snapped, and Jonathan sat up ramrod straight, shaking his head frantically.

"There is absolutely no way I'm lettin' them sleep in our room!" Apple cried.

"I want to go home, please," Jonathan said weakly, to no one in particular.

"Chastity and Jonathan are both welcome to stay if they want to," Father William interrupted firmly.

"No, we need to go home soon," Jonathan said, raising his voice for the first time since we'd arrived. "Mama expects us home soon."

"She doesn't even know we're gone," I protested.

"Jonathan, can I talk to you?" Beatrice asked suddenly. My brother blinked, then nodded, got to his feet, and followed her into the living room. I watched them talk by the Christmas tree, saw him whisper something, blushing furiously, and saw the understanding expression that crossed her face, the gentle way she patted his shoulder. Father William was completely distracted by his daughters, so I slipped out of my chair and snuck closer, hiding behind an armchair, just barely out of sight.

"...feel safe at home?"

"Yes, ma'am."

"Are you sure? I've just noticed you seem a little jumpy around us, and your sister's said some things that worry me."

"It's fine. Everything is fine."

"I'd really like to help you if there's something going on, dear."

"There's nothing."

"Jonathan..." Beatrice trailed off, then cleared her throat, continued in a carefully controlled, painfully gentle tone, "I know this is embarrassing, but we've noticed that the two of you don't... your hygiene isn't... it just seems like you're not really bathing that often."

"We bathe." It was true, we did bathe- but only when Mama remembered to buy soap, and even then, we tried not to use it too fast, plus Jonathan still only let me shower once a week, petrified that Mama's boyfriends would want me. He got more and more nervous as he got older, crying that he wasn't pretty anymore and if he wasn't pretty, they'd want me instead. I had to constantly reassure him that he still looked like a little girl, that no one would ever be interested in me, that he was the prettiest boy they'd ever seen.

"You can tell me if someone's hurting you," Beatrice said, and I ached with the sincerity, wanted to run to her and scream *yes Mama's hurting us we live in a rotting gingerbread house her boyfriends pay to hurt my brother he wants to die I want to kill them you have to help us you have to believe me-*

"No one's hurting us."

"I want you to understand that I'll go to the police if you're in danger," Beatrice said earnestly, and with that, I knew we were screwed. "I *will* tell them, you just have to say the word- because they're not gonna investigate if you deny everything, sweetheart."

"I'm fine," Jonathan said hoarsely. I knew he was thinking of Mama's cop boyfriend, a bearded, heavyset man who made Jonathan wear lingerie, who was constantly threatening to kill me if Jonathan told anyone about Mama's boyfriends, who showed up at random and wolf-whistled if he saw me, told me I was as pretty as my big brother. There were only four cops in Adabelle, and I had no doubt he'd make good on his promise if Beatrice went complaining to him.

"I wish y'all would spend the night. We can go to the store if you need-"

"No," Jonathan said quickly. "No, I just want to go home, please."

"Well, we got both of y'all a gift. At least take those, you can open them tomorrow."

"Alright," Jonathan mumbled. "Thank you, ma'am."

"Don't let Mama see," Jonathan reminded me as we walked down our driveway in the dark, carrying our presents. "She'll lose it if she finds out strangers are giving us gifts she can't afford."

"They're not strangers."

"They're strangers to her. And to me." Jonathan was clearly uncomfortable with the presents, and he set them both aside once we were safely in our room, hidden behind a box. "*Don't* tell Mama."

"Merry Christmas," I responded.

"You, too," Jonathan muttered, stretching out on our mattress before snuggling up to me as usual. I really wished he wouldn't sleep so close to me, but I never said anything-the last thing I wanted to do was make him more insecure than he already was. My brother fell asleep within minutes, but I laid awake for quite some time, letting my imagination turn piles of boxes into monsters for me to fight off. If I was a brave knight, I'd have a noble steed, a big black horse who'd carry me all across the land. Jonathan had once told me that horses had a soothing effect on people, and I liked to imagine the horse would calm him the hell down.

As I lay in the darkness, pretending to be safe in my brother's arms, pretending we could protect each other from Mama and her boyfriends, I wondered if it was possible for any of them to actually be arrested. Even at six years old, I knew that was a ridiculous idea; small-town cops protect their own, but I still wished they'd all go to jail and we could live with the Forge family, take real showers with nice shampoo, eat every day, wash our clothes with detergent, help Father William build up his congregation, and I'd have a sleepover with Priscilla every night.

I imagined growing up in their home, closer than sisters, taking ballet lessons with Priscilla, Jonathan in the audience at our recitals, graduating high school and leaving Adabelle for good, so I could be a world-famous ballerina and Priscilla could be a mortician, although she was really much too vibrant to be confined within the cold white walls of a morgue.

Once he confirmed Mama was getting high on the porch, Jonathan carefully closed our bedroom door and gestured for me to open my gifts- I had one from Priscilla and one from her parents- with a finger to his lips for me to keep quiet. I tore into the wrapping paper with gusto, Priscilla's first, and found a little canvas painting of two pink blobs on what was probably a stage, covered in an obscene amount of hot pink glitter.

"It's me and Priscilla," I explained to Jonathan, who tilted his head, squinted at it, shrugged.

"If you say so. Open the other one."

"Can we put it on the wall?"

"Sure, if you tell Mama you painted it in school."

"Okay." The next gift was a Butterfly Princess Barbie doll, brand-new, still in her box. I stared at it in awe, touched the plastic cover almost reverently- I'd never even dreamed of receiving a *new* toy. Unless you counted pots and pans from the kitchen, empty beer cans Jonathan drew faces on, or a rag he'd stitched into an odd sort of stuffed blob, I'd never had toys at all. I hadn't even looked in the toy aisle when we visited the store, not wanting to be disappointed.

"That's pretty," Jonathan commented, looking over my shoulder. "Want me to take it out of the box for you?"

"No."

"You can't play with it unless-"

"She'll get dirty if you take her out," I said firmly. I'd already decided I'd never take Barbie out of her perfect pink box, never risk her beautiful pink dress getting soiled or gnawed on by rats, I wanted to keep her pristine forever. "She's safe in there."

"Alright."

"Open yours!"

Jonathan sighed, glanced back at the door. "What if Mama comes in? I can open it later-"

"Open it *now!*"

"Opening it now," he muttered, obediently peeling the wrapping paper off. He was frustratingly slow, carefully lifting the tape so it didn't tear, unfolding the pretty snowflake-patterned paper, and finally setting it aside neatly, as if he wanted to save it for something. His gift was a book.

"What's it called?" I demanded, leaning in closer.

"*Trash*," he answered, holding it out for me to examine before opening it, reading the note scribbled in the front cover aloud. "'Jonathan- you won't find anything like this in the local library. Dorothy Allison is my favorite author of all time, and I think you'll love her. Love and merry Christmas, Beatrice (and William).' The 'and William' is in parentheses."

"Why won't you find it in the library?"
"Not sure."
"That's so nice of them."

FOUR

When we returned to school, Lily Faith Albrecht had a brand-new bracelet she showed off to all her friends, but I had Priscilla's painting hanging on my wall and a Barbie hidden under the truck. Priscilla stomped into class wearing her little pink cowboy boots, a puffy lime green coat, and violently orange dinosaur patterned overalls, exclaiming that I should have been allowed to sleep over on Christmas Eve.

"Your brother's so bor-*ing*," she sighed dramatically, throwing herself into her chair so violently she knocked it over and fell to the floor. She popped right back up and sat down a little less aggressively. "Why didn't he wanna stay?"

"Um- no reason," I said awkwardly. I told Priscilla a lot of things, but I could just imagine Jonathan breaking down in tears if he found out I'd told her about his bedwetting problem. It wasn't anyone else's business.

"Exactly! No reason, he was just bein' mean!"

"No, he's not mean. He was- I mean, there was a reason- he's scared of getting in trouble with our mama."

"Is y'all's mama mean, then? 'Cause if she is, y'all should both come live with us. We'll be real sisters!"

"We can't."

"Why not? Don't you want to?"

"Yeah, but… it just wouldn't… we can't."

"I'll pray about it," Priscilla declared. "I'm gonna ask God every night, okay? And you go home, and you do the same thing!"

"Why do you want to be a mortician?"

We were lying in Priscilla's backyard, trying to catch our breath after an incredibly enthusiastic game of tag, and I couldn't help asking about her career plan. It seemed a bizarre choice for such a perky child, and Jonathan was right when he muttered that it was strange for a kid to even know what a mortician was, let alone aspire to be one.

"When we lived in Gatlinburg, we were right next to a funeral home," Priscilla said, chewing her hair. "I don't remember it very much, it was forever ago, but I remember the mortician was always super nice and super happy, and when I asked him why he said it was 'cause he appreciated life more than most people."

"That doesn't make any sense."

"Sure, it does. Like, I know we only have a little while for playdates on Sunday, so I have to make the most of it. If you see dead people every day it reminds you to make the most of your life, 'cause you don't have long. Right?"

"I guess."

"And I wanna do something nice for people after they've gone to Heaven. I can be the last person to be nice to them. Isn't that special? One last nice thing."

"I guess it does sound nice, when you put it like that."

I tried not to go back inside when Mama's boyfriends came over. Jonathan had made it very clear that my job was to hide in the truck, ignore them if they called to me, keep away from them at all costs, no matter what. They were dangerous men who wanted to hurt me, or nice men who paid for our food depending on how out of it Jonathan was- he often went into a sort of deliberately oblivious trance, mumbling that everything was fine, Mama loved us, her boyfriends were nice men who wanted to help us, everything was *fine fine fine completely fine*, but I still needed to stay in the truck.

I tried not to, but there were some days when the ugly, creeping curiosity washed over me, and I had to slip back into the house, had to listen at the door and let the anger build in my chest, the impotent rage, and the desire to rip Mama's boyfriends to shreds. The things they said were so disgusting I wondered how the words didn't burn coming out of their mouths, how they could stand to look at themselves in a mirror afterwards. Sometimes I thought Jonathan was a trembling wreck, sometimes I wanted to slap him and yell at him to get it together, but when I heard what they said to him, I understood.

That day was the same as any other curious day at first, slipping through the back door, reflecting that we needed to patch the torn screen and then deciding there were already so many damn bugs in our house it didn't matter, approaching our bedroom on tiptoe. I could hear Mama on the front porch, yelling at no one, high as hell and pounding her fists against the railing. From our bedroom, I could already hear the preacher ranting about sin above Jonathan's broken sobbing, and for a second, I wondered why I could make it out so well, but then I saw our door was still open.

I should have turned around and run right back outside. It was bad enough to see him *after*, every week, multiple times a week, broken and bleeding and lost inside himself, but I had to. I don't know what made me do it, I don't know what made me come inside in the first place, I just kept walking forward until I stood in the doorway and- watched.

I was only there for a split second, couldn't bear any longer than that, but I saw the preacher's hips thrusting in time to his words, ranting that Jonathan was going to Hell, he was a faggot, a sodomite, he was damned for all eternity, how dare he allow this, how dare he tempt good Christian men like this, he was a whore and a bastard and a seductress bound for the lowest ring of the inferno.

What burned into my mind, though, what I still see on the back of my eyelids some nights, was the expression on Jonathan's face, the complete emptiness. I'd seen him catatonic before, but there was *nothing* behind his eyes in that moment. He was crying, eyes fixed on the ceiling, pained, broken sobs choked out of him, completely limp in the preacher's grip, eyes dead, glassy with tears, empty as a doll's. Neither of them ever saw me, the preacher too caught up in my brother's body, Jonathan lost in a world I couldn't imagine, and I ran after just a few seconds, didn't leave the truck until Jonathan came to get me hours later.

It wasn't long afterwards that Jonathan met me at the elementary school entrance in tears, trying and failing spectacularly to get himself under control. Priscilla and I ran up to him, concerned, and I threw my arms around his waist at once.

"What's wrong?"

"One of my teachers- my book- the book her- I'm sorry," Jonathan sniffled, wiping at his eyes as he took a deep, steadying breath. "My… my teacher, last period, saw me reading that book Mrs. Forge gave me for Christmas, and he just *stole* it. He took it away from me- we weren't doing anything, other people were reading, too- he said it was inappropriate. Said it was pornographic. And he won't give it back, he said I have no right to bring it to school, no right to have it *at all*- he called Mama to tell her what I was reading."

"Oh, shit." Mama hated the phone ringing at all, was constantly threatening to rip it out of the wall, but the landlord insisted we had to have it in case he needed to call us.

"She's gonna *kill* me," Jonathan moaned.

"What'd he have to go and tell her for?" Priscilla demanded.

"He said she needed to know what I was reading. Said parents have a right to know- to choose what their kids read."

"Priscilla!" We all jumped at Apple's voice, and Jonathan reached to pet my hair when she stomped up. She gave him a contemptuous look, pointedly held out her hand to her sister. "We need to go, Priscilla. People are gonna talk if they see me hanging around this freak."

"Don't be mean, his teacher made him cry," Priscilla scolded.

"Yeah, I was there." Apple looked Jonathan up and down, her face softening for just a second, but then she grabbed Priscilla's wrist in a bruising grip. "We gotta go."

Jonathan panicked all the way home, but by the time we got there, Mama was drunk on the couch, the phone call long since forgotten. It was never brought up again, but he never got his book back, either.

FIVE

My seventh birthday was just two weeks after Priscilla's, so she insisted on a joint birthday party. We were born in July, and I was glad for the excuse to see her- Beatrice or Father William, or sometimes even Apple, who was warming up to me after realizing I was apparently sticking around, picked me up twice a week plus Sunday mornings for summer playdates, but it wasn't the same as seeing her every day in school. Although I didn't tell her parents, I'd never had any kind of birthday party before, and I was so excited it made my head spin.

"What kinda cake do you like?" Priscilla asked, haphazardly slapping blades of grass into the giant mud pie she was making on her parents' garden table.

"Um- I don't know. What kind do *you* like?" The only time I recalled eating cake was on Lily Faith Albrecht's birthday last year, when her mother brought an apple cake for everyone in class and Lily Faith made a point of telling me I wasn't supposed to have a slice, but the teacher told her to share with *all* her classmates. I was the only one who saw Lily Faith throw her own portion away, her eyes blazing with pure fury and hatred.

"Strawberry!"

"Because it's pink?"

"Uh-huh!"

"That sounds perfect."

"And Daddy's gonna make a pizza. He worked in an Italian restaurant when he was a kid, didja know that?"

"No."

"Yeah, it's crazy! Maybe it was owned by the mob," Priscilla suggested, eyes sparkling. "He worked in the kitchen, so he makes really, really good Italian food- but you know *that*."

"Oh, yeah." Father William's homemade spaghetti was not even in the same category as Jonathan's pathetic attempts to turn penne pasta and canned tomatoes into a meal.

"The whole congregation is coming, and Apple Pie, and Jonathan, right?"

"I'll invite him."

"That should be everybody, then."

She never mentioned it, seemed completely unbothered by it, but I was Priscilla's only friend. Maybe it was her wildly colorful, mismatched outfits often consisting of too-big t-shirts from her parents' closet, maybe it was her insistence on saying grace before eating lunch, maybe it was her minor obsession with death, or maybe it was just because I was her best friend, but Priscilla was exactly as unpopular as I was, and I selfishly preferred it that way. After all, no one in their right mind would choose me if there was any other option.

"You're invited," I said, trying to mimic Priscilla's enthusiasm as I handed Jonathan an aggressively glittery card.

"What is this?"

"An invitation to our birthday party."

"*Our*?" Jonathan scowled at the invitation, seeming monumentally offended by the simple, pleasant message-

Please join us for Priscilla and Chastity's 7th birthday, July 8th, at the Forge home. Priscilla and I had both scrawled our names at the bottom, her in pink crayon, me in slightly darker pink crayon. "You two weren't born on the same day."

"No, but we were both born in July."

"What the hell do you need to share a party for?" His breath was starting to hitch, and I quickly patted his hand, hoping to calm him before he completely lost it.

"We just thought it might be fun."

"We can have fun here. I'll make it special."

"I want a *real* party. You can come too; I *want* you to come!"

"You like her more than me!" Jonathan wailed, tearing the card in half, and throwing it aside. "I *hate* Priscilla, I hate her and her sister and her stupid fucking parents! Everything was fine until they showed up, now you love her more and you wish she was your sister, and you don't even *care* about me!"

"That's not true!"

"Yes, it *is!*"

"I don't love anybody more than you, I *don't!* I can love more than one person!"

"You always want to be with her!"

"Because I hate our *house,* Jonathan! I hate our fucking shithole house, I hate Mama, I hate her boyfriends, but I never hated *you!*"

"You hate me," Jonathan sobbed, obviously not listening.

"I *don't* hate you; I just wish you were normal," I muttered. I knew full well it wasn't his fault he was like this, but I still resented it, wished he could have been more like Apple. Yes, she pushed her sister around, yes, she was an obnoxious, bratty teen, but Priscilla never had to baby her, never had to walk on eggshells to keep her calm, keep her fragile psyche from shattering even further.

"I'm not going to your stupid party," Jonathan announced, gasping for breath, and rubbing at his face.

"Fine," I snapped, and he looked shocked, started crying even harder.

"I hate Priscilla," he choked out. "I wish she was *dead*."

True to his word, Jonathan refused to attend the party, choosing instead to wash the sheets with more aggression than usual and curl up alone in the truck bed. I crawled in to hug him, kiss his cheek, and he relaxed slightly, gave me a weak, hopeful smile.

"You changed your mind?" he asked eagerly. "Because I was thinking we could-"

"No, I'm still going. They're all expecting me." Jonathan's face fell, and he practically shoved me away, wrapping his arms tighter around his knees.

"Get lost, then," he snapped.

"I love you," I offered miserably.

"No, you don't."

"Where's your brother?" Beatrice asked when I hopped in the car. "Doesn't he want to come over?"

"He's, um, he doesn't feel good."

"Oh, no! Well, does he need some kind of medicine, NyQuil or Tylenol or anything? We'll send some home with you."

"Uh- sure. Thanks."

"Too bad," Priscilla said morosely. "I wanna set him up with Apple Pie. If they get married, we'll be sisters-in-law."

"That's not exactly how in-laws work, honey," Beatrice laughed.

"I don't think they like each other," I added.

"They will once they get to know each other!"

Most of the congregation was chattering about their grandchildren in the living room, while Father William kneaded pizza dough in the kitchen. "Here come the birthday girls!" he cheered as we walked in, and Apple gave a deeply uninterested "yippee", raising her glass of sparkling cider. She was wearing an almost ethereal dress, loose and flowy, like something out of another time, and her hair caught the light as she leaned against the counter.

"Where's your psycho brother?" Apple asked me, tossing back the rest of her cider like it was a shot.

"He didn't want to come."

"You said he was sick earlier," Priscilla chimed in.

"Oh- yeah- he didn't want to come because he's sick."

"Uh-huh," Apple muttered, already tuned out. I was suddenly desperate for her attention, so I hopped up on the barstool next to her.

"Thanks for coming," I said genuinely.

"My parents made me, and I wanted cake."

"Still."

"You smell like shit." With that, she tossed her hair, which smelled of jasmine, and clicked out of the kitchen, slightly unsteady in her heels. I'd never seen her wear heels before, but they looked nice on her.

"...and many more!" Everyone clapped as Priscilla and I blew out the pink candles on our pink cake, even Apple, who looked more interested in hurrying things along so she could eat than anything else.

"What'd you wish for?" Apple asked a few minutes later, mouth full.

"To be best friends with Chastity forever, and to be a mortician, and for *her* to be a ballerina, and also I want a unicorn," Priscilla said at once. Before I could even open my mouth, Beatrice wagged her finger playfully at Apple.

"Now, you *know* it's rude to ask the birthday girl what she wished for!"

"I could've guessed all that anyway," Apple huffed, but when her mother wasn't looking, she reached forward to ruffle Priscilla's hair. "What about you, Chastity? I'll keep it a secret," she promised in a deadpan tone that didn't inspire much confidence.

"No, I didn't wish for anything," I said quietly. Really, I'd wished for quite a lot- I wished Jonathan was happier, I wished he was normal, I wished Mama would overdose and die, I wished her boyfriends would burn to death and go to Hell forever, but none of those were very pleasant wishes. "Well- I guess- I wanna be best friends forever, too."

"I knew it!" Priscilla squealed, throwing her arms around me.

"No unicorn for you?" Apple asked drily.

It was late by the time I got back, but I was scared Jonathan would be up all night worrying if I didn't come home, so I reluctantly turned down Priscilla's increasingly insistent sleepover invitations.

"Bye, Chastity! See you Sunday!" she yelled out the car door, waving wildly. I'd asked to keep all my presents at her house, and her parents had exchanged a nervous look, but ultimately agreed.

"Can I *please* drive you to your house?" Beatrice begged, looking suspiciously into the pitch-black woods.

"No, thanks. I know the way."

"I'm just worried it's not safe. I won't see your house in the dark, I promise- and if your mama asks, can you tell her it's just some stranger who made a wrong turn and left right away?" I hesitated, considered her offer carefully, and finally got back in the car.

"It's just at the end of the driveway," I mumbled, wringing my hands in my lap until we reached my rotting gingerbread house, melted into the darkness. The light switches were covered up by boxes, and all the lightbulbs were broken or missing anyway, so if we needed anything at night, we just used flashlights- or, in Mama's case, stumbled aimlessly through the dark and ended up passed out in the middle of the living room for someone to trip over come morning. "Well, thanks."

"Anytime, dear." Beatrice watched me get out and didn't drive away until I was inside.

"Jonathan," I called, walking into our bedroom and feeling my way to the mattress. He was curled up on his side, and for a second, unable to see his face in the dark, I thought- *what if it's not him?* What if I was touching some changeling, something that stole my brother's body and left me here alone? "Jonathan?"

"Chastity," he mumbled, still mostly asleep. He rolled over and held his arms out, like a child asking to be picked up; I laid down next to him and let him hold me. Jonathan sighed into my hair, as relaxed as he ever was. He always seemed happiest in those moments between sleeping and waking, just tired enough to forget his life. I considered getting him up to make him use the bathroom but didn't want to deal with his tears if he got embarrassed, so I just nuzzled my face into his neck.

"You fell asleep waiting on me," I said, slightly hurt. I could just imagine Jonathan crying himself to sleep while I was off having fun without him and felt guilty for a second before reminding myself he was invited, he *chose* not to join us. It wasn't my fault he couldn't share.

SIX

Until that year, we'd always spent our summers together, acting out fairytales in the woods, building strange toys out of random junk found in the yard, and generally entertaining ourselves as best we could. We never bothered walking into Adabelle, considering it too much effort just to go to the library; by the time school started up again, Jonathan and I were half-feral, isolated not only from our peers but from the whole world. The first and only summer I spent with Priscilla changed all that.

For one thing, we played together three times a week, but for another, I started bringing back books for Jonathan to read. Joyce Carol Oates, Shirley Jackson, Anne Rice, Bret Easton Ellis, and of course Dorothy Allison- Beatrice read voraciously, and nothing she liked could be found in the Briar County library. At first, Jonathan refused to read anything she sent home for him, but he quickly gave into boredom in my absence and, with nothing better to do, he began reading Beatrice's books.

Jonathan had always been clingy, but he was like a barnacle that summer, following me around every waking moment I wasn't at Priscilla's, demanding my attention, begging me to play with him, let him read to me or tell me a story, offering me little homemade gifts that we both knew were just repurposed trash.

"Chastity, I found a snake skeleton in the woods!"

"Chastity, come look at the stars with me!"

"Chastity, listen to this, it's from *We Have Always Lived in the Castle*."

"Chastity, you should sleep inside again."

"Chastity, I'm all alone."

"Chastity!"

"Chastity!"

"Chastity!"

Even with my limited knowledge of the real world, I knew it was pathetic for my almost-adult brother to grovel so desperately for my affection, to greet me in the driveway like an overeager puppy and offer to do anything I wanted, but I tried not to think about it, told myself it was fine, Jonathan was just lonely. And so, over the course of a week, the idea that Jonathan needed to befriend Apple rooted in my head and stayed there.

"Remember when you said we should set Apple and Jonathan up on a date?"

"No, but that's a great idea," Priscilla said eagerly, practically throwing her plastic teacup down to listen.

"Jonathan's really lonely, because we're hanging out so much," I said, fidgeting with the handle of the toy teapot. "I just think if he had a friend, too, he'd…" *Stop bothering me so much.* "...be happier."

"I bet he would! And Apple Pie doesn't have any friends, either, y'know. She says nobody wants to hang out with the new girl, especially 'cause we're not Baptist. She cried herself to sleep last week, somebody at school told her we're all goin' to Hell."

"Oh, Jonathan cries himself to sleep all the time! They can bond over that."

"You bring your brother next time you come over, and I'll get Apple Pie out here, and then we'll make them talk and they'll get married," Priscilla exclaimed.

"If you just come with me today, I promise, I'll never ask again. I'll never bring up church again, c'mon."

"You'll never go to church again?" Jonathan asked hopefully, eyes lighting up.

"That's not what I said. I'll never *ask you* to go to church again."

"They don't like me. I don't *want* to go. Why can't we both stay-?"

"I'll sleep inside with you again," I offered, and his face brightened a little. "Just come to their house this one time, okay?"

"And you'll come back in for the rest of the summer?"

"Yes," I said, already regretting my end of the bargain. "Deal."

Apple and Jonathan sat across from each other at the garden table, Apple staring at him with a look of cold disgust, Jonathan avoiding eye contact as always, Priscilla and I watching with bated breath. We were possibly the most unsubtle matchmakers on the planet, certainly the most misguided.

"Apple Pie likes reading," Priscilla announced.

"Don't call me that."

"She reads Jane Austen," Priscilla continued, as if her sister hadn't spoken. "Don't you like reading, Jonathan? D'you read Jane Austen?"

"He's read Jane Austen, they have all her books at the library," I confirmed. Jonathan pulled his knees to his chest and hid his face, ignored me when I poked his shoulder.

"Hey, you're having a playdate! You need to *say something*," I hissed, but he just whined, curled into an even tighter ball.

"This is ridiculous," Apple snapped. "I didn't even wanna talk to this lunatic-"

"Use your nice words!" Priscilla shouted.

"Why the fuck did you invite him over if he's not even gonna say anything?!"

"'Cause y'all need to be boyfriend and girlfriend so you're not lonely anymore!"

"I am *not* gonna date some inbred fuckin' freak!" Apple stood abruptly, batted away Priscilla's hands when she tried to grab her shirt, and stormed inside without another word.

"Well, shit," I said, kicking at the dirt.

"Use your nice words," Priscilla repeated dejectedly.

Jonathan spent the rest of the playdate in the same position, and when Father William called that it was time for us to leave, I approached my brother like he was a wild animal, rubbed his back softly and murmured, "We're going home now, Jonathan. You want to go home, don't you? I'm sorry I made you come over here, I thought you'd make a friend."

"Sorry my sister was nasty," Priscilla added, patting his head. Jonathan whined, twitched concerningly, and I quickly pushed her away.

"He doesn't like anybody else touching him. Jonathan, hey, can you look at me? We're going home now. You want to go home, don't you?" When he just kept whimpering, I looked to Father William for help, gesturing vaguely. My embarrassment over Jonathan's bizarre behavior was rapidly drowned out by concern for his well-being, especially since he hadn't been around anyone but myself, Mama, and her boyfriends all summer.

"Are you okay, sweetheart?" Father William asked cautiously. He walked slowly towards us and reached to put a hand on Jonathan's shoulder, but I made a frantic *stop* motion, knowing the last thing my brother needed was a grown man touching him. "Do you want to tell me what's going on? Did something happen?"

"Can you get Beatrice?" I asked suddenly. Father William hesitated.

"Of course I can, honey. Is Jonathan more comfortable around women?"

"I think so."

"Okay." He looked more than a little unnerved, but he hurried inside to find his wife, who trotted outside with a glass of water and a false smile.

"Jonathan! What's going on, buddy? Do you want some water? How about you sit up for me, huh? That doesn't look very comfy!"

It took almost twenty minutes, but Jonathan finally stood up, twisting his hands in his shirt. Beatrice breathed an audible sigh of relief as she offered him the water, but he just ducked his head, avoiding her gaze.

"Let's get y'all home, then," she murmured, trying to smile at me.

"Why'd you freak out like that?" I asked, slowly adjusting to the smell of our house. I'd spent most of the summer outside, only running in to use the bathroom and occasionally shower. Jonathan picked me up when we got home and hadn't sat me down since, carrying me on his hip as he wandered through the trailer in a daze, occasionally humming snatches of a lullaby. He didn't start talking again until he was cooking dinner.

"I don't like that family," he said softly. "I don't want to read books from them anymore."

"They're nice to you."

"They're trying to take you away from me." He sounded just like Mama at that moment, screaming that Jonathan thought he was my mother, *you're tryin' to steal my baby!*

"I think they're trying to take me away from Mama, not you."

"They can't. If they put us in foster care, they'd split us up, and foster parents are worse than this."

"That's what Mama says."

"Yeah, it is," Jonathan snapped, "and she's right. There's no funding in any of those social programs, they just put kids wherever, and I'll be eighteen next year, so even if they *did* put us in the same house I'd get kicked out and you'd be alone. Besides, they have to work with the cops, and the cops in Adabelle are…"

"I know. Don't think about him," I soothed, patting Jonathan's smooth cheek. "Priscilla's parents are nice people, okay? They just want to help."

"They want to take you away from me."

SEVEN

"Does your mama have a boyfriend?" Beatrice asked with the carefully practiced smile she always wore when she wanted to know something about my home life. I'd picked up on it by then, put a wall up right away.

"No."

"We were just wondering why Jonathan's nervous around men."

"He's not."

"You told us he was."

"Well- he's just- he's not- um- Mama doesn't have any boyfriends," I stammered, fidgeting with my sleeve. "Jonathan's kind of weird in the brain, don't worry about anything he does."

"That's not a very nice thing to say about your brother," Beatrice scolded gently.

"Everybody says so."

"Well, we shouldn't repeat things that aren't true just 'cause everybody says them. I think Jonathan's a very smart young man."

"Yeah, he is smart," I agreed.

"And you're very smart, too, but even very smart people need help sometimes. So, if you ever feel unsafe, you can tell us, okay?"

"I don't, but I will if I do. Thanks."

"Chastity?"

I peeked out from under the truck when I heard Jonathan's voice ring out across our backyard. It was easy for me to fit under there, and the grass was so long I was perfectly concealed; underneath the truck, there was nothing but soft, sweet-smelling dirt, and the long grass surrounding it kept everything cool and dark. I'd brought my Barbie out, still in her box, and kept her safe under there. The box was starting to get wet, and I worried it would fall apart soon, but for the time-being she was safe.

Mama's boyfriends rarely talked to me. Every time we heard a car turn down our driveway, Jonathan rushed me out to the truck and went to wait on the front porch, keeping them busy enough that they weren't interested in me. They all knew I was around, somewhere, but none of them had gone looking, and ever since the run-in with the farmer I stayed hidden for the most part. I'd stopped sneaking inside to listen after seeing Jonathan with the preacher, too.

"What?" I yelled back, crawling out of my safe little cave. "I thought you said one of Mama's boyfriends was driving up."

"Well- yes- but it's the cop," Jonathan said, and as I got closer, I saw how twitchy he was. "And he's not here for *that,* he's got a social worker with him."

"What's a social worker?"

"Someone who's supposed to protect kids. She won't come inside, though, and Mama's passed out. She wants to talk to us."

"With the cop?"

"They work with the police." Jonathan shrugged helplessly, shook his head. "It won't make any difference, so just talk to her. Don't tell her anything, he'll get mad if you do."

So, I followed Jonathan to our front porch, where an immaculately dressed woman was standing stiffly, looking at the random trash strewn around our porch and yard. She tried to smile when we walked out, but did not, I noticed, shake my hand when I held it out.

"Chastity and Joseph?" she asked.

"Jonathan," I corrected.

"Well, I'm Mrs. Everett, and I just wanted to ask you two a few questions, okay?" She had a distinct Yankee accent.

"Okay."

"Y'all ain't in trouble, now," the cop added, smiling at Jonathan. "I'm just here to make sure ever'thing goes nice and smooth." Jonathan shuddered and stared at the floor.

"So, Joseph, you said your mother is asleep right now?" Mrs. Everett began. Jonathan nodded mechanically. "That's good. We prefer to talk to children without their parents present, at first, but of course if she was awake, we'd have been happy to see everyone at the same time. Now, would you say you feel safe with your mother?" Another nod. "Joseph, dear, I need a verbal response, please."

"I feel safe," Jonathan said hoarsely.

"And you, Chastity?"

"Sure, I feel safe, but his name is-"

"That's great. How often do you two eat?"

"Um- twice a day?" Jonathan offered meekly. The cop laughed and shook his head.

"Did you forget how to count, boy? Y'all eat three good meals a day," he corrected.

"We eat three times a day," Jonathan repeated immediately.

"And when was the last time you had a bath?" Mrs. Everett looked us over, obviously taking in how dirty we looked. Beatrice and Father William constantly tried to convince me to take a shower at their house or bring my laundry when I came over, but I steadfastly refused, knowing Mama would be furious if she found out.

"Yesterday," Jonathan mumbled.

"We have shampoo," I added, since we were apparently just lying to the social worker.

"That's great. Can you tell me what happens when your mother gets mad? How often does she get mad at you?"

"Oh, Martha's the sweetest woman you'll ever meet," the cop laughed, staring meaningfully at Jonathan.

"Um- yeah. Yeah, she, um, she doesn't... she doesn't..."

"Mama doesn't get mad at us," I said helpfully.

"How did you get that bruise on your face, Joseph?"

Jonathan froze, glanced at the cop, then back to the floor. "I don't... remember," he managed. Anyone with half a brain could tell he was lying, but Mrs. Everett just nodded.

"I'm so clumsy, sometimes I wake up with bruises and I couldn't tell you where they came from for the life of me," she said. "Does your mother have a boyfriend?"

"No," I said, answering for Jonathan, who'd started whimpering.

"Has anyone ever touched you inappropriately?"

"No," I said.

"Joseph?" Mrs. Everett prodded. "Has anyone ever touched you inappropriately? I need to hear from both of you."

"You know no one has," the cop said. There was a cold, deadly note in his voice, and Jonathan gagged, pressed a hand over his mouth, then doubled over and vomited.

"Oh, my God," Mrs. Everett muttered, disgust evident in her voice. I wanted to throw something at her- it couldn't have been more evident we were being abused, but all she wanted to do was rattle off a list of scripted questions, accept our obviously false answers, ignore the cop coaching Jonathan directly in front of her. I never knew if he bribed her or if she just genuinely didn't care, but she couldn't have been that oblivious. Years later, I would track her down on Facebook and find she'd quit her job with CPS, started campaigning for parental rights, claiming foster care was always worse, real parents always knew best, and I wondered how many other cases she'd thrown away.

"I think that's as good a stoppin' point as any," the cop laughed. "Jonathan's a little *off*, Mrs. Everett, don't mind him."

"I thought his name was Joseph."

Mama brought me along to Winn-Dixie with her, said we weren't bonding enough, and that meant walking down the road with her for an hour and a half. "We gotta get us a car, huh, baby girl?" she commented, panting, when we reached Adabelle proper. "Maybe fix up that truck in the backyard, how 'bout that? Get your brother to do it, might's well make hisself useful ever' once in a while."

"Doesn't he pay the rent?" I asked softly, knowing I was risking her anger, but I couldn't bring myself to care. This was just a week after the social worker came and went, and the cop had been crueler than ever the next time he saw Jonathan, choked him until he passed out and left him so sore he was still limping heavily.

"Bein' a whore ain't nothin' to be proud of," Mama snorted. "Jonathan oughta learn some real skills 'fore he moves out- if he ever moves out, Lord knows that child cain't take care of his own self. Touched in the head."

Mama kept up a running dialogue under her breath as we walked through the store, triple-checking every price in one aisle and throwing random items into our basket in the next, digging her nails into my arm when I tried to stop and admire the shampoo bottles.

"Can we get-"

"Soap works just as good."

By then, I was old enough to be ashamed of my mother, to understand why the other shoppers were casting sideways glances at us, so when I heard Father William's familiar laugh from the cereal aisle, I grabbed Mama's hand and whispered, "I feel sick. Can we go home?"

"We gotta get pasta. I'll getcha a Coke if you're patient, you like them orange flavor ones, right?"

"No."

"Yeah, I remember you do."

I tried to hide my face as we walked past the aisle, but Apple recognized me, called out to me at once, "Hey, Chastity!"

"Hey," I mumbled, looking up to see Mama turning to stare at Father William and Apple, both of whom looked more nervous than I'd seen them in a while.

"Who're you?" Mama asked, balancing her shopping basket on her hip.

"Ah, I'm William Forge, and this is my older daughter, Apple. My younger girl is best friends with Chastity, here," Father William said politely, holding out his hand to shake. Apple winced at the sores on Mama's face and stepped back, half-hiding behind her father.

"Y'ain't told me 'bout no best friend," Mama said coldly. "Why'd y'wanna hide her from me? She someone you shouldn't be hangin' 'round with?"

"No, she's nice," I said to the floor. "I- I mentioned it, I told you."

"I'd remember that. You and your brother's both *liars*," she spat.

"Ma'am, please, I'm sure there's a misunderstanding," Father William cut in nervously.

"Shut the hell up! You don't tell me how to raise *my* child! I don't want y'all 'round this girl no more, y'hear? Chastity, you *stay away* from these assholes," Mama yelled, dragging me off before I could say another word. She started smoking as soon as we got home, and by the time she sobered up she'd forgotten ever meeting Father William, but I don't think he ever forgot her.

"This is completely ridiculous," Beatrice whispered, the tendons in her neck standing out in sharp relief. I'd slipped inside to use the bathroom, leaving Priscilla to sort the cool rocks we'd found, and come across her parents murmuring in the kitchen. "Did they even talk to the kids?" She was waving a letter around like she wanted to hit someone with it.

"They have to. I'm pretty sure CPS has to at least *talk* to them before they throw a case out," Father William responded softly.

"They don't bathe, they hardly eat, Jonathan's completely traumatized, and they think everything's just fine and dandy?"

"You've seen how scared they are to talk to us, and they actually know us. I can't picture either of them speaking to strangers about it."

"I just *know* their house is a complete wreck. There's a point where CPS steps in if the house is bad enough- and you met the mother last week."

"I don't know what to tell you, honey," Father William said. "We can always try again, and we'll keep inviting them over-"

"Their mother is on *meth!* She's addicted to meth, and they're just letting her keep these kids in her house, doing God knows what! And- and Jonathan's scared of men, you saw, and he told me he still wets the bed, that's why he wouldn't sleep over- those are both signs that- I'd bet you anything someone is sexually abusing that child."

"Beatrice, honey, you can't know that," Father William said quickly. "We don't need to jump to the worst-case scenario, okay? We'll reach out to CPS again, but you'll drive yourself crazy assuming the worst."

"He's so tiny," Beatrice said, her voice raising slightly. "He looks like a little boy."

"You don't know that's what's happening, Beatrice, *please*. Tell you what, I'll go directly to the police tomorrow, okay? They can make CPS take another look; I don't think they'll listen if we just keep badgering them. I promise this is gonna work out just fine, honey. Take a deep breath." Beatrice inhaled raggedly, clenching her fist tighter around the letter. "That's it, there we go. Tomorrow, I'll talk to the police."

EIGHT

It would be nice to say that Father William convinced the other cops to actually investigate, or that Beatrice got ahold of a better social worker, but my life was never a fairytale. No knight in shining armor came to rescue us, and they eventually gave up, went back to simply inviting us over as often as they could, offers that Jonathan always declined. Each of Mama's boyfriends came over at least once a week, and I often came home from Priscilla's to find money on the table, Mama passed out drunk or pacing the backyard, high as hell, Jonathan catatonic in our bedroom.

The preacher came over a week before we were supposed to go back to school. I hid under the truck for almost an hour, distantly heard Jonathan screaming but had learned by then to tune it out, didn't go back inside until the preacher drove off. I'd gotten used to finding Jonathan immediately after Mama's boyfriends left, usually curled up and dead silent, but that day he was still spread-eagled on the mattress, moaning in agony.

"What happened?" I demanded, rushing to his side. Jonathan didn't answer, just twitched weakly, gasped, and I started looking him over for injuries. By then, I was so desensitized that I didn't register the blood trickling from his penis as an emergency, just looked for something more obvious, started to panic when I couldn't see anything. "Are you just freaking out? Jonathan, what's *wrong?*"

"Hurts," he whined, unhelpfully.

"*What* hurts?"

"My…" Jonathan gestured weakly between his legs, face flushing bright red, and I finally realized he'd always been bleeding from the anus before; this was new.

"What happened?"

"He… he put a wire in… it *hurts-*"

"Well, did he take it out?"

"I think- so?"

"That's fine, then. You'll feel better soon," I decided. "If you can't walk, just lie still for a little bit, and then I'll help you clean up."

"It hurts," Jonathan repeated, eyes glazed over. He was, somehow, even paler than usual, almost gray, covered in a sheen of sweat, eyes glazed over, but I convinced myself it was nothing, sat next to him and stroked his hair until he threw up and I had to roll him on his side. I was expecting him to get better after a few minutes, but the bleeding didn't stop and he just kept crying, until finally I noticed his lower abdomen was swollen and, with great reluctance, got up to call 911.

"My brother's bleeding," I whispered, trying not to wake Mama up. "He's bleeding from, uh, from his, y'know, boy parts, and his tummy is swollen. He can't move, he says it hurts too much." I gave the operator our address as quickly as possible, then hung up and ran back to Jonathan's side, held his hand until the ambulance showed up. "I'm gonna go meet them," I said, kissing his sweaty forehead before hurrying outside.

Right away, I almost regretted calling. The paramedics were looking at our rotting gingerbread house with open disgust, making a show of sidestepping the trash in our yard, and I saw them taking in my torn, unwashed clothes, my greasy hair, the dirt smeared on my face from crawling around under the truck.

"He's in our bedroom," I said, trying to ignore the way one of them gagged as he was led inside. "Sorry, I know it smells bad- um, watch out for boxes."

"Are your parents home?"

"Mama's sleeping."

Jonathan screamed when the paramedics arranged him on the stretcher, reached out to me blindly, so I trotted along next to them squeezing his hand, determined not to cry. *I* was the tough one; it was only Jonathan who fell apart.

"You wanna ride with him?" the taller paramedic asked, draping a shock blanket over Jonathan's nude body. I guess they thought nothing in our house was clean enough to cover him with.

"Yes, sir."

I'd never been to a doctor before, but I was pretty sure Jonathan had, when he was very young. I knew he was seven years old when Mama took him away from her parents' house to move in with our daddy, eight when she started having her boyfriends around, so it must have been before then, before our daddy got her hooked on meth.

"Where's your mama, sweetheart?" A nurse with Dolly Parton hair and tie-dye scrubs smiled down at me, holding a clipboard with all the information she needed to give Mama, and I couldn't help rolling my eyes. Maybe I was spending too much time with Apple.

"She doesn't care. I need to know what happened." I tried to sound like an adult, but the nurse just laughed at my stern little voice.

"Of course she cares, sweetie. Is she in the bathroom?"

"She didn't-" I bit my lip, then tried to smile. "Actually, can I call her? She's at home."

"Sure thing. Tell her Jonathan's gonna be okay, but she should probably come see him pretty soon, just 'cause it's scary to be alone in the hospital."

Beatrice practically sprinted into the waiting room, looking as frantic as if Jonathan were her own son. "Chastity, baby, what happened? I know you didn't have time on the phone, but is there- oh, pumpkin, I'm so sorry- is he okay?"

"He's hurt really bad," I said quietly, unsure if I should divulge any further information. After the social worker, I was fully convinced nothing could be done, and I had no intention of saying anything without Jonathan's explicit approval. "Ask the nurse, she won't tell me."

"Okay. Can you at least tell me what happened leading up to-?"

"He, um, he just- he got hurt. I dunno. I don't *know!*"

"That's alright," Beatrice said quickly. "It's alright not to know, okay? That's just fine. Let's take a deep breath, now."

The Dolly Parton nurse trotted over within a few minutes, smiling hesitantly at Beatrice. "You must be Mama!" she chirped, but there was something false in her voice, a wall that hadn't been there before.

"Oh- well, no, I'm a family friend. Mrs. Caldwell is, um, she's… she's unwell."

"She sent you in her place?"

"Uh, yeah."

"Alright. Can you be very good and wait here, sweetie?" the nurse asked me, her smile plastered on like the Barbie safe in her box under the truck. "I need to talk to your friend, and we'll be right back."

"I want to know what happened!"

"I'll tell you in a little bit, okay?" I crossed my arms and glared at her back as she walked away, watched Beatrice's face drain completely of color when the nurse spoke softly to her, bit my thumbnail off so violently I drew blood. Within minutes, the nurse was back, Beatrice looking faint behind her, and she cleared her throat before cautiously telling me, "Your brother has what's called an *internal injury*. He's gonna be just fine, he just needs a very minor surgery, and we have to keep him here for a week or two."

"That doesn't sound fine."

"I know it seems scary-"

"When can we see him?" Beatrice interrupted, hoarse.

"After the surgery."

"Is that happening now?"

"Yes, ma'am, but in a few hours, you can go-"

"Is there a social worker here? I don't want Chastity going back to her house tonight." She spoke in an awful sort of monotone, barely concealed rage simmering just under the surface, and I shuddered.

"Of course, and once he's out of the ICU you're more than welcome to spend the night with him."

Beatrice just nodded and collapsed into the wildly uncomfortable chair, pulled me into her lap on instinct. "I need to make a call," she mumbled, sounding like a stranger. "Come with me, honey. I don't want you on your own right now, so just cover your ears while I call William, okay?"

"Okay." I didn't even bother with the pretense of covering my ears, just stood next to her and blatantly eavesdropped, watched the phone shake in her grasp.

"William, we need to contact CPS again," she hissed as soon as he picked up. "I can't tell you everything, Chastity's right here, but we need- they can't go back to that house. I was *right*. The nurse said they'll try to talk to him when he wakes up, ask him who did this, but it's completely- it's- I don't know who the hell we have to talk to, but we can't just let- I'll explain tonight. No, he's staying for a few weeks, Chastity's coming home with me."

For once, Apple didn't complain about my presence in her house. Priscilla didn't know anything beyond *Jonathan is in the hospital,* but she practically tackled me when I walked through the door, exclaiming that everything was going to work out just fine. "We'll have to pray for him," she declared, shuffling into the living room.

"Great idea," I mumbled.

Apple left the door open a sliver when we went to bed, and I lay awake in the dark, listening to Priscilla's unfairly steady breathing. My brother was alone in the hospital, he'd had *surgery,* and I wasn't there when he woke up. It was ridiculous that I wasn't allowed to stay with him, I thought, and the doctors were stupid for not healing him faster so I could hurry up and take him home. I vowed I'd never let him sleep alone again so long as God returned him safe and whole. I'd heard Father William say you couldn't bargain with God, but I didn't see the harm in trying.

When the kitchen light turned off, Apple slipped out of bed, and I watched her in the darkness for just a moment before trailing after her, silent as a ghost from years of practice. Her bedroom door was well-oiled, and the hinges never creaked, but even if they had, her and Priscilla were such deep sleepers you could have thrown the door open at 2AM and they wouldn't know. She noticed me once we reached her parents' bedroom door but made no comment, just raised a finger to her lips and beckoned me closer. We didn't even have to press our ears against the door to make out what they were saying.

"I want custody of those children," Beatrice sobbed. "This is our fucking fault; we should've tried harder to-"

"Honey, we went to CPS, we went to the police, I don't know what else we could have done." Father William was just as choked up as she was, and I was shocked, for a moment, to hear a grown man crying so openly. "What exactly happened?"

"I don't even want- it's just horrific." Beatrice took a deep breath, then said, slowly, carefully, "His bladder is ruptured, and his urethra's- injured, I don't know how badly. Someone forced a, a long wire, a coat hanger or something, some kind of *rusted*- into his- up his-" She took a deep breath, and I heard her gagging before she continued, "They've already called the police. Someone's gonna be over to talk to him once the anesthetic wears off- I mean, he'll still be on painkillers, but someone will talk to him. The nurse said it'll be someone from Adabelle, so he feels safer."

"We'll talk to them again, too. This *never* should have happened."

"Can we fit all the kids in one room? Chastity and Priscilla can share a bed, and if we get a cot or something for Jonathan, that should be fine. There's space, isn't there?"

"I think so."

From there, the conversation devolved into logistics, and Apple eventually took my hand, walked me back to my room. She closed the door fully behind us and sank into the fetal position on the floor, looking almost like Jonathan.

"Would he have stayed with us?" she asked softly, startling me out of my own dark daydreams. "If I was nicer, d'you think he'd of stayed here?"

"No," I said, after a minute of honest deliberation. "He was scared to leave our house."

"Who did it?"

"I don't know." The lie left a bitter taste in my mouth, but I'd promised myself never to tell without Jonathan's permission.

Jonathan was pale and still but fully conscious when I entered his hospital room the next morning, hand-in-hand with Beatrice. "Chastity!" he exclaimed once he'd placed me, lighting up. "I missed you!"

"Are you feeling better?" I took in the machines, the IV drip, the bloody urine in his catheter bag, and, bizarrely, the bruise on his cheek. It was totally innocuous compared to everything else, but for whatever reason, it stood out in sharp relief. Beatrice held me back when I tried to climb into the hospital bed with him.

"I guess so. I had surgery, you know."

"Yeah, I know. That's crazy."

"Why's Beatrice here?"

"I just wanted to check on you," Beatrice said quickly, smiling. Jonathan didn't look very appreciative.

"I don't wanna talk to anybody but Chastity," he mumbled, words slightly slurred. "Go away."

"Don't be *rude,* Jonathan," I scolded.

"No, no, it's fine. I can understand that. I'll just sit over here, and you won't even notice me, how 'bout that?"

"Go away," Jonathan repeated, groping clumsily for my hand. "Can you spend the night?"

"I'm not old enough."

"That's stupid. I want you here."

"I want to be here, too."

Before we could get any further, the door opened again, and when Jonathan yelped like a kicked puppy I turned around with a sinking feeling in my chest, locked eyes with Officer Albrecht. He smiled at me, took his hat off theatrically, and approached my brother's bedside. Another cop was with him, looking bored with the entire situation.

"I heard there's been some sorta commotion?" Mama's cop boyfriend said, laying a hand on Jonathan's shoulder, holding him to the hospital bed just the same as he held him down to the mattress. "You gotta kidney stone or somethin'?"

"No," Jonathan muttered. For the first time in my memory, he spoke to the cop with open disdain, obviously aided by the drugs in his system.

"Well, what happened, then? Hurt yourself?"

"The preacher hurt me." Jonathan's voice, slurred and confused as it was, rang loud and clear in the hospital room. Beatrice inhaled sharply through her nose, clenched her fists in her lap, and the Dolly Parton nurse, reading his chart, whirled around to stare at him.

"The preacher?" The cop sounded as casual as ever, and his partner didn't even react. "Brother Mitch, down at Adabelle Southern Baptist?"

"Yes. You *know*," Jonathan snarled. There was a feral gleam in his blue eyes, suddenly, something I'd never seen before, and I stepped forward like a shark sensing blood, eager, awake, enthralled. "You *know,* you motherfucker. You pay Mama, too."

"Alright," the cop said, chuckling, "I think I know what happened here. Whatever y'all got him on must be pretty good stuff if he's this out of it."

"I've heard patients say crazy things," the nurse laughed. "Poor baby."

"Hear him out a minute," Beatrice chimed in. "Jonathan, honey, you're a little confused- can you tell us who actually hurt you?"

"Oh, sure. Tell us all about it, son, and then you can tell us how you saw aliens in the woods," the cop laughed.

"You raped me," Jonathan said, and the cop's face shifted, ever so slightly. "You and the preacher and the landlord, you *all-*"

"Okay, that's enough," the cop's partner interrupted. "I'm sorry, but we really don't have time to listen to some kid's drugged-up ramblings."

"But-" I stopped myself, looked up at the cop, still pushing on Jonathan's shoulder, dangerously close to his thin, delicate neck. Obviously, he wouldn't have actually started choking him in front of everyone, but I was only a child, I knew he was a bad man, a dangerous man, I saw the fury in his eyes, I saw my brother dead.

"But what?" The cop's voice was deceptively calm, smooth, pleasant.

"N-nothing. You're right. He's… confused."

"Chastity?" Jonathan whimpered. I avoided his gaze.

"He's just confused," I repeated, voice empty.

Beatrice took me to the hospital every day, and as they slowly lowered the dosage of painkillers, Jonathan got more and more sullen towards her, eventually refusing to speak at all if she was in the room. She started leaving us alone with the nurse, occupying herself in the hospital cafeteria, and I was eventually allowed to crawl into bed with Jonathan and snuggle up to his side. After four days, Mama showed up in the hospital, looking surprisingly alert. She was still twitchy and nervous, but she didn't seem actively drunk or high, at the very least.

"Officer Albrecht told me what happened," she said, picking at a scab on her wrist. The Dolly Parton nurse was staring at her with open disgust. "He give me a ride over here, wants to talk to you in a minute, Jonathan."

"Okay," Jonathan mumbled, docile as ever.

"How old is you, now?" Mama stepped closer, squinting at him. "Thirteen?"

"I'm seventeen, Mama."

"But you're so small," she said blankly.

"Well, I'm seventeen."

"You're so small," Mama repeated, so quiet I could barely hear her. She approached the bedside and slowly, delicately, brushed Jonathan's hair back, ran her thumb over the faint stubble on his jaw. "Y'ain't never had a beard before."

"I'll shave," Jonathan said quickly, gripping me tighter. "I'm sorry, Mama, I haven't- only because I'm here- I'll shave as soon as I-"

"It's fine."

"Your heart rate's picking up, sweet boy," the nurse chimed in suddenly, scurrying over to check Jonathan's heart monitor. "Maybe you should take a nap for a little bit, huh? Doesn't that sound nice? I think he needs rest; you'll have to give him space, ma'am." Mama barely got a chance to speak before the nurse was ushering her out, babbling that rest was vital in recovering from emergency surgery.

We laid in silence until we heard the nurse arguing with someone in the hall, and seconds later the cop walked in, whistling. "Needed to talk to you alone for a few minutes," he explained, leaving the door barely cracked. "Just so we can get a full understandin' of what happened here. Chastity, you can stay if you want, it don't matter. Now, Jonathan, I believe there's been some confusion on your part." The cop sat on the edge of the bed and rested his heavy hand on Jonathan's chest. "You were on a whole cocktail of painkillers last we spoke, and you said some pretty crazy things, things that, frankly, could've got you in a lotta trouble if I weren't so nice. It's a serious crime to lie 'bout an officer of the law like you did. But, lucky for you, I *am* a nice man, so I'm here to give you a chance to set the record straight before anyone does anything too hasty."

"Set the record straight?" Jonathan was breathing slowly, obviously trying not to cry.

"That's right. See, here's what I think happened- your mama got herself hooked on meth when you was real little, right?"

"Daddy got her into it," Jonathan corrected quietly. "And it was Daddy's idea to use me for-"

"Now, hold up there. I don't care who started what, all I know is, y'all live with your meth head mama in a trailer full of garbage, ain't been kept up in God only knows how long, you got no money, you're hungry, you're dirty, blah, blah, blah. And you're a smart kid, Jonathan, so you wake up one day and think- how can I make some money to feed my baby sister? Maybe you heard about it on the radio or read it in one of them books you always got your nose stuck in, but either way, you're desperate enough to take yourself on down to the truck stop out by the highway and pick up some nice men, make 'em pay for your time."

"I didn't-"

"Yeah, you did. You thought you'd make some easy money, be a good boy and help your fam'ly out, and it didn't go so well for you this time. You had a rough customer, some stranger who'll never come through town again, told you he wanted to try somethin' new, he'll pay extra, so you bring him home, let him do what he wants, and next thing you know…" The cop shrugged and smiled. "That's what *I* think happened. 'Cause if you go tellin' ever'body in town Brother Mitch was playin' some kinda fucked-up sex game with you, well, there ain't a soul in Briar County who'll believe that."

"It's tr- it- it's true," Jonathan whimpered, pressing himself further back into bed.

"Now, what sounds more likely to you, Jonathan? A man ever'body in town adores, a man who's been preachin' God's word for nigh on forty years, payin' to fuck some white trash bastard child, pushin' a *wire* up his dick 'till his bladder tears, or some kid was in over his head with a random pervert and got a little confused on painkillers?" The cop's hand moved to my knee, suddenly, and he smiled sweetly at Jonathan. "And don't forget, boy, if you try to take this to court, it'll take up a hell of a lotta time. You'll lose in the end, after makin' every last detail of your pathetic little life public, and while you're off fightin' Brother Mitch's lawyer- 'cause I know at least three good lawyers who'd defend him free of charge- your baby sister's home alone."

I smacked the cop's hand and yanked the blanket up to cover my knees, but Jonathan had started crying as usual, pulled me closer to him, and hid my face in his neck. "I won't tell," he sobbed, burying his face in my hair.

"Is that a promise, son?"

"I'll n-never tell, I *promise*."

NINE

Beatrice and Father William were all too ready to believe Jonathan had been prostituting himself, and even though they wrote to CPS twice more, our case was never picked back up. A dirty house didn't qualify as abuse, and the cop insisted Mama was a perfectly attentive parent, always there when we needed her. After Jonathan's hospital stay, I once again refused to spend the night at their house, and my playdates with Priscilla dropped off to Sundays after church. My brother was clingier than ever; when we weren't in school, we were joined at the hip. The preacher never came back, and Jonathan said the cop and the landlord were gentler now, but nothing else changed.

The only difference in our lives was minor: suddenly, Apple wanted to be Jonathan's best friend. She sat next to him in every class and at lunch, walked with him in the halls, fought anyone who tried to harass him, and joined Priscilla in offering us rides home from school. All of this, and Jonathan still made no secret of hating her, either ignoring her completely or muttering that he didn't need to be babysat, that she treated him like a child.

"She needs to get some damn friends," Jonathan whined as we walked home from the bus stop, kicking a rock down the road. I stifled a laugh, remembering Mama yelling at Jonathan to get some friends his own age when she saw us playing make-believe in the front yard, and didn't dignify his hypocrisy with a response.

"Well, she's really nice to you. I bet you'd like her if you tried-"

"She's nice *now*. Her fucking parents *told her* what happened, they told her I- they had no right to tell her! She's just sorry for me, she'd still be a bitch if she didn't know how I got hurt!"

"They didn't tell her, she overheard."

"Well, they didn't have any right to talk about it all! They're not my parents! Apple tried to give me money yesterday, you know, for groceries. She thinks I'm a whore."

"She's worried about-"

"I don't want any of them worrying about me," Jonathan snarled. "The cop told me he *talked* to her parents, said we made a deal that he'd- he'd talk to Mama and the landlord and make sure we have enough money, said he wasn't going to arrest me *this time*, he'll make sure I don't do it again, and they think he's some kind of *hero*."

"They're good people," I said softly, and Jonathan just scoffed, but I was right. Beatrice and Father William were fundamentally good, kind people, and like all truly good people, they were blinded by naivety. They couldn't process what had happened to Jonathan, so when they got a neat explanation blaming a faceless stranger, exonerating Mama of everything but neglect, they jumped on it without question. Good, kind people couldn't live in a world where mothers whored their children out while cops bribed social workers to look the other way, where preachers hid behind holiness and got away with murder.

"You spend too much time with her," Jonathan sniffled, wrapping himself around me like a koala.

"I'm *sorry* I got back late," I sighed, reaching to pat his arm. Priscilla and I had gotten caught up in a new board game after church, and once dinner rolled around Father William insisted I eat with them, so it was dark out by the time they brought me home. Jonathan was already in bed, rolled away when I first tried to talk to him but quickly latched onto me.

"It's not fair! You're always gone, I'm all alone at school, then on the weekends you leave, too, it's not *fair!*"

"Jonathan, come on, you don't have to cry about this," I pleaded.

"I'm so lonely," he sobbed, tightening his grip on me. "I wish you'd never met Priscilla; I wish she'd just die! Everything was fine before-!"

"You're jealous of a second grader."

"Because she's *ruining my life!*"

"Jonathan-"

"I want you to stay home next Sunday."

"I'm not gonna stay home."

"You love her more than me!"

"I do *not,*" I said emphatically, dead tired of having the same conversation every week.

"You do! You wouldn't even care if I died."

"I'd kill myself if you died." I don't know that I really understood death at that age, but I truly meant it. I couldn't imagine a world without my brother.

"What if Priscilla died? Would you kill yourself then?"

"No. I told you; I love you more than anyone else. Doesn't that make you happy?"

"You don't show it," Jonathan muttered, but he did sound a little brighter, and he stopped crying after a few minutes, nuzzled his face into my hair with a contented sigh. "I love you so much, Chastity. You're the *only* person I'll ever love."

"I lo-"

"I wish you loved me as much as I love you."

"Whatever, Jonathan," I muttered, too exhausted to deal with him.

Jonathan became dreamy and dissociated as autumn dragged on, often staring off into space with a faint smile, refusing to speak to anyone but me. His English teacher sent a letter home to Mama suggesting he see a therapist, but he just set it on fire, watched it burn with a manic gleam in his wide blue eyes. The cop and the landlord still came, and in the aftermath of their visits Jonathan crawled under the truck with me, still bleeding, still naked, and laid shivering in the dirt for hours before I could coax him back inside to wash off.

"Are y'all going trick-or-treating?" Jonathan asked out of the blue, barely glancing at me as he hung our sheets to dry.

"Me and Priscilla?"

"Priscilla and *I*. Talk right."

"Fuck off," I muttered.

"What?"

"Yes, *Priscilla and I* are going trick-or-treating."

"You never asked *me* to take you-"

"Oh, my God, *shut up!*" Jonathan flinched back, whimpering, and I felt a little like I'd just kicked a puppy before the frustration that had been building in me for weeks boiled over again. "Shut *up* about Priscilla! You're right, I *do* like her more than you, I do! All you ever do is cry, and then you want me to fix everything for you, you come crying to me about every little thing- someone pushed you in the hall, Mama yelled at you, you pissed the bed *again,* and by the way we share the same bed and it's *gross,* Jonathan, every little fucking thing makes you cry and it's my job to make it better! I'm *tired* of you!"

Jonathan stared at me blankly, tears streaming down his cheeks, and for a second, I thought I'd gotten through to him- but then his face crumpled up and he started sobbing so hard he fell to his knees, so hard he gasped for breath, and the shame rose up in my chest immediately. I'd always known my brother was fragile, always accepted my job fitting his broken pieces into some kind of coherent order, but I'd never resented him so much until I met Priscilla, until he developed this pathetic, possessive jealousy, this raw desperation to keep me with him.

"No, I- I'm sorry," I stammered, hurrying forward to stroke his hair. Jonathan latched onto me as always, buried his face in my stomach, and I let him cry, rocked him as best I could. "I didn't mean it, Jonathan. I know it's not your fault."

"Happy Halloween!" Priscilla bellowed, hugging me so aggressively we both fell over. Father William had made costumes for us and Apple, who was reluctantly taking us trick-or-treating; I was Dorothy, Priscilla was Glinda the Good Witch, and Apple was "Dorothy's farm neighbor", a costume which consisted of her regular clothes and a nametag reading I LIVE IN KANSAS.

"Sorry Jonathan couldn't come," I said.

"Does he still think I don't like him?" Apple asked nervously, fidgeting with her braid.

"No, he knows you're sorry."

"I invited him, at school, but he didn't say anything. He isn't talking at all-"

"Let's go before it gets too dark," I interrupted, determined to forget about my brother for one night. I'd left him in our bedroom, playing with the odd stuffed toys he'd sewn together from scrap fabric around the house, and that was where I wanted him to stay.

"I heard somebody put razors in a candy apple and they gave it to a kid and then the kid died," Priscilla informed me as we walked down the street, a few paces ahead of Apple.

"I don't think that's true."

"Well, I'll ask Daddy. He'll know. We have to check our candy and make sure none of it's opened after we get it, 'cause of the razors in apples and I guess also regular poisons too."

"I'm pretty sure nobody's trying to poison us."

"There was a guy who poisoned his own son on Halloween," Apple chimed in, startling us. "He put cyanide in Pixy Stix, gave it to his son and some of the kid's friends, and I think his daughter, too, but none of them ate it except the son. He wanted to collect on a life insurance policy."

"So, if anyone's planning to murder us with candy, it'll be your daddy," I told Priscilla drily.

"Nah, we don't have life insurance," she said brightly. "Hey, I found an old photo the other day! It's just Mama and Daddy and Apple watching TV in our old house, when Apple was our age, so I was gonna move on 'cause we were going through all the old photo albums, but then Mama told me they were watching Live Aid, which is a concert that happened on TV, I mean live but also broadcast, and Queen was there, and they were watching the Queen part."

"That's *so* cool," I exclaimed, whirling around to look at Apple. "Was it really good?"

"Yeah," she said boredly. "I mean, I don't really remember. Would've made more of an impression if I was there in person."

"Still, that's so *cool!*"

"It got recorded, so we can watch it when we get home," Priscilla offered. "At least the Queen part."

Priscilla's living room had shag carpet, and when I remember that Halloween night, the last night we spent together, I remember the feel of the carpet first. Beatrice promised to get me home at a reasonable hour, assured me there was more than enough time to watch Queen's taped Live Aid performance, and so we flopped down in front of their old TV set, still in our costumes, and watched Freddie Mercury perform, just as rapt as her parents had been in '85.

She was always happy, but she looked happier than ever that night, singing along at the top of her lungs until she got up to dance, pulling me around the living room in a wild, completely offbeat waltz, both of us shrieking with laughter and finally falling down to the thick shag carpet, still giggling, "We Will Rock You" playing as loud as her family's TV could go, and I loved her with all my heart.

At seven years old, Priscilla wanted to be a mortician. She wanted to move back to Gatlinburg and take over her former neighbor's funeral home, she wanted to do it for free rather than take money from grieving people, and she wanted to do it as a final kindness to the departed. She wanted to be my best friend forever, told me we'd build a little house together, a pink house with a stable for unicorns out back, because, she reasoned, if narwhals were real and horses were real you could surely combine the two. She never hurt anyone, and she deserved a happy life more than anyone I've known since.

When Beatrice dropped me off at home, driving carefully down the driveway so I wouldn't have to walk in the dark, I found my bedroom empty, a note from Jonathan saying he'd gone for a walk and would be back in a few hours. I sat up in a blind panic, imagining all the things that could kill him, picturing his frail body crushed under the wheels of a truck, broken in the morgue, and as I fell asleep from sheer exhaustion my fears blended with memory. I saw the preacher running his hands over Jonathan's bloodless face, reaching into the gaping wound in his chest to fondle his heart, throwing him in a shallow ditch for the crows to rip apart and no one ever knowing, no one ever looking but me-

-and Jonathan shook me awake with the rising sun, the heavy smell of smoke clinging to his clothes, caught in his hair. "Chastity," he whimpered, tightening his grip on my shoulder, "Chastity, I did something wrong."

TEN

Jonathan refused to say what he'd done, just mumbled that he needed to shower, so I followed him into the bathroom. His hands shook too badly to undress himself; I made him sit on the toilet and took his clothes off, frequently pausing to pat his cheek and reassure him he was perfectly safe when his breath hitched, and he slapped my hands away. Once he was actually naked, Jonathan was meek and pliant, but getting him undressed to bathe was damn near impossible.

In the shower, he sat at my feet and let me wash him, leaning his head against my legs like a tired dog. "There, isn't that all better?" I asked gently, running my fingers through his hair. We didn't own a hairbrush, and while my hair was short enough that it really didn't matter, Jonathan's fell past his shoulders, so I was always trying to untangle it in the shower. "You're being so good," I cooed, rubbing his shoulder before tilting his head back to wash his face. That awful blank stare was back, and I performed my customary check for injuries, but found nothing new.

Jonathan didn't speak once he was out of the shower, just snuggled up to my side in the truck bed, shrieking wordlessly if I tried to pull away. "You're acting like a crazy person again," I told him, wishing I could grow up faster so holding him wasn't quite as awkward. Jonathan only squeezed me tighter, whimpering, and I resigned myself to lying in the truck bed all day.

I started trying to coax him inside once night fell, and after several minutes I was able to start guiding him back to our bedroom, holding both his hands and constantly telling him how well-behaved he was, how proud I was that he was listening so nicely, all the while feeling like our ages were reversed. We had just laid down when we heard the car, and Jonathan cried out, pulled me closer.

"It's too late for Mama's boyfriends," I said, squirming uselessly against him. He didn't let go until someone knocked timidly on the door and Father William's shaky voice rang out, calling my name. "Get *off!* They've never come here before; I need to see what they want!"

Jonathan stayed in bed while I picked my way through the dark maze of our rotting gingerbread house, gumdrop couch attracting flies, hard sugar windowpanes shattered on the sticky floor, praying Mama wouldn't wake up. Father William was alone on the porch, looking like he'd aged a thousand years in a day, and he patted my head like an automaton.

"Priscilla is dead," he said hoarsely. The words rang in my ears, echoed through my heart but didn't register as real in my mind, and I just stared up at him, his shadowed face ancient in the dark.

"But she's my age," I said.

"Our house burned down. Priscilla is dead." The words were rehearsed, forced out with agonized calm, and he patted my head again, like he had no idea what else to do with his hands. I imagined him repeating it in the car, *Priscilla is dead Priscilla is dead Priscilla is dead Priscilla is dead.*

"That's not true," I insisted, and for the first time in months I began to cry. I cried quietly, nothing like a normal seven-year-old or my histrionic brother, just stood impossibly still with tears streaming down my face.

"I'm sorry," Father William said, his voice breaking. "It was very- fast. It was very fast, and she didn't suffer. Beatrice is at the hospital- Apple's still in the burn unit- I just had to tell you. Priscilla loves- she *loved* you. And we didn't want you to hear it from anyone else." I'd soon find out he was lying, that the fire had started in her bedroom and quickly burned out of control, that Priscilla didn't die for five hours after arriving in the hospital, burned so severely the doctors knew they couldn't save her, so they just tried to drug her into oblivion until she finally succumbed to her injuries.

"She can't be dead," I said stupidly. Father William just patted me again and walked away without another word, not looking back even when I started screaming after him, "You're lying! You're fucking *lying to me!*"

Jonathan yelped when I kicked him in the chest but didn't actually move, just stared up at me with wide, confused eyes, like he genuinely didn't understand why I was hurting him.

"What the *fuck* did you do?!" I demanded, falling to the floor next to our mattress and battering his chest with my little fists, an inhuman scream shaking my entire body. Jonathan let me hit him, didn't move a muscle to push me away, and when I was finally done, I collapsed backwards, tangled my hands in my hair and gasped for breath, rocked myself slowly back and forth, slapped Jonathan across the face when he reached to help me. "Priscilla is dead," I moaned, pulling my hair so hard I yanked several strands out.

"I- I didn't mean- I didn't *want*-"

"You *murdered* her!"

"I didn't! I just wanted them to leave," Jonathan whined, grabbing for my arm again. "I thought they'd go back to Tennessee if-"

"You killed my best friend!"

"I didn't! I didn't mean to, it's not my fault!"

"I'll tell the cop. I'll call him right now, and he'll take you to jail and *hurt* you. He'll make you *sorry!*"

"No, no, Chastity, no-!"

"I hope he rapes you again," I spat, "I hope he rapes you until you *die.*" Jonathan shuddered convulsively, pressed himself back into bed and just stared at me, wide-eyed, until I finally went still and just sat there, staring at him. "I could really call him," I said softly.

"D-don't," Jonathan stammered, reaching out to me. I let him take my hand that time.

"I could. I might."

"I'm sorry."

"Shut the fuck up!" I barked, and he nodded weakly. "You're my brother. The only reason I won't tell is because you're my brother."

Apple never came back to school. She was in the hospital for months, but I never visited, too afraid I'd blurt out the truth, and I never spoke to her parents again for the same reason. They were too wrapped up in their own grief to seek me out. Jonathan, for his part, became completely submissive to me, agreed to everything I said without question, and if he ever voiced an opinion I disagreed with, or I just wanted to see him grovel, I threatened to tell the police what he'd done, getting increasingly creative with descriptions of what would happen to him in prison.

For whatever reason, arson was never officially suspected. At the time, I assumed it was because the Adabelle police were reluctant to do their jobs in general, especially when the victims were Episcopalians from out of town, and I later learned arson is notoriously difficult to prove. I now believe it was a combination of both factors.

I began talking to Priscilla around Christmas. I never did it around other people, but when I yelled at Jonathan to leave me alone, I watched him scurry off and then started whispering to a dead girl, at first just commenting on how pathetic he was, but my little insults quickly turned into full-blown conversations. I was as bad as Mama, talking to thin air and pausing for answers.

The landlord came to see Jonathan on my eighth birthday, so I ambled out to our daddy's truck, murmuring softly to Priscilla, "They'll lose interest pretty soon, you know. He'll be eighteen in a month, and they just won't care anymore. I don't know what we'll do then, but-"

I was interrupted by a sharp cry from the kitchen and hurried back inside, peeked around the corner to see the landlord holding Jonathan on his lap. He was mostly dressed, pants pushed down slightly, while Jonathan was completely nude, bruised and battered in his arms. The landlord moved his hips lazily, holding a sharp little knife to Jonathan's stomach and thrusting upwards more aggressively each time he cut him. Occasionally, the knife ventured lower, and Jonathan yelped when the landlord nicked his genitals, but it was otherwise a completely silent affair.

I patched him up afterwards, washed all the little cuts with soap and warm water, wished we had bandages to cover the deeper ones.

"I love you," Jonathan said quietly, trying to hug me. He seemed completely out of it.

"Love you, too," I mumbled, detangling his hair. "Don't you want a haircut?"

"I love you," he repeated.

"That's great, buddy."

"Why'd you do it?" I asked the day after Jonathan turned eighteen, resting my head on his chest in bed. "Why didn't you start the fire in their living room? You're not stupid, Jonathan."

"I don't know," he answered. He sounded genuine. "I wasn't thinking. I just… hated her. I guess that was it."

"But you didn't mean to kill her."

"No."

"You wanted her dead, but you didn't want to kill her *yourself*."

"I guess."

"Where are you going to college?"

"I'm not," Jonathan said, sounding surprised. "I need to stay with you."

"I think you really, *really* don't."

"Of course I do. I can't- I don't know how- I need you."

"You need to learn to take care of yourself."

"I need you," Jonathan insisted, holding me tighter.

Gradually, Mama began to notice how I bossed Jonathan around, how much he relied on me- I was barely eight years old, but as he got more and more absentminded I took care of him, reminded him to eat, watched him carefully when he used the stove (assuming we could get it to work), helped wash our soiled sheets every morning, picked out his clothes and helped him get dressed. I didn't believe Jonathan really needed my help with every little thing, and it started off with me just pitching in here and there, until we both got used to the new routine.

"Be more careful," I admonished my brother, pressing the least dirty towel we owned to a gash on his ankle. He'd tripped over something on the porch and cut himself on what looked like the remnants of a metal lawn chair.

"My bad," Jonathan said awkwardly.

"It's not that deep, so we don't need to bandage it, but it could've been a lot worse."

"I just wasn't paying attention-"

"I know, I'm telling you to pull your head out of the clouds and stop-"

"What's goin' on out here?" Mama drawled, wiping her runny nose on her sleeve as she stepped onto the porch. Jonathan went stiff, but I just shrugged, lifted the towel so she could see.

"He's hurt."

"Hurt bad?"

"No, ma'am."

"Well, that's good. Look, I gotta talk to you, Chastity. *Just* Chastity," she added when we both stood up.

"How long will you be gone?" Jonathan asked nervously, grabbing my arm. I'd stopped sleeping in the truck bed, so we were constantly together, and I was starting to worry about how he'd react when we had to go back to school.

"A few minutes, Jonathan, for fuck's sake."

"But I'm hurt-"

"You'll live."

I slouched in the single kitchen chair with my arms crossed, watching Mama with what I hoped was an intimidatingly blank expression, but I probably just looked pouty. She tried to smile at me, remembered her teeth were rotting, and stopped, cleared her throat. "Your brother's listenin' to ever'thing you say."

"He listens to everything you say, too."

"But he ain't scared of you."

"Oh, yes he is," I muttered, reflecting on how easily I could make Jonathan cry and beg for forgiveness just by grabbing the phone and threatening to tell the cop what he'd done. It would have been nearly impossible to prove anything at that point, but neither of us knew that.

"Y'all got a real good relationship," Mama said cautiously, trying to smile with her mouth closed. "I just thought I'd ask you to tell him, so he hears it from somebody he trusts- Brother Mitch wants to see him again." My breath stuttered, and I stared at her with blatant hatred, jerking upright.

"No way in fucking hell is-!"

"Chastity, please, calm down! Look, we need the money real bad, it'd only be once, and he promised to be gentle this time-"

"Jonathan almost *died*. He would've died if I hadn't-"

"But he's fine now, isn't he? He's just fine, and anyway Brother Mitch is really a nice man, he won't hurt him again. I already told him yes."

"So, I have to tell Jonathan?"

"He trusts you," Mama said weakly, wrapping a strand of hair around her fist and tugging.

Jonathan reacted to news of the preacher's upcoming visit with an empty *that's fine* and stopped speaking for the rest of the day. I couldn't convince him to eat that night, stopped short of threatening him and just agreed to go to bed early. My brother fell asleep at once, but I laid still in his arms, listening to him breathe, trying to ignore the awful stench of our bedroom that you could never quite get used to, until my eyes finally drifted shut around 1AM.

It wasn't the first nightmare I'd had about Priscilla, but it was certainly the most vivid. I never thought or dreamed of the fire itself; all I could imagine was what she must have looked like afterward, dying in the ICU, surrounded by doctors who knew it was a lost cause, who couldn't help or put her out of her misery, who just watched and drugged her and waited while her parents prayed for her to die faster.

I saw her skin blistering off the bone, her eyes melted in their sockets, her pink unicorn-patterned nightgown melted into her blackened flesh, her little hands spasmed into fists they couldn't unclench when she finally died, her mouth open to scream, the numbed but present agony she must have been in for *hours*. And in the bed next to her, I saw my brother after his surgery, pale and bruised and terrified, both of them together under unforgiving hospital lights.

ELEVEN

Whether the preacher actually was gentle, I don't know. I didn't hear Jonathan screaming, but he was bleeding when I found him, dead-eyed and unmoving. It took two hours to coax him into the shower, and I had to bathe him once he was there, softly reassuring him the entire time. Everything was normal until I moved the washcloth between his legs, and he instinctively shoved me, covered himself with his hands, and started bawling again.

"I won't hurt you," I said desperately, patting his shoulder. Jonathan just shook his head, sobbing, and I couldn't get him to move his hands. "Please, baby, I won't hurt you. I won't let anyone hurt you again." It wasn't exactly what I'd meant to say, and it was a completely empty promise, but Jonathan looked up at the words, met my eyes eagerly.

"You won't?" He sounded stupidly hopeful. I should have just told him I'd misspoken, but I couldn't stand the thought of him crying again, so I nodded.

"I won't," I promised.

Jonathan usually forgot things I told him when he was freaking out, but he latched onto my promise like a little dog with a chew toy, kept asking how, exactly, I intended to fulfill it. "The cop's coming later this week," he reminded me, tying a length of string into a complicated knot for no real reason.

"Well," I said awkwardly, trying to sound more confident than I really was, "well, uh, obviously… obviously I'll make sure he doesn't…" From the house behind us, Mama knocked something over and swore at the top of her lungs, and a switch was flipped in my head. I'd thought of it before in the half-realized way children do, but until that moment, I'd never seriously considered it. Still, when I spoke, it was with complete conviction. "We'll just kill Mama."

"What?" Jonathan froze, stopped playing with the string and stared at me, unable to process the brazen suggestion.

"We'll kill Mama," I repeated, increasingly confident. "If she's dead, she can't invite her boyfriends over, and without them, nobody can hurt you- except those assholes in school, I guess, but I can't do anything about them."

"We can't-"

"You killed Priscilla," I reminded him, hot rage flaring in my tone for a split second. "You had no problem murdering my best friend, so don't sit here and tell me you can't kill Mama."

"I didn't murder her-"

"We're going to kill Mama, or else…"

"Okay," Jonathan said quickly. His spinelessness really was concerning.

We had no neighbors for miles. Frankly, I was pretty sure we didn't even have an address. People hunted in the woods all the time, so no one would question a gunshot, but we didn't own any firearms. Our daddy had owned guns, but he took them when he left, and Mama's boyfriends didn't think she was stable enough to be trusted with one. What we *did* have was a hunting knife.

"What if she wakes up?" Jonathan asked, shuffling his feet nervously and trying to hand the knife back to me.

"Slit her throat." My voice was high-pitched and soft, unmistakably a child's voice, and Jonathan shuddered. He'd just turned eighteen but looked about four years younger, a delicate blue-eyed doll clutching the handle of an old hunting knife in small, trembling hands. "She won't wake up if you're fast enough."

"I didn't *mean* to kill Priscilla."

"Don't talk about her," I snapped, and Jonathan nodded rapidly.

"I just mean I've never-"

"It's *easy*. It's like cutting into a ham or something," I assured him, as if I had any experience with either. "Look, I'll be with you, okay? Right next to you. And remember, if you *don't* do it, everything stays the same."

"I know. I know, I'm ready."

Mama's room was dark, and we both gagged at the stench- it seemed impossible that her room could smell worse than ours, but somehow it did, and neither of us was too keen on finding out why. She was passed out drunk, the rise and fall of her chest so shallow it was barely noticeable, vomit dried on her face. I patted Jonathan's arm encouragingly, led him up to the bed by his sleeve and stood back, gesturing towards our mother's prone figure.

Jonathan's hands shook, and he paused, looking to me for help. "Hurry up," I hissed.

"But what if-?"

"What do you think she'll do if she wakes up right now?"

That was enough. In the blink of an eye, Jonathan drove the 10-inch blade into Mama's neck, yanked it sharply to the side and pulled it out again, then panicked and stumbled backward, shoving me behind him. Mama must have been deeply unconscious, because she never woke up, and we watched her bleed out in fascinated silence.

She'd looked like a zombie for years, and I could see her coming back from the dead, meth sores widening into gaping wounds, imagined dirt under her cracked, yellow nails as she clawed her way out of whatever shallow grave we buried her in. I was old enough to know zombies weren't real, but I still didn't like the thought of her staying in one piece, I knew I'd dream of her coming back home for months, I could never sleep easy with her buried in the woods.

"We can't just bury her," I announced, tugging on Jonathan's shirt to get his attention.

"Huh?" He was starting to cry, but I ignored it.

"We can't bury her like this. What if she- what if someone finds her? Then you'll *really* go to jail."

"What do we… do, then?" Jonathan blinked, wiped his eyes. "She's already-"

"Cut her up and bury her in different places."

"No-!"

"Do it, or you're going to get raped in prison."

Jonathan walked forward on shaky legs, shook Mama's shoulder as if she might still be alive, and hesitantly brought the hunting knife back to her neck. "Should I start here?"

"Yes, but take her outside first," I said impatiently. "Here, go get a towel to wrap around her neck, then we'll drag her to the backyard. And when we're done, we'll burn her sheets."

"Why?"

"So we don't get blood everywhere, idiot. Hurry up!"

It's funny; when I heard Priscilla was dead, I lost my mind, screamed at her grieving father that he had to be lying, tried to beat Jonathan up, considered jumping in front of a car to join her in Heaven, but I felt nothing watching my mother die. All the years of abuse played in my mind like a film reel as Jonathan sawed the knife mechanically back and forth, panting with exertion, never increasing or decreasing his speed.

"How old were you when her boyfriends started coming around?"

"Eight," Jonathan said softly, pausing to wipe the sweat from his brow. "Except they were Daddy's friends, back then. It was his dealer, and it was only supposed to be one time."

"Do we still have Granny's phone number?" We hadn't seen our grandmother in at least a year, but I figured she'd have to take us in if Mama disappeared.

"I think so. Why?"

"We'll have to live with her."

"We can't stay here?"

"No, Jonathan. We don't have any money," I explained, as patiently as possible. *You're the adult in this situation, not me!*

"That's right," he muttered, resuming his gruesome task. Finally, Mama's head was severed, and he looked to me for guidance.

"Cut her arms off next."

It took hours, but we finally had her in enough pieces to manage. I grabbed her head by the hair, and that was what I always remembered, the weight of Mama's decapitated head. I didn't look at her face, just dragged it along the ground as we walked through the woods, searching for a spot to bury it. I was convinced we had to bury everything a good distance apart, although in hindsight, that would only make it look more like murder if anyone found part of her. It made sense to me at the time, though- smaller pieces meant less chance of someone finding her, and more importantly, it was impossible for her to come back.

"Do you feel any different?" Jonathan asked, following me with the shovel.

"No."

"Are you sure? Because I-"

"I didn't kill her."

"You made me do it!"

"Shut up, Jonathan."

Granny answered her phone on the first ring. "You've reached Barbara Caldwell," she chirped, and I could just see her grinning, always thrilled to chat with just about anyone.

"Hi, Granny. It's Chastity- oh, and Jonathan's here, too."

"Chastity! Oh, darlin', it has been *too* long! How's you doin'?"

"Well, that's why we're calling. Mama sort of… I don't know. She went out two nights ago, and she hasn't come back since."

"She left you *alone?*"

"I mean, Jonathan's here."

"Exactly. You ought to of called sooner, darlin', I'd've come and picked y'all up straight away. Now, I'll see if I remember the way to y'all's… house..."

"We can walk into town," I said quickly.

"That'd be a real big help. Don't bother bringin' no clothes, I got some things I think oughta fit y'all- has Jonathan growed any?"

"Uh, no."

"Well, ever'thing'll be just a tad big on him, then. Oh- are y'all spendin' the night?" she asked hopefully.

"Yeah. Um, Jonathan still wets the bed, though."

"*Chastity!*" Jonathan shrieked.

"That's fine, ain't his fault. So, I'll see you at Winn-Dixie in a couple hours, how 'bout that?"

"Perfect."

Iphigenia Strangeworth

TWELVE

"Remember our story," I reminded Jonathan as Granny's car pulled into the Winn-Dixie parking lot. "Mama went out two nights ago, we don't know where to, and we don't know where she is now. We're worried she's dead in a ditch somewhere, but we don't *know* she's dead. Got that?"

"Yes."

"You don't sound very confident. Just don't say anything, okay?"

"Okay."

Granny jumped out of the car before we could even approach, hurried over in her little kitten heels, briefly stumbled back when she smelled us before plastering her smile on and pulling both of us into a hug at once. She was not a tall woman, but she was significantly taller than Jonathan, practically towered over me.

"It's been too long! That crazy woman just wouldn't let me see y'all, I dunno *why* when all I want's to help, and-"

"I won't go to church," Jonathan blurted out. I wanted to slap him.

"What?" Granny asked blankly.

"I won't go to church. I *won't*."

"Alright," she said after a moment, shrugging. "You don't gotta. I'd sure like it if you did, of course, but I won't force you. How 'bout you, Chastity?"

"I'm Episcopalian."

"What's Episcopalian?"

"Like Catholics, but also hippies."

"Oh." Granny's smile fell for a second, then she cleared her throat and continued, "Whatever you are, I'm so glad to see y'all again. You've gotten so big!"

"I'm eight now, and Jonathan's eighteen."

"Really! Why, y'all's gonna be taller'n me 'fore I know it!"

"I think he's done growing."

"Well, then you'll be taller'n *both* of us, and Grampa, too, how 'bout that? Are y'all hungry? I seen a *French Chef* rerun last night, had a recipe for a real fancy, uh, a French stew with red wine, called a beef... somethin', I weren't plannin' on makin' it but if y'all's here I might as well, huh? And we can get some other stuff, too."

Granny kept up a constant, one-sided conversation as we walked through the store, instructing us to go find this or that, ignoring Jonathan's humiliated expression when she threw a package of Goodnites into the cart, waffling over brands of cat food, and finally stopping at the exit to chat with the cashier for almost half an hour.

"Y'all just talk so darn fancy," she said brightly once we were back in the car, grinning at us in the rearview mirror. "I wish I sounded half as smart!"

"It's only because Jonathan reads so much."

"I really oughta read more, I just never did too good in school- well, I left after the fourth grade- so I ain't the best at it, but I love stories. My mama used to make up fairytales for us when we was kids, I loved that. And your grampa's a real artist, he does taxidermy, he makes some *beautiful* things, and I decorate cakes real nice, so don't think we're total savages! What all d'you read, Jonathan?"

"Oh, he'll read anything."

"That's good, that's real good. Smart boy," Granny said, beaming.

We'd only met our paternal grandparents a few times, but Grampa hugged us like he'd known us all our lives when we walked through the front door of their little house. It was old and the paint was peeling, but it was clean, it smelled nice, there was no trash in the yard. Jonathan stiffened when Grampa hugged him, grabbed my hand once he was released.

"It is *so* delightful to have y'all over! I see Barbara went crazy at the store again, but she's a fantastic cook, I guess it's worth the money." He winked conspiratorially, as if we were all hiding Granny's grocery bill from someone. "Now, y'all are goin' into… what, kindergarten and seventh grade?"

"Third grade and senior year," I corrected.

"Alright!"

"Do y'all have shampoo?" I asked. I never showered at Priscilla's house out of fear that Mama would find out and go into a rage, but Mama was scattered through the woods behind our trailer, Mama couldn't do a damn thing about it now.

"Do we- what?"

"Do y'all have shampoo?"

"Yeah, honey, 'course we got shampoo," Grampa said, exchanging a concerned look with Granny. "Y'all ain't got no shampoo back at your house?"

"No. Mama says it's too expensive. Can we take a shower?"

"Sure. Whyn't you go ahead and get cleaned up, then Jonathan can go after you."

"We usually just shower together," I said, frowning.

"Uh… I think y'all's a little too old for that. Go on, bathroom's right this way, we'll talk to your br-"

"I can't leave him alone," I told them, tightening my grip on Jonathan's hand. "It's fine, it's normal for us. He's scared of people."

"He can wait in the guest room, then," Granny insisted. "I don't think y'all need to shower together anymore."

"Fine."

I took my time in the shower, washed myself off before I finally grabbed the shampoo bottle and just held it for a long, sweet moment, admiring the pretty roses on the label. I opened it with reverence and inhaled deeply, then finally poured some into my hand, giggling uncontrollably at the feeling. I spent several minutes playing with my hair, and when I finally rinsed it out, I reached to turn the water off, then changed my mind and washed my hair again.

It was strange to actually feel clean, stranger still to dry off with a soft, clean towel. I tossed on the old-fashioned nightgown Granny had given me to wear and practically skipped out of the bathroom, twirling flamboyantly to make the skirt flare out.

"You can't wear that," Jonathan said immediately, genuine panic creeping into his voice. "We don't know that old man at all. You look like a girl, and you- you're too clean- we're in his house, he'll have a key if we lock the door-"

"He's our grandfather," I said in my most calming tone. "It'll be okay, Jonathan. We can go back to the house and get our clothes in a few days, and we'll actually wash them, and then I'll look like a boy again- I won't grow my hair out, okay? You can keep cutting it however you want."

"Can we put a chair in front of the door tonight? Just in case?"

"Yes, Jonathan, of course we can."

"This really is fantastic," Granny gushed, watching us eat with a proud gleam in her eyes. "I cain't believe that nasty- I mean, uh, sorry, just- well, we been wantin' a relationship with y'all for I dunno how long. Since Jonathan was borned, at least. It was your other grandparents who didn't want us to see you at first, and I can understand that, our son really wadn't- uh- he wadn't the right fit for Martha, we'll say. But after they got married, we thought we could be more involved, she just wouldn't let us. 'Course neither would our boy."

"Do you know where he went?" I asked, curious but not exactly dying to know the answer.

"Couldn't tell you," Granny shrugged. "He ain't spoke to us since he left home to marry your mama."

"Prob'ly dead," Grampa added helpfully. Granny smacked his shoulder lightly.

"Don't go tellin' 'em that, Arnie. Maybe he got hisself clean." She sounded so doubtful I wondered why she even bothered to lie in the first place. "So, how long you said she been gone?"

"Two days," I said, trying to seem nervous.

"Been more'n twenty-four hours, then- that's how long you gotta wait to report a missin' person. I'll go on down to the police station tomorra and let 'em know."

"Okay. That's perfect."

"I'm sure we'll find her real soon, but maybe y'all could stay a while once we do, anyway," Granny said hopefully.

I don't think the police ever even looked for Mama. If anyone cared, it would have been her cop boyfriend, albeit only because she was the one giving him access to my brother's body, but he didn't put up much of a fuss. Maybe it was because Jonathan was just getting too old for him. Our grandparents believed Mama had run off somewhere, and they were more than happy to take us in despite our considerable issues.

Once it became clear that Mama wasn't coming back anytime soon, I convinced Jonathan to wait in our bedroom- our grandparents had, with reluctance, accepted that we were just going to share a bed- and found Granny cleaning the kitchen, humming along to the radio.

"Are you going to make Jonathan leave?"

"Oh, Chastity! You gave me a good scare, baby, I ain't heard you come in! What was that, now?"

"Are you going to make Jonathan leave? I know he's eighteen, but he can't live alone, he's still in high school, and besides he's…" I waved my hands around; unsure what Jonathan was. "He can't take care of himself."

"No, no, 'course not. I always forget he's eighteen, he's such a tiny little thing. Don't you worry none, we'll take good care of y'all both." Granny bit her lip, set her washcloth down and turned to smile at me. "Is Jonathan alright? Mentally? We cain't afford to send him to no special school, but we could homeschool him. 's only for a year, right?"

"He does well enough in school."

"Oh, you're just the cutest thing! So… so *formal!*" Granny giggled. "If he's doin' alright, that's good. That's really all we want. I know we don't know each other too well yet, but your grampa and me both wanna change that. We ain't got no other grandchildren- that we know of- and we thought we'd never get to know y'all, so this is… this means a lot. Jonathan can stay here as long as he needs."

"I appreciate that."

The only thing I brought over from our previous home was the Butterfly Princess Barbie Priscilla's parents had given me for Christmas. Her box was dirty and starting to mold, so I finally, with great reluctance, took her out- only to put her under a glass case on Grampa's advice. "Keeps her safe much better'n cardboard will," he said, ruffling my hair. "That's one purty doll you got, huh? Where'd you get her?"

"My best friend's parents."

"Really! Y'ain't never mentioned no best friend before, what's she like? Does she want to come over for supper sometime?"

"She's dead."

"O-oh." Grampa obviously didn't know what to say to that. He coughed, cleared his throat, scratched his beard, and finally muttered, "I'm so sorry, Chastity."

"She burned to death in a house fire." *A house fire my brother started. What if I told you he murdered her, disfigured her sister for life? What if I told you he killed Mama? What if I told you I made him do it?*

"I- oh- sweetheart, I-" Swallowing heavily, Grampa fixed his gaze on the floor. "She's in Heaven now, Chastity. She's up there with Jesus, watchin' over you. Y'know that, right?"

"I know."

"Good."

THIRTEEN

When school started back up, Grampa offered to drive us in his truck, so we ended up squished together in the cab with me in the middle. No matter what I said or did, Jonathan was terrified of him, couldn't be convinced he had good intentions. He hadn't said a word to either of our grandparents since announcing his refusal to attend church, and while I obligingly bonded with them, Jonathan hid in our room with a book.

"I like being closer to the library," he admitted a few nights after our arrival, "and I like being clean all the time. And obviously it's better without Mama's boyfriends."

"And we got food!"

"We *have* food. Talk right, these people are a bad influence on you."

"They're nice, Jonathan. Be *nice*. You need to talk to them more."

"I don't trust that man," he insisted, pulling his knees to his chest. I couldn't exactly blame him for being hesitant- if I'd been sexually abused for a decade, I wouldn't have been eager to befriend random men either.

"You don't have to trust him, okay? Just be civil. We can still keep the door locked at night."

Nights had gotten significantly better since we got a real bed. I still remember falling asleep in my grandparents' house for the first time, Jonathan clinging to me, too scared to close his eyes. I could look out the window and see the moon, the whole house smelled pleasantly of old wood, the mattress and pillows were so soft I could just sink into them, and Jonathan was wearing a diaper, so I wasn't going to wake up soaked in piss again. We'd locked the door and pushed a chair under the handle, just in case, and I had to remind my brother of that several times before he finally fell asleep.

Waking up dry and comfortable was incredible, too; our old mattress hurt my back, but at our grandparents' house I could roll right out of bed feeling actually refreshed, and instead of washing the sheets Jonathan just had to change. It was so much more convenient, so much better in every possible way, and I never wanted to leave.

Jonathan had been nervous about going back to school for months, at one point admitting he'd liked having Apple around to protect him, prompting me to kick him in the shins and yell *whose fucking fault is it she's gone?* I still woke up every Sunday thinking Beatrice would be by soon to pick me up for church, and when I realized she wasn't I woke Jonathan up to bully him, tell him he deserved everything Mama's boyfriends had done, he was a pathetic excuse for a man, call him a coward, a monster, a slut, anything I could think of until he was in hysterics, crying too hard to even ask for forgiveness.

On my first day of third grade, Jonathan walked me to the elementary school entrance as always, then just stood there holding my hand, obviously unwilling to leave.

"Jonathan, you have to go to school now," I said patiently, feeling, as always, like his mother.

"I know," he mumbled, but didn't move.

"So, you need to let go of me and go to the high school. Right now."

"I know. I will."

"Right *now,* Jonathan. You look crazy- they're only going to treat you worse if you keep standing here holding onto me." Finally, he left, and I hurried inside.

"Holy shit," Lily Faith Albrecht said, staring at me. I blinked at her, and she giggled. "You look really… clean."

"I moved in with my grandparents, they have better soap. And shampoo, and everything."

"How come?"

"My mama left."

"That's right." Lily Faith's eyes were sharp and cold as a shark's. "My *daddy* told me 'bout that. He was friends with your mama, and he's a cop. He said she's prob'ly dead somewhere." She spat the word "daddy" out like it burned her mouth, and I remembered how furious she always looked at the end of every school day, the wild, unrestrained glee that lit her face as she walked through the classroom doors every morning.

"I hope so."

I was never popular, but I wasn't exactly bullied, either. Lily Faith and her friends stopped making their nasty little comments once it became apparent that I genuinely didn't care, so I was completely left alone at school. I'm convinced it was because I was so quiet, because I just didn't give a damn- they certainly talked about me behind my back, but there was no fun in teasing someone who gave no reaction beyond a blank stare. Jonathan might have had an easier time if it wasn't so ridiculously easy to make him cry, and, admittedly, so *fun.*

Outside of school, Jonathan occupied himself with his books, and I started following Grampa to his taxidermy shop.

It was a tiny old wood building a few yards from his house, and while he was initially worried I'd be scared or put off, he quickly started teaching me the ropes. Before long, I could preserve birds fairly well, and by the time I started middle school I'd graduated to rodents. Grampa's creations were stunningly lifelike, convincing enough you'd think they were still alive on first glance, and I was proud to learn from him.

Jonathan still refused to speak more than a few words at a time, but he slowly, cautiously, took to following Granny around the house like a shadow, watching her cook and clean and copying everything she did, trying to be helpful in his own way. If Granny acknowledged him, he ran back to our room, so she just pretended he wasn't there, smiling wider than usual. Eventually, he started standing over her shoulder when she embroidered in the evenings, watching carefully, until she set aside a wooden hoop and length of fabric for him.

"Say, Jonathan, I'm headin' out for a huntin' trip this weekend," Grampa said carefully over dinner, not long after my tenth birthday. "You'll be twenty next week, right?" I nodded for him, and Grampa smiled hopefully. "High time you learned how to handle a gun, then. How 'bout it?"

Jonathan stared at him like a cornered dog, starting to tremble. I could almost hear his thoughts- alone, in the woods, with an armed man who he still believed wanted to rape him. He shook his head, whimpering, grabbed my hand under the table and looked to me for help.

"He doesn't want to," I said, as if that wasn't obvious.

"Oh," Grampa muttered dejectedly.

"But I could come," I added quickly. Grampa brightened up, and Jonathan tightened his grip on my hand, breath hitching.

"You can't go," he hissed that night, clinging tightly to me in bed. "He'll murder you and rape your corpse and-"

"Shut up, Jonathan. Grampa's perfectly safe."

"He *isn't*," Jonathan insisted. "He's not, you can't trust him!"

"Why? Because he's a man? *You're* a man."

"It's different, he's- he's not- I'm not like him. I'm *not* like Mama's boyfriends."

"Neither is he."

"He is."

"Do you think every other man is like Mama's boyfriends?"

"Yes," Jonathan answered without hesitation.

"Okay, well, you're wrong, so shut up and let me sleep."

"You can't go."

"You don't tell me what to do."

Jonathan cried when I left with Grampa, looking so distressed I considered backing out, but instead I just reached up to pat his head. I'd had a growth spurt, and Jonathan was only 5'3; I reached his shoulder by then. He didn't get any taller, but I ended up being 5'5 and never failed to remind him of my 2-inch height advantage.

"Now, normally I'd get up a hell of a lot earlier, but when I was younger'n you my daddy made me get up at the ass-crack of dawn for our first huntin' trip, and I hated it for *years* after. You gotta learn to like it *before* you wake up at five in the damn mornin'," Grampa said brightly as he drove out of town. "I reckon you'll be a great hunter, y'know. You're real quiet, that's important- well, not as quiet as your brother, I guess. Is he… is there somethin' we're doin' wrong?"

"No. Jonathan's just really skittish."

"You can say that again, boy." Grampa wasn't senile, but I looked masculine enough that he often seemed to forget I was female, and happily treated me as the good son my daddy hadn't been. He was awkward around Jonathan, unsure what to do with my immature, effeminate brother, and rarely interacted with him again after inviting him on the hunting trip. Luckily, Granny doted on Jonathan, generally treating him like a child or small dog.

He brought me to an old, tiny hunting cabin in the middle of the forest, threw his arms out dramatically as we stepped across the threshold. "Ta-da! Now, we ain't spendin' the night here, I think your poor brother'd have a heart attack if y'all was apart that long, but this here's where my old man used to bring me once I started appreciatin' the sport more. Well, I dunno as it's much of a sport, mostly just a-sittin' around waitin', but, y'know. Anyway, just wanted to show you so's you know it's here." The cabin had two rooms, and there was an outhouse several yards away. It was the definition of rustic- no running water, no electricity, nothing.

We sat in the woods for hours before a deer walked by, and Grampa helped me aim my gun but moved back to let me pull the trigger. I missed. Although neither of us actually shot anything, Grampa was in high spirits as we drove home, explaining that the real joy of hunting was just sitting out in nature. "We'll go fishin' once it gets a little warmer," he said cheerfully. "I tell you, I ain't never caught a fish in my life, but really it's all about relaxin' next to a river with a flask- wait, how old is you now?"

"Ten."

"Yeah, that's plenty old enough to have a drink now and again."

"They got them head doctors over in Statesboro," Grampa said with forced casualness as I helped him skin a dog. People brought him their dead pets to stuff, which Jonathan found creepy, but I understood perfectly- why would you ever want to bury someone you love? I had never visited Priscilla's grave, couldn't help but imagine her trapped underground, alone in complete darkness. Granny'd had several cats over the years, all of which were now stuffed and arranged around the house, some of them stretching, some napping, some just sitting up. Her current, living cat, Snowball, seemed unbothered by them.

Snowball was a massively fluffy and ironically pitch-black Persian cat- where Granny got him, I have no idea- who adored me, but ran away every time Jonathan tried to pick him up. They'd liked each other until Jonathan hugged him too tight and got a nasty scratch down his cheek for it. Once, when Snowball ambled past me to stare curiously at a stuffed cat, I muttered "You're next," sending Granny into a hysterical laughing fit.

"Head doctors?" I asked, not looking up from the dead dog.

"Yeah, y'know, they're called, uh… psychiatrists." Grampa looked pretty proud of himself for remembering that one. "They talk to you; give you medicines to fix whatever's wrong in your brain. I ain't never knowed nobody who needed to see one, but maybe it'd help your brother."

"Nothing can fix Jonathan."

"Aw, don't say that. Whyn't you ask him 'bout it, see what he thinks? If he could talk more, I bet he could get him a job somewhere in town, go to college, somethin' like that. Don't you think he'd do good in college, all that readin' he does?"

"He wouldn't go unless I could come, too. Besides, he's terrible in school." Ever since the preacher put him in the hospital, Jonathan's grades had been slipping; after the fire, he stopped turning in assignments, refused to answer when called on, hid in the bathroom during lunch and frequently skipped school all together, insisting he was sick. Now that we lived with our grandparents, he wasn't allowed to stay home unless he actually had a fever, but he still refused to put any effort into his schooling.

"That's the thing, I think he sorta… he depends on you a little too much. You don't gotta spend your whole life takin' care of him, and he can cook and clean and all, I'm sure he can learn to live on his own."

"I'll ask him," I said, but I never did. He would have said no anyway, and regardless, I liked taking care of Jonathan- for the most part. I also truly believed it was impossible to fix him. I could imagine him pretending to be normal, but everyone would have seen right through it. There was no point.

"Would you ever want to move out, honey?" Granny had sat Jonathan down at the kitchen table, sent Grampa out to the taxidermy shop and let me stay in the room only with great reluctance and because Jonathan wouldn't sit still without me there. He shook his head at the question, tightening his grip on my hand.

"You promised you wouldn't make him leave," I said coldly.

"No, no, I don't want him to leave! Actually, it's really the opposite- I wanna file for guardianship. I been lookin' into it, and I cain't adopt you, Chastity, 'cause we don't really know where your mama's run off to, but Jonathan, you're a legal adult. Your mama doesn't have a say in your life anymore, and I just think- I think it might be better for you, in the long run, if you have someone to… help you make hard choices. Medical choices and things like that."

"What exactly would you do?" I asked, rubbing Jonathan's hand with my thumb.

"Just what I'm doin' now, basically. Provide food, shelter, all that kinda thing, and if you need help makin' really difficult choices in the future, I can do that. *And,* if y'all's mama- or daddy, I guess- came back, they wouldn't be allowed to talk to you."

"That sounds good," I said, and Granny chuckled.

"It's up to Jonathan, sweetheart, but I'm glad you approve. Jonathan? What do you think?" My brother blinked, crossed and uncrossed his legs, looked to me for help, and finally nodded slowly. "Perfect," Granny sighed. "I'm'onna make sure you're safe, I promise."

126

FOURTEEN

I was fourteen when I started visiting the graveyard. It was a historic little cemetery just down the road from our grandparents' house, no longer maintained- the new cemetery, where Priscilla was buried, was on the other side of town- and I went in the middle of the night, sneaking out the window while Jonathan slept. Granny kept offering to buy us separate beds, saying we could still share a room if we wanted, but we both firmly refused.

Jonathan had always slept soundly, so it was easy to just slip out of bed, slowly pry the window open, and hop into the garden. Our grandparents' house was only one story, just like Priscilla's. As far as I knew, Beatrice and Father William had divorced two years after her death, and Beatrice went back to Gatlinburg with Apple. Father William moved to Louisiana.

Adabelle was such a safe town no one ever locked their doors- I knew the Forge family hadn't- and I felt totally comfortable walking around at night. Jonathan would have freaked out if he knew I was doing it, but since he was responsible for the only murders committed in Adabelle for 50 years, I didn't think his opinion counted for much. Aside from my brother and I, Adabelle was safe, at least in terms of homicide rates.

My favorite grave was towards the back of the cemetery. It was a young woman's headstone, someone named Mary Laura Nichols who died at age 20 in 1903, and I liked it purely because of the little poem engraved under her name and dates.

Remember me as you pass by
As you are now, so once was I
As I am now, so you must be
Prepare thyself to follow me

I imagined Mary as a clever, sharp-tongued woman. In my mind, she died of something like consumption, some old-fashioned and suitably romantic wasting disease, and I pictured her facing death head-on, proud and noble in her sickbed. The cemetery was so overgrown there were no paths left, but I remembered the way to her grave, I'd cleared out a little spot in front of it to sit and rest. Sometimes I talked to Priscilla there.

I was talking to Priscilla the night I ran into Lily Faith Albrecht, telling her about the latest problem with Jonathan-he was suddenly taking Snowball's dislike of him personally and crying when he couldn't force the cat to like him. "I'm trying to make him understand you can't *make* an animal like you; he's just scaring the poor th-"

"Who's there?" Lily Faith called suddenly, making me jump. I recognized her voice, but it was so unexpected in the graveyard I took a minute to place it.

"Chastity Caldwell," I answered after an awkward silence that must have been pretty eerie for her.

"*Chastity?* What're you doin' out here so late?" She sounded personally offended, like she thought she owned the cemetery.

"What are *you* doing out here?"

"Just walkin'." Lily Faith picked her way through the brambles surrounding Mary's grave and sat uncomfortably across from me. "I ain't never seen nobody else out here before."

"I come here a lot. This is my favorite grave, look at the poem." She shined her flashlight on the headstone, smiled faintly once she'd read it.

"That's real nice," she murmured appreciatively.

"What on Earth made you want to come here?" Lily Faith was the most popular girl in the freshman class, already on the cheerleading team, bright and blonde and bubbly.

"Had to be alone."

"In the middle of the night?"

"Why's it matter?"

"I just didn't expect to see you out here."

"It's nice, that's all. Don't it feel- I dunno- peaceful?"

"Yeah," I said softly, surprised to hear Lily Faith Albrecht, of all people, giving voice to something I'd always thought. "The air's different."

"Full of ghosts," she laughed. "Your weirdo brother ain't here, is he?"

"He's asleep."

"Good. Is he still livin' with you? In y'all's grandparents' house?"

"Yeah."

"Ain't he, like, twenty-somethin'?"

"Twenty-four. Yes."

"He got him a job?"

"He does all the cleaning, now, and most of the cooking, but he can't really… he's scared to leave the house, and he can't talk to anyone but me."

"So, he's still crazy."

"Jonathan's not crazy," I lied.

"Sounds crazy to me."

"It's none of your business."

"Alright, alright, damn." Lily Faith adjusted her legs, cleared her throat. "Did you ever find out what happened to your mama?"

"No."

"I'm sor-"

"Don't." I was too surprised by her presence to lie, and I thought, curled up in the dark by Mary's grave, I could be at least a little honest. "I hated her."

"I hate my parents, too," Lily Faith offered quietly after a brief pause. "Y'know my daddy, right? He's a cop."

"Yes."

"Yeah, well, he's a bastard. And my mama don't care none, just so long as he's beatin' on me 'stead of her."

"I'm sorry," I told her. She just nodded, and we sat in silence after that, listening to the wind rustle through the trees.

"You'll never guess who started being nice to me," I told Jonathan, watching him pet the taxidermized cat he'd become fixated on after Snowball bit him the other day.

"Who?"

"Lily Faith Albrecht." Jonathan shuddered at the name *Albrecht,* scowled at me.

"The cop's daughter?"

"She's… better than I always thought. He beats her, you know. I think he probably does worse-"

"Don't you *ever* go to her house." For the first time in years, Jonathan sounded stern, authoritative, and even he looked a little startled at himself.

"I'm not fucking stupid, Jonathan, I have absolutely no intention of going over there. It's not like we're friends, she's just nicer than she was when we were kids."

"Can't you be friends with *anyone* else?"

"Worry about yourself before telling me how to live my life," I said coldly. Jonathan fell silent, resumed stroking the cat, cooing softly to it after a few minutes. I sat back in Granny's overstuffed floral armchair and watched him, taking in how feminine he still looked, his delicate little hands methodically petting the dead cat, his porcelain skin, jet-black hair, and soft red lips making him look like a fae creature in the dim evening light.

"Snow White," I said softly. Jonathan either ignored or didn't hear me.

It was a stretch to say Lily Faith and I were friends at school- she wasn't cruel anymore, but she almost never spoke to me. At most, she waved in acknowledgement or asked what I was reading. When we met at Mary's grave, though, we sat in a much more companionable silence, only occasionally breaking it to start short, quiet conversations.

"You know how my grandfather's a taxidermist?"

"Yeah."

"Well, he stuffs all of Granny's cats after they die. She'll only have one *living* cat at a time, but there's a ton of dead ones around the house. The current living cat is Snowball, and Jonathan scared him a while back- he was freaking out and hugged him way too tight, so the cat hates him now."

"Does he need, like, therapy?"

"He's fine. Anyway, he's been petting one of the stuffed cats and acting like it's still alive. It's in our room now, on the bedside table."

"That don't sound fine."

"Maybe he's a little crazy, but he's not hurting anyone." *Anymore.*

I don't know if it was the lingering effects of childhood malnutrition or just genetics, but I didn't start menstruating until I was almost fifteen. It was sweltering hot in Grampa's taxidermy shop, and the familiar smell of blood was starting to make me sick, so I stepped outside for a second. It wasn't much better in the Georgia heat, but I could at least breathe through my nose without wanting to vomit. When I noticed the wetness between my legs, I stiffened up, surprised- I'd started to notice a not-unpleasant damp feeling when I watched Lily Faith in her cheerleader outfit at our pathetic high school football games, but I was the furthest thing from aroused in that moment.

"I'll be back," I called to Grampa, who responded with a distracted grunt, elbow-deep in a deer carcass. Jonathan and Granny were in the living room, embroidering in silence across from each other, and I hurried awkwardly past them into the bathroom, slamming the door behind me. I inhaled sharply when I saw the blood, carefully touched myself to confirm where it was coming from. Jonathan had bled from his genitals after his bladder ruptured, and now that I was thinking about it, there *was* a faint, dull pain in my abdomen.

"Jonathan, come here," I called, poking my head out the bathroom door. My brother trotted over like a loyal dog.

"What's wrong?" he asked, not caring that I was naked from the waist down- until he noticed the blood smeared between my thighs and froze, opened his rosebud mouth to speak, closed it again.

"I'm bleeding," I told him, as if he hadn't noticed. "I think my bla-"

"I'll *kill* him," Jonathan said hoarsely, reaching for the doorknob. Too late, I realized how it must have looked to him, how vividly he remembered bleeding after Mama's boyfriends left, how he still believed Grampa wanted to hurt us.

"No! No, Jonathan, he didn't touch me, this is something else- it's like when your bladder ruptured, I think, if your appendix can just explode then maybe-"

"*Don't lie to me!* All that time alone with him, is this the first time? Has he done it before? I'll kill him, I'll fucking *kill him!*" I grabbed Jonathan before he could open the door, tightened my grip on his narrow waist as he screamed like a wounded animal, struggling uselessly- he never ate much, remained small and frail all our lives, and I'd gained muscle helping Grampa in the taxidermy shop, lifting weights in the school gym. I worked out with the intention of protecting Jonathan, not restraining him, but I didn't mind doing both. My pants were still around my ankles, so I stepped out of them and planted my feet more firmly.

"Listen to me! It's not him, something's wrong with my bladder or my stomach or something, I need to go to the hospital-!"

"*I'll kill him!*"

"What the hell are y'all doin' in here?" Granny threw the door open, and I squeezed Jonathan warningly, worried he'd lash out at her- he was already clawing violently at my arms.

"I'm sick," I yelled over Jonathan's wordless screaming. "I'm bleeding." Granny just stared at us, watching in mute horror as I wrestled Jonathan to the ground and shoved my knee in his stomach. We must have looked insane, fighting in the bathroom with me half-naked, but she just forced herself to smile.

"Looks like you're on your period," she said awkwardly.

"What?"

"Well, you… you're bleedin' down there." We were both yelling to be heard, so I elbowed Jonathan sharply in the ribs, making him gasp for breath and, for at least a minute, stop shrieking.

"Yeah, I think my bladder ruptured. That happened to Jonathan one time."

"Huh? No, sweetheart, it's totally normal. I thought your mama must've told you- is he alright? What happened?"

"He thinks someone hurt me." Granny's eyes widened in understanding, and she gingerly knelt next to Jonathan's head, stroked his sweaty hair back. We never told her anything explicitly, but she'd read between the lines, clearly knew or suspected what had happened to my brother.

"Jonathan, sweetie, didn't anyone ever tell you? Women bleed like that once a month. Our bodies store up blood in the womb to feed a baby if we get pregnant, and it all has to come out if we don't. That's all, nobody touched her. Your mama really never told you?"

"No," I said, feeling like a moron.

"Well, it's nothin' to worry about," Granny said softly. She kept petting Jonathan until his breathing evened out. I got up cautiously, helped him stand before redressing. "I'll buy you some pads tonight, okay, sweetheart? D'you mind wearing one of your brother's diapers in the meantime?"

"Sure. How long does it last?"

"A few days, maybe a week."

"Every *month*?"

"Yeah," Granny laughed nervously. "We got the short end of the stick, huh? You're lucky you don't have to deal with this, Jonathan."

Sex education was not taught in Briar County. There had been a brief period in 1995 when a science teacher pushed for it to be added to the middle school curriculum, but it didn't even get past the school board. Parents didn't want their children learning about *that* from teachers, teachers who probably had some kind of political agenda they wanted to force down our throats, and besides, what sort of pervert cared if kids learned about sex anyway?

And what *kind* of sex? Were they going to teach us about sexual perversions, fetishes, and homosexuality like those big city schools? Sex was between married, opposite-sex couples, no one else. Teaching teens about condoms would only encourage them to have sex outside of marriage. They were pushing sexual matters on innocent children; they were *forcing* us to learn things we shouldn't. Even when the proposed course was dialed back to a frank explanation of how puberty changed the body, parents were opposed; that was for them to teach their children when the time was right.

The offending teacher was branded a groomer and promptly fired, and there was no further suggestion of sex education in Briar County. Teaching children about sex was essentially mental rape, robbing us of our innocence at a young age, and only a pedophile would want little girls understanding menstruation before they were ready. It was up to parents to decide what their children knew and when, not teachers. Sex education was just child grooming, malicious left-wing indoctrination.

Jonathan's understanding of sex was very simple- he believed sex and rape were the same thing, a man holding you down and violently penetrating you. He was vaguely aware that vaginal intercourse was how women got pregnant, and assumed all pregnancy was the result of rape. All my life, he'd done his best to instill in me what he considered a healthy fear of sex, emphasizing that I, unlike him, could get pregnant.

Pregnancy would be nine months of increasing violation, a parasite living inside my body, feeding off of me until I give birth, which would, Jonathan assured me, be agonizingly painful. We weren't entirely sure how an entire baby could fit through the vagina, but I had the idea that it would probably break your pelvis. By Jonathan's logic, all mothers hated their children for putting them through such pain, for reminding them of the violent rape they'd endured every time they laid eyes on us.

I can't overstate how horrified Jonathan was when he started going through puberty. Mama had always made it clear her boyfriends were only interested in children, so Jonathan shaved every inch of his body, pitched his voice higher, and ate even less than usual in the hope he wouldn't get any taller. If Jonathan grew up, Mama's boyfriends would lose interest in him and move on to me. We'd both seen their eyes on me already.

Jonathan completely panicked when he started having erections, dealt with it by taking ice-cold showers and pinching himself with his fingernails until he drew blood. He was so convinced something was wrong with him that he actually went to the school nurse about it, but she just snapped at him for asking her vulgar questions, told him she could lose her job for discussing anything like that with a student. Mama's boyfriends mocked him, forced him to ejaculate during their encounters and took photographs to prove he enjoyed it. For my brother, sexuality was inextricably linked with pain and humiliation, and no one ever corrected that belief.

I believed everything Jonathan told me about sex until we moved in with our grandparents. At first, I was as wary of Grampa as Jonathan was, convinced he'd raped Granny and wanted to do the same to us, but I pretended to trust him. I was certain they'd get rid of us if we both acted like frightened feral dogs, so I had to be the stable one, I had to make them believe Jonathan was harmlessly insane and I was an essentially normal child, we were no trouble at all.

The first time Grampa invited me into his taxidermy shop, I assumed he was going to rape me. I'd spent my life believing rape was both natural and inevitable, and had in fact been surprised Grampa waited so long to get one of us alone. I didn't tell Jonathan we were going out into the taxidermy shop- he'd paid the rent with Mama's boyfriends, so it was only fair I take my turn with our grandfather.

When all Grampa did was proudly show off his latest creation, I didn't know how to react. He held up the stuffed raccoon with a wide, mostly toothless smile, and I just stood there stupidly, waiting for the other shoe to drop. Finally, I cautiously reached out to touch the raccoon. "Where'd you find it?"

"In the road, poor thing. He was squashed purty flat, but I salvaged what I could and sorta pieced together the rest- this in the middle here's actually from another raccoon I skinned a while back. I ain't named him yet, though. Got any ideas?" I just blinked. "He looks like a Harold, don't he?"

"Uh- sure."

"Harold, then."

The other shoe never dropped. Within a week, I felt pretty confident Grampa didn't want to hurt me, and with-in a month I was certain he'd never hurt Granny, either. Jonathan couldn't be convinced, but I slowly developed a tentative affection for our grandparents that blossomed into some kind of love by the time I reached high school. While Jonathan quickly grew to adore Granny, he always hated Grampa, and he never actually spoke to our grandmother beyond a few muttered words here and there.

"I don't think you should read this," the librarian said, frowning at the copy of *It's Perfectly Normal* that Jonathan was trying to check out. He just blinked at her, glanced over to me for help; although we'd been coming to the library for years, he'd always had trouble speaking to people other than me, had loved the library mainly because no one required him to talk. Once he graduated high school (and refused to walk across the stage, petrified of having so many eyes on him), Jonathan pretty much stopped leaving our grandparents' property. He went outside to mow the lawn, weed the garden, finish any other tasks Granny needed done, but the only other place he really went was the library- and only if I accompanied him.

"He can read whatever he wants," I said shortly.

"This isn't appropriate," she insisted. Mrs. Springs had been a librarian all my life, and had lately been having issues with Margaret, a younger librarian who kept ordering "offensive" books.

"I want him to read it." I'd asked Margaret if they had any books about puberty, and she proudly directed me to *It's Perfectly Normal,* exclaiming that she'd fought Mrs. Springs tooth and nail to add it to the collection. Unfortunately, she was nowhere to be found when we tried to check out.

"Jonathan, sweetie, wouldn't you rather read something nice? You were reading *Little Women* a few days ago, do you want to read something else by Louisa May Alcott?" She spoke slowly, and Jonathan ducked his head to avoid her intense eye contact.

"He turned twenty-five last week, he can read whatever he wants," I snapped, shoving the book at her. "Just scan it."

"I'm not comfortable letting either of you read this," Mrs. Springs sniffed.

"I'll have Margaret check it out if you won't. It's important."

"What could possibly be so important in here?"

"I want to know more about periods."

"Don't say that so loud! If you have any questions, you can ask your grandparents."

"Give us the fucking book!"

"Chastity!" Mrs. Springs looked stunned, and an old woman I recognized from Father William's church turned to stare at us. Jonathan stepped closer to me, grabbed my hand. "What's gotten into you?"

"I just want to check out a book," I gritted out. "You're a librarian. Give me the book."

"Jonathan isn't mature enough to read this," Mrs. Springs said firmly.

I slapped Jonathan across the face when we got back to our bedroom, making him yelp and stumble backwards, staring at me with wide, hurt eyes. "Why'd you do that?" he demanded, tearing up.

"What the hell do you mean, *why'd I do that?* The librarian won't let us check out a book for fucking middle-schoolers because you've made her think you're a goddamn retard! Have you ever even spoken to her?"

"When I was younger," Jonathan said quietly, rubbing his cheek.

"Oh, but now that you've got me to talk *for* you-"

"Why are you being so mean? I didn't do anything wrong!"

"Everyone in town thinks you're insane! You're a grown-ass man, Jonathan, you can't keep hiding behind my skirts all the time!" I wasn't sure why my anger had flared up so suddenly, but it died down the second Jonathan started weeping, bringing his hands up to cover his face. "No- no, don't cry, come on…"

"You're *mean*," he sobbed, and I pulled him into a hug, sighing as he hid his face in my shoulder.

"I'm sorry," I said, gruff and reluctantly. "I just wanted us to learn more about puberty and all that stuff. It's the librarian's fault, not yours, okay? We'll talk to Margaret next time, she'll let us check it out. Come on, Jonathan, I'm not mean. I take good care of you, don't I?"

FIFTEEN

"Mrs. Springs is a cunt."

"Who?" Lily Faith asked, pulling up blades of grass. We were leaning against Mary's headstone together, and I tried to ignore how fast my heart beat every time her arm brushed up against mine.

"The old-ass librarian. She thinks Jonathan's crazy."

"Well, he is."

"He's not *that* crazy. She wouldn't let us check out a sex education book, said he's *not mature enough* to read it." I put on a mocking, high-pitched voice, and Lily Faith giggled. I blushed, quietly proud to have made her laugh.

"Don't he know already? I mean, Lord almighty, he is *gorgeous*."

"Not exactly," I said quietly. "He didn't understand what was happening when I got my period. I mean, I didn't know either, that's why I wanted the book."

"My mama explained when I got mine. Said it was God's way of punishin' women, that and childbirth- y'know, 'cause Eve et the apple. Original sin and all that."

"I'm pretty sure that's wrong."

"Well, Jonathan ain't mature enough to get that book checked out, so I guess we'll never know," she joked. "Hey, y'oughta try out for cheer this fall."

"*What?*"

"Cheer. Cheerleading."

"I heard you," I said, suddenly feeling dizzy. "I'm just a little confused. I don't think I'm really- I mean, I don't *look* like a cheerleader."

"You would if you fixed your hair." Lily Faith brushed a lock of hair behind my ear, letting her hand linger for a second. "And shaved your legs, but you could always wear leggings if you don't wanna. You're real strong, you'd be good on the bottom of the pyramid. We need strong girls, 'cause we don't got no boys."

"Uh- I'm not sure. I'd have to go to practice, wouldn't I?"

"Yeah, but it ain't too long, and it's fun."

"Maybe I'll give it a shot-"

"I'll teach you! If you can do a backflip, they'll let you on. Whyn't I come on over to your house tomorra, and we can practice in the yard?"

"Sure," I said, swallowing hard. "My grandparents are super friendly, just so you know."

"That's fine. That's good!"

Lily Faith showed up around noon, wearing hot pink, coordinated workout clothes. Granny greeted her at the door with a pitcher of sweet tea, grinning so wide her cheeks must have hurt.

"Oh, sweetheart, it is *so* good to meet you! Chastity's so focused on school, she ain't never brought home no friends before- are you real, uh, academic like that?"

"Yes'm," Lily Faith lied smoothly. I was fairly confident she'd never done homework a day in her life. "Y'all got a lovely home."

"*Thank* you! So, you're a cheerleader?"

"Yes'm."

"How fun! Chastity's real strong, I bet she'll be great at all the flippin' and floppin' you girls do. I never was very athletic myself, but Arnie actually ran track in high school. And how's your parents doin'?"

"Oh, um, good," Lily Faith said, stiffening up.

"Great!"

"Perfect!" Lily Faith clapped dramatically, and I gave her a weak thumbs-up, sprawled on the ground. I'd finally managed to land a backflip, but it tired me out so much I just threw myself down to rest in the grass. "Just keep practicin' that, we'll have you on the squad in no time at all!"

"Can't wait."

"You'll love it." She joined me on the ground, poked my side playfully. "You'll look *good* in the uniform."

"Will I, now?"

"Yeah." A slight blush rose on her cheeks. "I just mean, y'know, 'cause you're real pretty. Not, like, in a weird way or nothin'."

"You're pretty, too," I mumbled. I knew I was good-looking, strikingly androgynous; if you saw Jonathan and I together, you'd think I was the boy. My haircut was still deliberately unflattering, but I had my brother's pretty features, high cheekbones, and big blue eyes.

"Well- thanks." Lily Faith cleared her throat. "You seen that new movie? The one with the guy? That one guy, y'know?"

"I don't watch movies."

"You're so fuckin' weird," she said fondly.

"Who was that?" Jonathan demanded later that night. He was sitting up in bed, holding the taxidermized cat on his lap and stroking her fur, scowling.

"You know that thing's dead, right?"

"Citrus is *not* dead," Jonathan said, his voice rising slightly. "She's sleeping. You're just jealous she likes me more than you."

"Alright," I said, deciding to pick my battles. I was never sure if he genuinely believed the cat was still alive, or if he was simply in denial and desperate for a pet's affection. "Sorry, Citrus."

"Who was that girl you had over?"

"A friend."

"You don't have friends." There was a dangerous note creeping into Jonathan's voice, and I remembered dancing with Priscilla in her parents' living room, singing along to Queen at the top of our lungs.

"I don't even care about her," I said, too quickly. "Come on, you know you're my favorite person in the world."

"Why was she here, then?"

"She wants me to join the cheerleading squad. They need strong girls for the pyramid-"

"Absolutely not," Jonathan snapped. "No way in hell are you going to put on a skimpy little costume and throw yourself around in front of a bunch of teachers and football players- you're not a fucking whore."

"It's just gymnastics with pom-poms."

"You might as well drop out and become a stripper! They'll just take it as an invitation to-"

"Jonathan, please, calm down. Let's be rational, okay? It's not an invitation for anything, it's a practical outfit for gymnastics."

"It's dangerous."

"So, do you want me to spend my whole life hiding inside with you, then? I can't do anything fun?"

"You can have fun without putting yourself in danger! Please, Chastity, *please,* you can't dress like that." Jonathan's voice broke, and I sighed, wiped the tears from his face.

"It would mean a lot to Lily Faith if I-"

"The cop's daughter? You invited *her* over? Did he give her a ride? Does he know where we live?"

"He already knew, Jonathan, he's a cop. He can just find out."

"What if he comes over with her?"

"Shh. Just lie back, you're hyperventilating. It's okay, baby, you're alright. You're alright."

"I don't want you around her," Jonathan sobbed, clinging desperately to my arm.

"Breathe, baby."

"She's not safe-"

"Breathe-"

"-not safe-"

"Can I wear the male uniform?" I asked Lily Faith, tracing the poem etched into Mary's headstone. "If I make the cheer team, I mean?"

"I guess," she shrugged. "You'd look cute in that, too."

"Thanks. Jonathan doesn't want me wearing a skimpy outfit."

"That's weird."

"He's scared for me; he doesn't trust men."

"Why not?"

I froze, dug my fingernail into a crack in the headstone. *Why not? Ask your daddy, Lily Faith Albrecht. Ask your preacher. Ask the social worker and the school nurse and his teachers, ask anybody who knew but didn't give a damn.* "He was molested when he was a kid," I finally said, slow and careful. If you'd asked me in the past, I would've said Lily Faith Albrecht was the last person I'd ever confess to, but after our nights in the cemetery she felt like the only person I could trust.

"That's awful," Lily Faith said in a strangled whisper. "Did you- were you-?"

"No. Mama had these boyfriends- well, she called them her boyfriends- men who came and paid her, when Jonathan was little. He never let them touch me, tried to make himself look younger as long as he could, cut my hair and wouldn't let me bathe. I hid out back when they came over. And then our mama left when I was eight, and our grandparents don't know about any of that."

"Oh." Lily Faith sat in silence for a moment, then took my hand. "I- if I tell you- can I tell you somethin'?"

"Anything."

"My daddy," she began, then coughed to cover up a sob, "my daddy, he… When I was younger, 'fore I hit puberty, he used to…"

"I figured."

"How'd you know?"

"Because he was one of my mama's boyfriends."

Lily Faith didn't speak the rest of the night except to mumble "good-bye", and she was distant the next morning at school. When lunch rolled around, though, she stopped me on my way to the library and demanded I eat lunch with her and her friends, a group of pretty, perky, popular cheerleaders. "You'll have to anyway, once you're on the team," she said, a dim sort of light returning to her eyes.

Missy, Peggy Lee, and Savannah were all nicer than I'd anticipated, certainly nicer than they'd been in elementary school. Peggy Lee clicked her tongue as soon as I sat down, reached over to pet my hair without asking, and sighed, "You got the purtiest hair I ever seen! So thick- you *got* to get this cut right."

"The way you dress, a man's cut would look better," Savannah said, eyeing me up and down. "Whyn't you go to the barber 'fore try-outs?"

"Sure," I agreed, slowly pushing Peggy Lee's hand away from my hair.

"Chastity can do a backflip," Lily Faith said proudly. "*I* taught her that."

"And you can pick us up, right? You look strong."

"Probably. I can pick my brother up." That was true- Jonathan had started staying up late with Granny, both of them bent over their embroidery until one or the other inevitably fell asleep. If Granny fell asleep first, Grampa laughed quietly, gently shook her shoulder until she blinked awake, yawning, and mumbled a vague justification before shuffling off to bed, but I never bothered trying to wake Jonathan up. I just lifted him into my arms, with some effort, brought him back to our room and changed him into a diaper, tucked him into bed like he was my child.

"Your brother still live in town? I ain't seen him lately," Missy commented, trying and failing to open the entire jar of applesauce she'd inexplicably brought to school.

"No, he goes to the library, I seen both of y'all there," Savannah answered for me. I hadn't noticed her, but I nodded anyway.

"He lives with my grandparents and I."

"That's nice they let him stay. My parents is always sayin' they's gonna throw me out on my ass the second I turn eighteen," Peggy Lee giggled, her hand drifting back to my hair.

"Only 'cause you're trouble," Lily Faith teased her.

"You got a haircut," Jonathan said as soon as I came home. He hadn't cut his hair in years; it reached his waist, and Granny liked to braid it for him, exclaiming that we both had such nice, thick hair. Sometimes he sat by the window and brushed it, looking like a princess in a tower, Snow White staring out the window of her stepmother's castle.

"Yeah. Lily Faith thought I'd look better for cheer if I-"

"I told you not to try out for that."

"*You* don't tell me what to do," I sneered. "Get back to me when you can go to the library on your own, baby brother."

"I'm still older than you," Jonathan protested, voice shaking. "I know what's best for us."

"The hell you do."

"I just want to protect you," he whined, reaching to pet Citrus. It was becoming an instinctive, obsessive habit; I worried the dead cat's fur would fall out.

"Well, I'll be wearing the boy's uniform, does that make you feel better? You're worried about the uniform, right? I'll be wearing pants and a t-shirt, total coverage. Lily Faith's friends all think I'm basically a boy."

"Don't you have to practice all the time? I'll miss you. And all you ever do when you're home is hang out with Grampa, you don't even care about me anymore!"

"I realize *you* don't have a life outside of embroidering and following me around, but I'm not centering my whole life around your bullshit," I snapped. "Why can't you just be happy I made friends?"

"Because I need you *here!* Why the fuck would you want to be friends with those shallow little sluts anyway?"

"They are *not-*"

"They're throwing themselves in front of a bunch of men, in their little micro miniskirts and- and crop tops," Jonathan snapped. "They're just a bunch of whores. I don't want you around-"

"Well, you'd know all about being a whore," I said coldly. Jonathan fell silent, staring at me with his pretty red lips parted slightly.

"It's different," he said weakly, pulling Citrus onto his lap. "They all *decided* to-"

"Oh, but you used to beg Mama to invite her boyfriends over."

"Because we were hungry, we needed money-"

"They made you cum," I spat, and Jonathan shrank back, hugging Citrus gently to his chest. "You told me, they jerked you off until you cried, they took photos- you little *slut*. Don't act like you're any better than them when all you'll ever be is a cheap fucking whore."

"You're mean," Jonathan whispered. He was starting to cry, but I couldn't bring myself to care.

"And what are you gonna do about it? Kill them? You gonna kill Lily Faith like you killed Priscilla? You're a murderer and a prostitute and a crybaby bitch, and that's all you'll *ever* be."

"Go away!" Jonathan suddenly shrieked, throwing a pillow at me. "Go *away! I* hate you! *I hate you!*"

"Fucking *fine!*"

I stayed in Grampa's taxidermy shop all day, carefully preserving a dead possum I'd found in the yard and thinking over everything my brother had said. He was right that I didn't really need friends, although not for the reasons he thought- as pretty as Lily Faith was, as much as I liked making her laugh, I couldn't have honestly said I was in love with her. The only people I'd ever loved were Jonathan and Priscilla- I had no understanding of romantic love.

I don't believe I was ever capable of loving anyone but Jonathan after Priscilla died. I loved my grandparents to the best of my ability, but even that was based more out of appreciation for how they'd helped us than anything else. I wanted to fuck Lily Faith, but I couldn't see myself marrying her, not least because same-sex marriage was still illegal in Georgia. I was neutral to her friends at best, mildly annoyed by them at worst. I wanted to join the cheerleading team purely because I had a childish crush on Lily Faith and wanted to be near her, wanted to see her prance around in a skimpy little outfit, that was all.

And I'd made my brother cry, upset him so much he actually yelled at me. I rarely felt guilty, but a deep, shocking shame washed over me that day. I'd never said anything like that to Jonathan before, would never have dreamed of it- why in the world had I gotten so angry? I didn't like Lily Faith *that* much. At the time, I chalked it up to simple frustration, but looking back I think I always went on the defensive when Jonathan mentioned my friends, I always remembered Priscilla with her whole life ahead of her and saw red.

Jonathan was quiet as we got ready for bed that night, made a point of pulling away when I tried to hug him. "Hey," I said quietly, squeezing his arm, "I'm sorry. I shouldn't have said any of that. You know I didn't mean it, don't you?"

"Sounded like you meant it," Jonathan muttered into his pillow.

"Well, I didn't. I was just mad; I didn't understand why you cared so much."

"You'll get hurt."

"I know. I know, baby. Listen, I'll tell Lily Faith I can't do it, okay? I won't do it."

"Really?" Jonathan rolled over to face me, and I could hear the smile in his voice.

"I promise. We'll spend more time together, too, how does that sound?"

"Perfect."

SIXTEEN

"I can't try out," I told Lily Faith at Mary's grave. If her face fell in the dark, I didn't see it.

"Jonathan convince you not to?" She spoke with forced casualness, projecting a calm, cool air.

"Yeah. It's really important to him, and he's my brother, so…"

"So? I don't get that, *he's my brother*. Y'know how, with science and shit, you're s'posed to question ever' little thing, figure out *why* things are the way they are- whyn't folks do the same with fam'ly? All I ever hear is *'cause I'm your daddy, 'cause I'm your mama, 'cause they're your fam'ly.* 'I'm doin' it for 'em cause they're fam'ly.' What's that *mean?*"

"Well- I- he *is* family," I said, awkward and unsure.

"Again, *so?* That ain't no kinda answer. Same as sayin' *'cause I said so* or *'cause it's just like that.* Don't tell me nothin'. What's he done to make you love him? You're related by accident. He don't deserve your love just 'cause y'all happen to be related." I could tell she wasn't really talking to me anymore, so I sat still and let her rant. "Ever'body's always sayin' I gotta love my mama. 'She gave birth to you'- who cares? That don't mean nothin' to me. Just 'cause she gave birth to me, I'm in her debt forever? I owe her love 'cause she *chose* to have me? The bitch makes it sound like I decided to be borned, like I made her do it!

"And speakin' of, she's always sayin' she loves me 'cause I'm her daughter. I *hate* that. She wouldn't give a damn 'bout me if we weren't related, that ain't real love. She loves her daughter, she don't love *me*. Fam'ly, fam'ly, fam'ly, all I ever hear's *fam'ly!* The hell has fam'ly ever done for me? Let 'em all rot in hell, all the good they ever did me!" Lily Faith stopped panting, and I rubbed her knee awkwardly.

"Jonathan's been good to me," I said softly.

"Good. Yeah, good. Sorry," she muttered. "I'm just- I'm tired. Look what my daddy done last week." Lily Faith turned away from me, took her shirt off, and in the moonlight streaming through the trees I saw thick, deep gashes across her back. They mixed with the twisting shadows cast by tree branches, seemed to dance over her skin, and I almost touched them before remembering myself.

"He's awful."

"I hate his guts," Lily Faith hissed. "*That's* what I mean. All these folks goin' on and on about fam'ly, they don't know. They think ever'body got fairytale fuckin' lives. Fam'ly," she muttered disdainfully. "Fam'ly ain't worth a shit."

"Would you want Missy to be your sister?"

"I think I'd hate her if she was," Lily Faith giggled. She hated everyone she was related to on principle. "But, I dunno, maybe a sister's different. Jonathan's basically a sister, d'you like havin' him around?"

"For the most part. I think it's better, having siblings. Spreads your parents out a little thinner. I mean, Mama pretty much hated him, but she beat me, too. Took the focus off each of us a little."

"I'm an only child. My mama says I was a difficult birth and a difficult girl."

"You always seemed spoiled when we were kids," I teased, and Lily Faith giggled again. Her laughter echoed off the headstones, alien in the abandoned cemetery.

"Oh, I was. If I wanted it and he could afford it, my daddy bought it for me. Ever' time he come into my room at night, next day he had some new toy for me. Did he bring Jonathan toys?"

"No."

"I think damn near ever'body in my fam'ly knew," Lily Faith said thoughtfully. "Nobody said shit, though. Nobody wanted to tell anyone how to raise their kids. I had this cousin, I forget her name, but we all knew her mama beat her. That woman had a temper hotter'n hell, and we saw how she yelled at her, shook her around, we saw the bruises. I asked my mama 'bout it one time, and she told me it wadn't none of my business how Aunt Arlene raised her kid. Told me the kid was a little bitch anyway, it was just discipline. My cousin ended up killin' herself just to get away, twelve years old and shot herself in the head."

"My God."

"Aunt Arlene still hates her. Always goin' on and on about how selfish she was, how she just devastated ever'one who loved her. Says she ain't never recovered- bullshit. Didn't nobody love that child."

I didn't try out for the cheerleading team, but I started going to more football games just to watch Lily Faith. We began meeting at the cemetery almost every night, talking more and more, and while I still didn't love her, warm lust built up deep within me all throughout our conversations.

"Guess what *I* saw last week," Lily Faith giggled. I wondered if she noticed her hand was on my thigh.

"Your raccoon?" She'd been seeing a raccoon wandering through her neighborhood at night lately and had made it her goal in life to befriend and, eventually, domesticate the creature.

"No, but I'm gettin' close, he'll be eatin' outta my hand soon. Missy and I took ourselves on down to the theater, they was showin' this movie come out last year called *28 Days Later.* We get there and right away the ticket taker says he cain't let us in, so I give him a twenty and he looks the other way. It's a zombie movie, it's real good. There's this gorgeous woman-" She cut herself off, coughed awkwardly. "I mean, there's other stuff, too. Zombies. Got a guy full naked at the beginning."

"You remember the pretty woman, though?"

"I guess. Yeah. I mean, she was just real strong, she had a machete. Cool to see women runnin' around with machetes, y'know? I'd like a machete. Where d'you get a machete?"

"Not sure. I bet you'd look good with a machete. If you had one. I think it'd look really good."

"I'd like one," Lily Faith repeated, awkward and halting.

After crawling back through our bedroom window and slipping into bed, I couldn't get Lily Faith out of my mind. She was beautiful, funny, and smarter than I'd given her credit for before- certainly not a genius, but clever, in her own way. I knew it was mostly her looks I was attracted to, though, and as Jonathan unconsciously cuddled closer to me, I imagined Lily Faith behind glass like my Barbie doll, eyes open and unblinking, pinned carefully to soft, velvety fabric.

If she were to die tomorrow, would I care? Maybe, if she burned to death like Priscilla, or shot herself in the head like her nameless cousin, died so she left behind an ugly corpse, maybe that would upset me. Lately, I'd started to understand Jonathan's obsession with Citrus more, saw the appeal in a dead cat over a living one. Citrus would never get old and cranky, Citrus didn't need her litterbox changed, Citrus couldn't run away if you wanted to pet her.

Priscilla was flawless in my memory, so perfect I surely must have exaggerated her. If she'd lived longer, she would have been just like anyone else, a flawed, fallible human, but now she was a ghost under my control, better than any living friend. I had built her up in my mind, forgotten any little arguments we might have had, forgotten anything imperfect about her. I just adored her completely. I didn't want to think about Lily Faith growing old and ugly, but I didn't want to picture her rotting, either.

If I could stuff her like an animal, keep her behind glass in a temperature-controlled room, wouldn't she be perfect? Maybe I couldn't actually fuck her then, but I imagined I'd do it just once, in Grampa's taxidermy shop, slow and gentle on the bloodstained old table. I pulled my nightgown up slowly and slid a hand between my legs, imagining Lily Faith cold and stiff underneath me, beautiful and perfectly preserved behind glass.

I was so caught up in my fantasy I didn't notice Jonathan stirring awake, but when he sleepily mumbled, "Chastity? What're you doing?", I quickly stopped, heart racing.

"Nothing, baby. Go back to sleep."

"You were doing *something*."

"Just scratching my thigh. It's too early to wake up."

"Were you?" Jonathan sat up, rubbing his eyes. "Didn't seem like-"

"Why do you care?"

"I'm just wondering," he said defensively.

"I was touching myself," I admitted, irritated. "Happy?"

"You were- what?" Jonathan looked shocked, and I had to wonder what the hell he *thought* I'd been doing. "That's disgusting, Chastity. You weren't- you *can't* be- you're joking."

"It feels good."

"It doesn't! It hurts, it's too- it's too *much*- it's bad for you, Chastity, don't ever do that again!"

"Jonathan," I said, soft and sweet, patting his shoulder soothingly, "lots and lots of people do it, okay? I was just thinking about- you know, about something that made me… that…"

"That's impossible. Girls don't want sex."

"You're wr-"

"You don't have any idea, Chastity, it *hurts*. And you could get pregnant, you know you can *die* giving birth, it'll ruin your life- it's-"

"It's another girl," I blurted out, and Jonathan froze.

"Huh?"

"It's Lily Faith. I'm not interested in guys."

"I don't- that doesn't- it doesn't work like that," Jonathan said, too confused to continue his hysterics. "You can't have sex with a girl, neither of you wants it. And neither of you has a penis."

"We've talked about how sex and rape aren't the same thing-"

"-they *are!*-"

"-if we both want it, we can figure out a way, alright?"

"No! No, you're wrong, the only people who want sex are men- rapists- you're *sick*," Jonathan yelled, practically falling out of bed in his haste to get away from me.

"Jonathan! Calm down, you'll wake Granny and Grampa up, you're overreacting!" I held my hands up, standing carefully and approaching him like he was a cornered animal, gently tucking his hair behind his ear. "Listen to me, okay? I'm not going to hurt you. No one wants to hurt you."

"You want to hurt Lily Faith."

"No, no, I don't. I think we both want to- do things- together. Can you understand that? It's because we're both girls," I said, thinking quickly, "so it isn't really sex. It's just… being good friends. I wasn't doing anything sexual, I just explained it wrong, I was tired."

Jonathan looked pretty doubtful, but I could see in his soft blue eyes how much he wanted to trust me. After a minute, he relaxed and nodded, allowing me to lead him back to bed. "Sorry for overreacting," he muttered guiltily.

"It's okay, you were scared. I should have explained myself better. Are you going back to sleep?"

"Yeah."

"Do you need to change first?" Jonathan squirmed slightly, avoiding my gaze. After all these years, he still clammed up when his bedwetting problem was mentioned, had outright left the room when Granny gently suggested taking him to see a doctor about it the other day. "Go change and then come back. It's Saturday, we can sleep in as late as you want."

"You know, Missy kissed me one time," Lily Faith said, apropos of nothing. There was no moon that night, so she'd brought her flashlight to the cemetery; I had an easier time navigating the darkness from years of sneaking through Mama's dim, crowded trailer. "At her birthday party last year."

"Did she?" School had just ended, and my own sixteenth birthday wasn't far off. Granny had been making vague implications that there would be some kind of special celebration, "accidentally" leaving issues of *Martha Stewart Living* lying around, open to spreads on cake recipes and party decor.

"Yeah." Lily Faith fidgeted with the hem of her jean jacket. She'd stolen it from Goodwill and embroidered roses all up and down the sleeves, thorny, crimson roses. I'd asked why she'd gone to the trouble of stealing it when her allowance was more than enough to pay for it, when she could afford to buy clothes at Walmart and didn't even need to set foot in Goodwill; she just grinned, stretched her arms out wide and proudly said, *I don't need none of my daddy's money, see? I got this all on my own.*

"Well, did you like it?"

"I guess I did," Lily Faith said cautiously. "She was a little drunk, y'know. Stole some whiskey from her parents- they got themselves a still. She was just playin', though, *she* didn't like it."

"I'd like it."

"What? Kissin' me, you'd like that?"

"Sure," I said, feeling myself blush. "You're really pretty. And, uh, smart."

"Oh, so are you," Lily Faith said eagerly, grabbing my hand. "You look like a boy- I mean, a handsome boy. One of them real pretty boys, like, uh, Gerard Way." Lily Faith had recently become more than a little obsessive about My Chemical Romance, a band her parents considered Satanic. "I like that, girls who look like boys and boys who look like girls. You and your brother are really somethin' else."

"I've never kissed anyone."

"Well, I've only kissed Missy. Clark likes me, but he ain't my type, y'know? Too big."

"The quarterback?"

"Yeah. Besides, my daddy says he's too old for me." Lily Faith laughed bitterly at the irony of that, then leaned in closer, so close I could smell bubblegum on her breath. "You'd be a better boyfriend than him, even if we couldn't tell nobody."

"I bet I would," I agreed. *I could keep you safe forever.*

"You can kiss me, if you want. I'd like that."

I kissed her gently, hesitantly. Neither of us knew what we were doing, so neither of us realized we were doing it terrifically wrong, and we were both giggling like crazy when we pulled away. Lily Faith had soft lips, to which she constantly applied beeswax lip balm in school, and her hands felt soft and dainty in mine.

"That was great!" she exclaimed, but I privately thought she moved too much, it would have been better if she was just- still.

"Happy birthday!"

I gasped in mock surprise when Granny woke me up with a Texas sheet cake, sixteen pink candles stabbed into it. I'd actually hated pink since Priscilla died, but I always wanted pink candles on my birthday cake, always waited a minute before blowing them out. *I wish Priscilla was a mortician, I wish we could be best friends forever, I wish I had a unicorn...*

"You didn't have to do anything," I laughed, wiggling out of Jonathan's grasp to sit up.

"You're like a little koala, aren't you, Jonathan?" Granny asked, scrunching her nose up in fond confusion. She still couldn't understand why we were so close, told me she'd pretty much hated her siblings, but had long ago accepted it.

"Happy birthday," he mumbled, still half-asleep. His hair covered his face like a curtain, so I brushed it back and poked his soft, alabaster cheek, grinning. Jonathan stuck his tongue out at me but joined me in an upright position, wrapped his arms around my waist again and rested his head on my shoulder.

"I brought a lighter," Granny chirped, setting the cake on the edge of our bed to light the candles. "Now, you can blow them out here, but I want y'all to come into the kitchen to eat, okay? I know Jonathan doesn't want Arnie in y'all's room, so he's waitin' on us out there."

"Sixteen!" Lily Faith cheered that night, hugging me.

"Four years younger than Mary, here," I said, deadpan.

"Damn, was that a *joke?* I didn't know you were capable of joking," she teased, flopping down on the grass.

"I have my moments."

"So, how was your birthday?"

"Good. Granny baked a cake and decorated the living room- I would've invited you, but it was supposed to be a surprise."

"And Jonathan didn't want me there."

"Well, yeah, there is that."

"He's a little antisocial, huh?"

"Just a little."

Lily Faith laughed, stretched out on the grass with her head on my lap. "You look like a faerie in the moonlight," she murmured. "Just like a faerie, walkin' outta the woods to steal my soul."

"I didn't know faeries did that."

"Oh, yes," she said dreamily, reaching up to touch my face, "in the old myths. If you tell a faerie your name, you're in their debt forever, and if you follow 'em into the woods for just one night, seven years pass without you in the real world. And you gotta leave iron scissors over your baby's crib, or else the faeries spirit it away and leave a changeling behind for you to raise. You look like a changeling, y'know."

"Do I?"

"Yeah. Too beautiful to be human," Lily Faith sighed. "Are you gonna steal my soul, Chastity?"

"I might. I haven't decided yet."

Lily Faith unbuttoned her jeans slowly, pulled me into a kiss and guided my hand between her legs. Our first time was clumsy, unsure, but by the end of it she lay sweaty and satisfied in my arms, chest heaving. "I love you," she murmured, then giggled, hid her face in my neck like she couldn't believe she'd said it out loud.

"I love you, too." The lie was heavy in my mouth, but I told myself it wasn't completely untrue. If she was dead and stagnant, eternally perfect, I could have loved her all my life, kept her behind glass like a butterfly, let her live on flawlessly in my mind. As she was, though, I couldn't feel anything but lust, and even that was tempered by the breath in her lungs.

SEVENTEEN

"Happy birthday, baby brother," I said softly, shaking Jonathan's shoulder.

"Don't call me that," he mumbled, yawning.

"I'm bigger than you. Little brother, how about that?"

"Shut up. I'm still older."

"How's it feel to be twenty-six?"

"The same."

"I don't think Granny's doing a surprise party this time." She'd attempted a surprise party for his twenty-first birthday, scaring him so badly he ran back to our bedroom and hid under the covers for almost five minutes. Jonathan didn't do well with people jumping out at him.

"Thank God."

"I asked her to bake a cake, though. You like those pretty cakes in her magazines."

"Oh, but those are hard to make. I don't want her going to any-"

"She loves baking, you know that."

"If she wants to," Jonathan said after a moment.

"Come on, up you get. Big day."

Jonathan patted Citrus's head as he walked to the bathroom, and I wondered again if he realized the thing was dead.

"I think Jonathan honestly believes that stuffed cat is still alive. He was just playing pretend at first, I'm pretty sure, but now it's like he doesn't know…"

"He really does need a therapist," Lily Faith hummed.

"Maybe. I'm scared they'd want to lock him up."

"They don't got insane asylums no more."

"No, but they have psych hospitals and care homes and things. He wouldn't do well there."

"I dunno, I think he might. Or maybe he just needs some kinda medicine."

"What would make *you* feel better?"

"Huh?"

"You and him- y'all went through the same thing." It was the first time I'd mentioned Lily Faith's abuse since she'd told me about it. "Will you ever forget it?"

"I don't know," she said, after a long, long pause that had me wondering if she'd just get up and leave the cemetery.

"What if he died?"

"That bastard's healthy as a horse."

"But if he did die, tomorrow, would you feel better? Don't you think it'd help?"

"Yeah," Lily Faith admitted. "I mean, yeah, 'course it would."

"If I tell you a secret, can you promise me you'll never tell, no matter what?"

"Yes," she said eagerly, linking her pinkie with mine.

"I'm serious."

"So'm I. I keep secrets real good, you know that."

"Jonathan killed our mama."

Silence fell, and when I looked down at Lily Faith's shadowed face, I saw no obvious emotion, no hint at what she was thinking. It was risky, confessing to her, but I truly trusted her by that point, I'd already told her almost everything else, everything except Priscilla. No one else would ever know about Priscilla- I could justify matricide, but Jonathan's murderous jealousy of an innocent child couldn't be explained away.

"Did he do it on purpose?" she finally asked, deathly quiet.

"Yes."

"I'll never tell," Lily Faith promised.

Over the next several months, our conversations kept turning back to the cop, what he'd done to Jonathan and what he'd done to Lily Faith. We stoked the fire of our hatred every night, letting it rage into an inferno or smolder like a candle, warmed our bellies with it, and I watched as Lily Faith quietly, slowly but surely, stopped praying for her father's death and began planning it out.

"My mama was drinkin' one night, drank half a bottle of wine all by herself, and he told her to stop, said she was wastin' money. I didn't even say nothin', I swear, I didn't say *nothin'*. I just sat there and watched him take the bottle and shatter it on the ground. I never said nothin', but he looked at me like I'd done somethin' wrong, made me kneel in the broken glass. I dunno why, he didn't say. Just made me kneel right there for an hour, and look, I still got the scars."

"He made Jonathan suck him off, but he pushed his cock so far down his throat he puked, and I heard him yelling all the way from outside, calling him disgusting, ungrateful. He made Jonathan eat his own vomit, told him if he threw up again, he'd kill him."

"We had this antique fire poker, and he used to threaten me with it all the time, used to say he'd put it in the fire, let it get to where it was glowin'-hot, then fuck me with it. He never did, but one time he said he really would, he stuck it in the fire, and I tried to run, my mama blocked the door, told me I was bein' *disrespectful.* He came up to me and I was screamin' my head off, thought for sure I was gonna die, but all he did was brand me with it. Here, on my thigh- see?"

"He handcuffed Jonathan to the porch and left him there over the weekend, naked. I brought him food and water, but I couldn't unlock the handcuffs- I tried to break the porch railing, it didn't work. It had just rained, and the mosquitoes bred like crazy under our porch, I remember Jonathan was imagining mosquitoes for months after, he'd just start hitting himself, scratching all those bug bites until he bled."

"My mama *knew,* she knew all along, but she never did nothin', nobody ever did a damn thing! They all knew!"

"A social worker came once, and he coached Jonathan on what to say right in front of her, but she didn't care."

"Nobody *ever* cared." Lily Faith's lips pulled back in a feral snarl. "Nobody cared 'cause he's my daddy, he's a cop, he's an *upstandin' citizen.* Nobody stepped in 'cause it ain't none of their business how parents raise their kids. There's a lady goes to our church, she used to live in Florida, and she was real active in that Save Our Children group, she's still goin' on and on 'bout how the gays is gonna molest kids, groom kids, whatever- always sayin' she cared so much about kids. So, I went up to her one day, 'cause I heard her say she cared, and I told her what my daddy'd done, and you know what she said? She called me a liar. She told me I was goin' to Hell for lyin' about my daddy like that."

"No one's going to do anything," I said softly. "You know that, don't you? Haven't you seen that? No one will ever do anything about it- and he's probably found some other kid by now."

"Maybe *I'll* do somethin'," Lily Faith murmured. "That bastard owns a fuck of a lotta guns."

She kissed me eagerly, sighed into my hair, and made halting, nervous love to me on Mary's grave. She shoplifted just to prove she could, just to have something she got all on her own. She practiced her cheer routine to My Chemical Romance and ran until she couldn't breathe, stood at the edge of the track drawing air into her lungs like a swimmer coming up from the depths. Lily Faith, who called me her boyfriend and asked me to bring her flowers, was the only living lover I ever knew.

Lily Faith sat down gingerly next to me, pulled an apple from the inner pocket of her stolen jacket and offered it to me with a grin, morphed by moonlight into something borderline inhuman, something feral and deadly. "My mama bought a bunch of 'em yesterday."

"It's pretty." I watched her face as I bit into the apple, let the stickiness coat my chin and didn't wipe it off.

"I like berries better, honestly. Blueberries are my favorite."

"Blackberries are mine."

"They're too much work, gotta risk cuttin' yourself to get at 'em."

"Just little scratches."

"Nah. Too much work," Lily Faith repeated. She grabbed the apple and took a bite, then shook her head at once, handed it back. "Blueberries are better for sure."

"Well, thanks. I like apples just fine."

"My mama used to make apple cake all the time. She had this fam'ly recipe, passed down from her mama, and from her mama, and so on, so forth. Tasted like heaven. I think she only made 'em every now and again when I was real, real little, but when my daddy started touchin' me, she started givin' me a slice of that apple cake every time. Soon as he left, she'd come into my room with a slice of apple cake, never said nothin', just left it on my bedside table and walked out. I et it with my hands. Got to where she was whippin' up an apple cake damn near every week."

"I'm sorry," I said quietly. When I saw Jonathan's injuries, when he told me what Mama's boyfriends had done, I felt like I never knew quite what to say. *I'm sorry* was always too little; Jonathan was bleeding out, and *I'm sorry* was a band-aid slapped over a severed artery, useless and almost insulting in the face of his pain, but it was all I could think to say.

It seemed impossible, sometimes, that Lily Faith and Jonathan could have endured the same violation at the hands of the same man but come out so radically different. Lily Faith was a wolf in a miniskirt, building up muscle under the guise of cheerleading, sharpening her claws on a nail file, hiding her teeth behind pink lipstick and bubblegum breath. Lily Faith slept with a stolen switchblade under her pillow, swore that it hadn't happened in years and would never happen again, she'd cut the bastard's balls off before submitting.

Where Lily Faith became a wolf, Jonathan remained a child, perpetually terrified and dependent, always jumping at shadows and running to me for help, crying, crying, crying at the drop of a hat. Lily Faith exploded outwards, made herself into something more than a girl, made herself strong for her own sake; Jonathan curled up so small he disappeared, bent, and broke under the slightest pressure, expected me to care for him, to be his mother, replace the one who failed him.

"I'm sorry, too," Lily Faith murmured. "I'm sorry for myself, and I'm sorry for your brother." She licked her lips, let her fingers ghost over my hand. "And I'm gonna make my daddy sorry he was ever born."

Lily Faith didn't come to school the next day. Her friends whispered among themselves, worried she was sick-*that girl ain't been sick a day in her life, it must be awful if she's skippin; school!*- but I just smiled, a small, self-satisfied smile I couldn't wipe off all morning. By lunch, rumors were spreading faster than wildfire, and by the time the last bell rang, everyone in Briar County knew Lily Faith Albrecht had murdered her parents.

The papers said she shot them in their sleep, but when I visited her before the trial, she laughed weakly and told me that was a damn lie. "I woke my daddy up, first. Mama, she slept right through her death, but I woke Daddy up- just for a second. Just long enough. I wanted him to *know*."

"I don't understand," Missy said, gripping her purse strap so tight her knuckles went white. "Lily Faith is so *nice*. I don't understand at all. I don't-"

"She just went crazy," Savannah told her dully. "Some folks do."

"D'you think we could of stopped it?" Peggy Lee demanded, tearing up her empty milk carton. "I mean, Chastity, you knew her real good, y'all were- *close*. Did you know?"

"No," I said, trying to sound stunned rather than bored. "I had no idea."

Jonathan never heard local gossip. He was scared of everything, and we were all happy to coddle him; maybe it wasn't healthy, maybe we should have made him face his fears, but Granny liked having him around and I knew trying to change the secluded life he was used to would only make him retreat more. He seemed content to exist in a sort of perpetual childhood, and no one wanted to traumatize him further by forcing him out into the world, even a world as small as Adabelle.

Grampa pulled me aside the day Lily Faith became an orphan, rushed me into his taxidermy shop the minute I got home from school. "You must've heard," he said without preamble.

"About Lily Faith Albrecht? Yes, sir."

"I'm so sorry, sweetheart. I know y'all was friends, I seen her over here a time or two." He cleared his throat, ran his fingers through his beard. "When I was your age, I was best friends with Bo Lawson, lived 'bout a mile down the road from my folks. Bo seemed like the sweetest boy you ever met, gentle as a kitten and just- so kind. He was smart, too, ever'body said he was gonna go off to college, maybe become a doctor. We loved Bo.

"And then one day, I find out Bo's under arrest, and there's all kinda rumors flyin' about why. I asked around long enough that I finally found out- he raped his neighbor, a little girl no more'n five years old. She was never the same after that, never really left her house again. Her daddy walked in on it and damn near killed Bo, beat him half to death 'fore he called the cops. I never could work it out in my head, how someone could seem so nice but turn out to be so rotten. Bo was just evil, just pure evil, and we never knew."

Grampa cleared his throat. "All I mean is- don't obsess on this, okay, honey? We cain't know why Lily Faith done what she done, all we can do's pray for her soul, hers and her parents'. You understand?"

"Yes, sir. Thanks."

"And- I dunno if we oughta tell Jonathan 'bout this. That boy's nervous enough as it is, I don't want him gettin' hisself all worked up over somethin' that don't need to concern him. Don't need him thinkin' Adabelle's a dangerous town."

"Of course not."

"Stop wiggling," I laughed, pulling Jonathan to my chest and wrapping my legs around his, locking him firmly in place. He squirmed weakly before giving up and relaxing against me.

"I'm trying to get comfortable," he said, and I let him go, poked his nose when he finally rested his head on the pillow. We lay facing each other, our lamp still turned on, neither of us remotely tired. I was still buzzing with the knowledge of what Lily Faith had done, concern for her wellbeing pushed to the far recesses of my mind, and Jonathan was just restless.

"I know a secret," I said quietly, reaching to play with his hair, spread across the white sheets like spilled ink. It contrasted sharply with the long white nightgowns he'd started wearing not long after we moved in with our grandparents, both because he thought they were more comfortable than pajamas and to hide the diapers he was still so ashamed of needing.

"What is it?"

"I can't just *tell* you."

"Come on, that's not fair. You can't say you have a secret and refuse to tell me anything," Jonathan whined, pouting, and widening his eyes. Granny always said his eyes could break your heart, breathtakingly blue and framed by long black lashes- *I'd have killed for eyes like that when I was young! You should've been a girl, sweetheart, you don't even need mascara.*

"Puppy eyes don't work on me, baby brother."

"I'm older-"

"The cop's dead." Jonathan froze, staring at me like he hadn't understood, so I repeated, slow and careful, "The cop is *dead.*"

"Mama's... boyfriend?"

"What other cop do we know?"

"He's dead," Jonathan repeated, a shocked sort of glee building behind those ocean eyes Granny fawned over so much.

"Yes, he's dead. He'll never hurt you or anybody else again, Jonathan. He is dead, dead, *dead.*"

Jonathan shrieked with delight, threw his arms around me, and just laughed, laughed until he cried, sobbing heavily into my chest but shaking his head when I asked if he was upset, and finally yelled, *"Thank God!"* So loud Granny knocked on our door to see if we were okay.

"Oh, we're fine. Jonathan woke up from a nightmare, he's just glad I'm here," I called, trying not to sound too happy.

"Well, alright. I hope he sleeps better the rest of the night."

"Thanks, Granny. We love you."

"I love y'all, too," she chirped.

"How did he die?" Jonathan finally asked, wiping at his eyes and sniffling, still grinning so wide it must have hurt his cheeks.

"Lily Faith shot him, and his wife, too. Shot them both in their sleep."

"Lily Faith? Really?"

"Yeah." For the first time since I'd heard the news, worry trickled in- was she all right? She'd go to prison, probably for the rest of her life, but that was fine. Prison wasn't so bad, and anyway, *I* hadn't pulled the trigger. I never made her do anything. If I encouraged her, well, that wasn't a crime, was it? She'd wanted him dead for years, all I did was push her a little further.

Jonathan fell asleep soon after, worn out from his fit of exuberance, and I was careful not to disturb him as I reached to turn the lamp off. Lying in the bedroom we'd made our own, I remembered all those years on the floor of the trailer, boxes stacked the ceiling blocking out all the light, Jonathan crying himself to sleep at my side. He wasn't really better, but the cop was dead, and that was enough for me, enough for now.

I kept fantasizing about Lily Faith in the weeks following her arrest. She was sentenced to life in prison with the possibility of parole, but I couldn't help wondering how it would have been if she'd gotten the death penalty. I didn't really *want* her dead; I just wanted to fuck her corpse. I imagined Lily Faith strapped to a metal gurney, sighing out her life minutes after the needle pierced her bicep, I imagined her cold and pale underneath me, forever young, beautiful, and all mine, all mine.

EIGHTEEN

After Lily Faith's arrest, I quietly slipped into the background at school, content to let her friends move on without either of us. I only visited her once, right before the trial, and after that I wrote her letters. She always wrote back right away, trying desperately to sound upbeat, and I kept them in a shoebox under the bed. I wasn't a hoarder, but I held onto physical memories.

My grades were perfect, and I was set to be valedictorian. Jonathan, who'd always been such a good student before the preacher put him in the hospital, had barely graduated; I remembered reading his report card and yelling that he was smarter than this, he could do better. It would have been comical to an outsider, a little girl yelling at her brother to fix his grades, but at the time I was just furious, furious at Jonathan for giving up on everything, furious at the preacher for hurting him so bad, furious at all the adults who refused to help him.

Grampa, who was willfully oblivious to the implications of my brother's androphobia, thought Jonathan had some kind of intellectual disability. He asked me about it once, in the gruffly nervous way I'd come to appreciate, "Chastity, is your brother, uh- is he retarded? I mean, shit, sorry, that ain't polite, there's a lady at church got her a re- um- got her an intellectual disabled child. Intellectually. She told me retarded ain't the right word no more. That's it, anyway, is that what Jonathan's got?"

"No. He's really smart."

"Oh," Grampa said, disbelievingly.

Granny, for her part, thought Jonathan was completely and benignly out of his mind. He never said more than a few words at a time, but he obviously liked being around her, eventually trusted her enough to curl up next to her on the couch when she watched her cooking shows. Our grandparents loved both of us, but I think Granny was always confused by my insistence on dressing like a boy, my complete disinterest in feminine hobbies, my perpetual singleness "when you're so pretty!", while Grampa couldn't find a way to get through to Jonathan, understood he was scared of him and didn't want to know why.

"Y'know, Jonathan," he began at dinner one night, clearing his throat, "that needlework you done for your granny's quilt sure is nice. You're real good at all that sorta thing. It's fine if you wanna marry a man." Granny choked on her water, Jonathan froze like a rabbit about to run, and I bit my hand so I wouldn't laugh out loud. "I- I just mean- well, they say in church it's a sin, but I had me a brother, Clancy, used to listen to the radio all day, he loved classical stuff. Mozart and all that. And later I found out he was a homosexual, and that's fine. He was a good man, he's gone on to Heaven now, I just wanted you to know-"

"Arnie," Granny interrupted, her lips twitching like she was trying not to smile, "you're embarrassin' the poor child. We'd still love you no matter what, Jonathan," she added hastily. "It *is* fine, but goodness, Arnie, a little warnin' next time?"

"Right," Grampa muttered.

"I'm never marrying *anyone*," Jonathan hissed that night, clinging to me fiercely. "I'd never marry a man. No one in their right mind would ever-"

"He's just trying to be nice," I said soothingly, stroking my brother's hair. "This'll be past your hips pretty soon, baby, want me to trim it tomorrow?"

"Never getting married," Jonathan repeated.

"You don't have to. No one's going to make you get married, okay? I promise, you never have to if you don't want to."

It sounds vain to say it outright, but Jonathan and I were always good-looking. He told me Mama used to be beautiful, bitterly muttered that she could have whored herself out if she really needed money, and when I saw old photos of our daddy in Granny's photo albums, I was shocked to see how handsome he'd been.

Lily Faith wasn't the only girl who liked me- I noticed Peggy Lee watching me on more than one occasion, and a girl in my algebra class whose name I've forgotten told me I carried myself like a man, giggled that she'd ask me to prom if she could. I showed up to prom alone, in an old suit dug out of Grampa's wardrobe, and ended up dancing with each of Lily Faith's old friends in turn.

"Boys would fight over you if you wore a little make-up," Granny told me cajolingly, smiling hopefully in the beauty section of Winn-Dixie.

"Girls are already fighting over me," I responded drily. She blinked, nodded, awkwardly patted my back, and mumbled something that might have been *how fun* before hurrying me into the soup aisle.

After my confession at Winn-Dixie and Arnie's stumbling acceptance of Jonathan's perceived sexuality, I noticed our grandparents slowly stopped going to church so often. They claimed they were just getting too old to make the drive every Sunday, but when they quit attending altogether, Granny admitted that she felt guilty listening to Brother Mitch rant about homosexuals burning in Hell. "He's fixated on it," she said, fidgeting with the lace on her skirt. "I sort of tuned it out before, I didn't really care, but with you and your brother bein'- well- it felt wrong. I love y'all more'n I love that church."

Even after she left the church, Granny's friends were always coming over for lunch, relaxing in the backyard with sweet tea and little sandwiches, giggling like girls. She was constantly inviting us to join her, but I always found some excuse to get away- I was never much of a people person. At first, Jonathan outright refused, but as the years passed and he slowly got used to Granny, he started joining them for a few minutes here and there, standing uncomfortably next to her chair at first, then sitting on her lap, until he was willing to stay the whole time, never speaking.

I watched one of their little lunches once, Granny and her three friends chattering about their gardens while she absentmindedly stroked Jonathan's hair, letting him hide his face in her neck. She applied rose-scented lotion every night, so her skin was soft and sweet-smelling, and she was a surprisingly strong woman; it must have been nice to curl up in her arms. Granny's friends infantilized him even more than she did, cooing that he was such a darling little thing and occasionally bringing him gifts I would have found insulting, crocheted toys and teddy bears and porcelain dolls he lined up on our shelves without complaint.

Jonathan always liked being fussed over. He played up his helplessness with me and happily let Granny think he was somewhat simple-minded, so she'd lavish attention on him, but he really did panic when left to his own devices. He needed someone, specifically a woman, to make decisions for him, tell him what to do, reassure him he was being good, or he completely fell apart- but if you told him something he didn't want to hear, he'd whine endlessly. I loved my brother to his dying day, but even I could admit he was beyond difficult.

"It's my *graduation*," I said through clenched teeth.

"We're having a graduation party here, aren't we?" Jonathan countered, tangling his slender fingers in Citrus's fur. "I don't want to go sit in a crowded auditorium all day."

"I'm asking you to do it for me. I graduated high school, that's a big deal, I want you to come support me."

"Can't I support you from home?"

"You go to the library once a week. I know you can go outside."

"The library's *quiet*."

"Fine," I said coldly. "Stay here if you want. See if I care."

I fell asleep on the couch that night, and when Jonathan shook me awake, I just waved him off, said I was more comfortable on the couch. It was a week before my graduation, and I knew how perpetually affectionate he was, how he needed me more than water, more than oxygen, more than anything. We both knew, by then, that it was impossible to prove he'd killed Priscilla, and he knew I'd never tell what had happened to Mama, but Jonathan was still so easy to control it didn't even feel like manipulation.

The next day, I ignored him when I got home from school, pushed him away when he tried to hug me and said I needed to work on a taxidermy project. I wouldn't hold his hand at dinner or sit with him and Granny afterwards, and when he tried to snuggle up to me in bed, I shoved a pillow between us and rolled away.

"Chastity?" Jonathan whimpered, shaking my shoulder. "Chastity? Chastity, what's wrong?" I closed my eyes, tried to fall asleep, but he only shook me more aggressively, starting to cry. "Chastity! Don't ignore me! I know you're awake, don't *ignore* me!" After damn near ten minutes of shaking me and pleading for attention, Jonathan finally gave up and just lay there sobbing hysterically, shamelessly crying like a baby; our grandparents must have heard him from down the hall, but they rarely intervened when he had his episodes, knowing I was the only one who could really comfort him.

Jonathan shook me awake in the morning, as gently as possible, smiling when I opened my eyes and leaning forward to kiss my cheek. "I'm glad you're awake," he said eagerly, practically bouncing in place as he sat up. "You were being so weird last night, are you sick? Do you feel-"

"Why do you care if I'm sick? You've made it pretty clear you don't care about me," I said, keeping my face carefully blank.

"Huh?" Jonathan looked horribly, painfully confused. "I care about you more than anybody."

"But you won't even do the *slightest* little thing for me," I sighed. "I just want you at my graduation, and you can't be bothered to go out of your comfort zone for even an hour. God, you're selfish."

"No! No, I'm not, I lo-"

"Save it. Obviously, you *don't* love me, so don't bother pretending. I'll talk to Granny about getting separate beds, since you hate me so much."

"*No!* I- I'll go. I'll do it, Chastity, please, don't- don't leave- I'm sorry-"

The second he agreed to go, I relaxed, smiled sweetly, and held my arms out. Jonathan latched onto me at once, whimpering, and I hushed him as I stroked his hair, rocking us gently back and forth. "You're all right, Jonathan. I knew you'd do the right thing, my sweet boy."

Jonathan sat between our grandparents throughout my graduation ceremony, frequently trying to climb onto Granny's lap like a kitten and being gently pushed back into his own seat. He looked almost as uncomfortable as Grampa did in a suit, neither of them used to formalwear. There were twelve people in my graduating class, and when we all bowed, I saw Jonathan cover his ears to tune out the clapping, watched with secondhand embarrassment as he tried to curl into the fetal position. Granny had to urge him to keep his feet on the floor, and I saw my classmates looking, giggling behind their hands. For the first time, I wondered if it might have been better to force him outside more often.

We tried to slip away as soon as the ceremony was over, but Peggy Lee ran up to us and hugged me, kissed both my cheeks "like they do in Europe!"

"Granny, Grampa, Jonathan, this is Peggy Lee Watson," I said, trying not to sound annoyed by her intrusion. "Peggy Lee, meet my grandparents and my lovely brother."

"*So* great to meet y'all!" she squealed, hugging both my grandparents but stepping back when Jonathan flinched away from her. "Chastity's so smart it's crazy, wasn't her speech awesome? How long did it take you to write that?"

"Oh, a while," I said. Really, I'd banged out the valedictorian speech in an hour, filled it with the sort of generically uplifting shit I heard on TV, tossed in a made-up Albert Einstein quote to see if anyone would notice.

"It was awesome," Peggy Lee repeated. "Are you comin' to Missy's after this? She's havin' a party to celebrate-"

"No, sorry," I interrupted, "we're having a thing at our house, just the four of us. Thanks for the invitation, though."

"Of course! Well, y'all have fun!"

"Peggy Lee seems awfully nice," Granny said at dinner, raising her eyebrows meaningfully.

"She's just a friend."

"Well, she'd be a good *girl*friend." Having long ago accepted that Jonathan was never marrying anyone, Granny was starting to unsubtly suggest I should hurry up and find a wife, start adopting children.

"Maybe. Yeah." I cleared my throat, set my fork down, and smiled. "But I'll be gone about two years. I thought I'd wait to tell y'all until after graduation- I'm going to college in Atlanta. I've already been accepted."

"College!" Granny squealed, practically dropping her glass.

"*Atlanta?*" Jonathan whispered.

"It's a mortuary school," I continued, "and I'll be getting an associate's degree. It'll only take two years."

"Now, what's a mortuary school?" Grampa asked.

"It's for morticians and funeral directors. Undertakers."

"Oh! Is *that* what you wanna do?" Granny asked incredulously, giggling to cover her alarm.

"Yes, ma'am. I want to do something nice for people after they've gone to Heaven," I said softly, remembering Priscilla's chipper little voice, *one last nice thing.* "I got a scholarship, but I'll still have to take out student loans and get a job while I'm there. I'll come visit every weekend, I promise- it's only three hours away." I really was sorry it wasn't closer, had in fact considered bringing Jonathan with me, but I knew he'd hate Atlanta. The noise and crowding of a city would drive my brother completely insane, I was sure of it.

"You're leaving," Jonathan said in a flat voice I'd never heard from him before. He let me cuddle him but didn't respond in kind, just laid completely still in my embrace.

"Only for two years, and I'll be back every single weekend, I promise. You'll see me every week."

"I want to see you more than that."

"Well, I want to be a mortician. Once I get my license, everything will go right back to normal, you'll see. I'll buy us a nice little house and-"

"You're *leaving*."

"If you want to come live in a big city apartment, you're more than welcome, but I don't think you'd like that very much. Would you?" After a long pause, Jonathan slowly shook his head. "Exactly. Plus, I'll spend the summer here- remember, it's only two years, it'll be over before you know it, and once I'm done, we're set for life. The funeral industry never goes out of business- all the customers are *dying* to get in." I nudged him with my knee, proud of myself. "Eh? Come on, that was funny."

"Every weekend?"

"Every weekend, baby, I promise."

"Every weekend," Jonathan repeated in a low murmur, finally nuzzling closer to me. "I'll see you every single weekend, and then you'll come home."

NINETEEN

There was a woman who loved me in Atlanta, a woman Granny would have been pleased with, a woman Jonathan would have murdered in a fit of jealous rage, a woman I couldn't bring myself to care about but strung along for two years just the same. She brought me peaches, said it was stereotypical but weren't they so good, weren't they so sweet, brought me peaches and fed them to me by hand. I licked peach juice off her fingers and thought about Lily Faith, still sending me letters even though I hadn't written back in months.

I never brought her home, told her my grandparents would never accept us with an air of brave, forced resignation, and when Granny hopefully asked if I'd met any nice girls in Atlanta, I told her no, I was so focused on my studies I barely had time for anything else. She slept in my postage stamp apartment most nights; hers was bigger, but her cat hated me.

"My brother loves cats," I told her after she pried her rotten Sphynx off me, sheepishly saying he was normally the sweetest little thing. "Our grandfather does taxidermy, and he thinks one of the stuffed cats is real. Nobody tries to tell him different anymore."

"Your family sounds so… whimsical," she laughed. She was born in Atlanta, had never lived in the country, and thought it charming that I had, found my slow drawl sexy and my childhood stories quaint. I lied to her about almost everything, claimed I was raised on a cute little farm straight out of a storybook, wrote Mama out like she'd never existed at all and made Jonathan seem more eccentric than deranged.

"Maybe your brother's autistic," she told me helpfully, curled up naked in bed. "You should bring him up here to get tested."

"He's not autistic, there's just something wrong with him. It doesn't matter." I became short with her if she brought up my family- sure, I could tell my folksy small-town stories, but Jonathan and my grandparents were none of her business. I didn't like her bringing them up out of the blue, and she realized that, quickly changed the subject.

Jonathan did better with the arrangement than I'd expected once he got used to it. Granny said he cried himself to sleep the first several nights, carried Citrus around and whispered to her all day, and had started sucking his thumb again, a habit Mama beat out of him when we were children. He was glued to my side when I came home, always hugging me, on my lap every time I sat down, invariably bursting into tears when I had to leave, as if it was some huge shock.

The woman who thought herself my lover was studying psychology, talked about regression and emotional immaturity, claimed she could probably help Jonathan if I'd just let her talk to him. She diagnosed everyone in her life with some mental illness or another, thought she could fix all my problems, and I wanted to laugh in her face every time she brought up her ideas about healthy coping mechanisms. *You want to be my fucking therapist, bitch? You think Jonathan's just immature; you don't know. Think I'm a nice woman, you don't know shit. I could tell you things you'd never forget, I could tell you things to make you change careers. Don't think you know a damn thing, little girl.*

When I moved back to Adabelle, a licensed mortician in the state of Georgia, I kissed her good-bye and told her she could find someone better. It was the only truly honest thing I ever said to her. She was a good woman who meant well, a woman who eventually settled down with a nice lady from West Virginia and adopted a girl with Down's syndrome. I forgot her name within weeks of returning home.

There was only one funeral home near Adabelle, and I was immediately hired on as an assistant. The old man who operated the place, Mr. Kaplan, had been desperate for someone to take it over after his death. "My son wants nothing to do with it," he said sadly, shaking his head as if this was a personal affront, "and I'd never sell to some big chain, so I really was getting scared. So good to have you here, Chastity!"

I wondered if Priscilla's old neighbor had been anything like Mr. Kaplan, a bizarrely jovial man who treated cadavers with the utmost respect, had a remarkable knack for setting grieving families at ease, and occasionally cracked morbid jokes that never failed to shock the listener into laughter. "You know, my son is a doctor," he told me once, grinning, "so I always say if *he* can't help you, I'm your next bet!"

"I'll live there in a few years," I told Granny, smiling sheepishly, "but in the meantime, do you think I could keep staying with y'all? Jonathan's coming with me when I move, of course-"

"Oh, sweetheart, you don't even gotta ask," she said, waving a hand airily. "Y'know we'll always want y'all here with us."

"It's unusual to see someone go into this career right out of college," Mr. Kaplan said, mopping the morgue floor while I scrubbed the gurneys. Both of us were obsessive about cleanliness. "What made you want to do it?"

"I had a friend," I said, surprised to hear the words coming out of my mouth, "when I was a little girl. She was the nicest kid you ever met, and she wanted to be a mortician, she said, because she wanted to do something nice for people after they died, and because her neighbor back in Gatlinburg- her family moved here so her father could plant a church- had been a mortician. I loved her." My voice rang out too loud, and I smiled weakly, shook my head. "I guess it's a pretty stupid reason."

"Not at all," Mr. Kaplan said gently. "Did she move away, or…?"

"She died. She died very young. I remember screaming at her father when he told me, screaming that he was lying- she was only seven years old. She was so much nicer than me," I said, clearing my throat, trying not to sound too sentimental.

"I'm sorry for your loss." Mr. Kaplan said that, or something to that effect, almost constantly, but it always sounded incredibly, heartbreakingly sincere.

"I don't know if she would have changed her mind, but I just thought I should..." I cleared my throat again. "Were you working here, then?"

"This would have been in the 90's? Yes, I was."

"Her name was Priscilla Forge, and she burned to death. Do you remember her?"

"*Oh,*" Mr. Kaplan said, briefly stunned. "Oh, my God, I'm so sor- yes, yes, I remember her." He looked like he might be sick. "I remember her very well. I guess if I worked in a big city I'd see worse things, but out here, that… I remember her."

"She had a closed casket," I said softly. Beatrice had picked me up for the funeral, held me on her lap and rocked us both back and forth the whole time, sobbing into her hand.

She insisted Jonathan come with me, saying Priscilla had liked him, Priscilla would have wanted him to attend, and he sat stiffly throughout the service, gripping his knees, never saying a word to Priscilla's parents.

"Yes. Her poor father asked if it was possible to make her look like she was just sleeping, those were his words. 'Can you make it look like she's just sleeping?' I had to tell him no, and he started crying right there in my office. He said he heard her screaming, but he couldn't get into her room, the fire was…" Mr. Kaplan cut himself off, looking horribly guilty. "I'm sorry, dear."

"It's fine. I already knew, I guess."

"Whatever happened to that family?"

"Her parents got divorced, and her mother and sister moved back to Gatlinburg- Apple was burned really severely, she almost died, too- and I'm not sure about her father. I'll have to look him up sometime."

"Well, I think it's wonderful that you're honoring your friend this way," Mr. Kaplan said, smiling gently. "I'm sure she'd be proud of you."

"Maybe."

"Will you take me to the library?" Jonathan asked hopefully when I got home, hugging me and quickly kissing my cheek.

"Sure," I said at once. "You can find a book on your own, can't you? I need to Google something." Our grandparents didn't own a computer.

"I'll just wait until you're done."

I sat Jonathan next to me while I searched for Father William, gently pulled his hand away from his mouth when he started absentmindedly sucking his thumb- apparently, we'd need to break that habit again. The urge to snap *you're thirty years old* briefly overwhelmed me, but I ignored it, murmured something about people staring as I wiped my brother's hand off on his shirt.

It took a while, but I finally found Father William's obituary. He'd died in 2004- I felt somehow surprised that I hadn't known, as if someone should have told me. It was a brief, impersonal piece, the sort of depressing obituary a stranger writes about someone with no friends. He'd given up the priesthood and become a grocery store manager, never remarried, or made any real connections, and ultimately hung himself, leaving a letter of apology to Beatrice and Apple.

I stared at the screen in complete silence, barely moving, white-hot rage coursing through my veins. Next to me, Jonathan braided and unbraided his hair, humming softly to himself, and for a second, I wanted him dead. "We're going home," I said shortly, grabbing my brother's dainty wrist hard enough to bruise.

"Why?" Jonathan whined, trying to tug his hand away. "I want to get a new book. You said I could, after you were d-"

"I said you could find one *on your own*. Fuck, Jonathan, can't you do *anything* without me? What's the plan if I die, huh?"

"I'll kill myself," he said at once, as if that were obvious.

"You think I want to spend my whole life taking care of some pathetic little freak?"

"You don't really think that," Jonathan said weakly, trying to hug me.

"Don't touch me! Just shut up, we'll talk when we get home." No one had noticed our little argument- the librarians were used to Jonathan's odd behavior, had seen me correct him before, so if they saw anything, they didn't register it as out of the ordinary.

My brother was quiet as we walked home, obediently followed me into our bedroom and tried to hug me again, whimpered when I shoved him away. "Take your shirt off," I ordered. He blinked, tilted his head.

"Huh?"

"Take your shirt off," I repeated, slower. Jonathan did as he was told, fumbling with the buttons until I stepped forward and practically ripped it off, threw it to the side. "Kneel by the bed."

"Why-?"

"Kneel by the goddamn bed, how many times do I have to fucking repeat myself? Are you retarded? I tell you to do something, I expect you to fucking do it! You make me take care of you, that's fine, but if you want to be treated like a child you damn well better *listen to me!*" Jonathan dropped to his knees next to our bed, tears already streaming down his face.

"I don't understand what I-"

"*Shut up!*" I undid my belt, then hesitated, sat on our bed, and announced, "I changed my mind. Take your pants off, then lie over my lap."

"No," Jonathan said immediately, picking up on where this was going.

"Fucking *yes,* you stupid little shit."

"I'll tell Granny."

"She's not home."

"When she gets home, I'll-"

"You go crying to Granny about this, and I'll tell the cops exactly where they can find Mama."

"You wouldn't," he said uncertainly.

"Really? Why not? I'll say you made me help. I was eight years old; *you* were the adult. I can't be prosecuted for shit, but you're a murderer- you're a murderer twice over. Shut the fuck up, take your pants off, and *lie down.*" Jonathan hesitated, crying freely, then slowly took his jeans off, stood shifting from foot to foot in his underwear. "Take that off, too."

"I don't-"

"Take it off." He did as he was told, quickly covering himself with his hands as if I hadn't seen him nude a thousand times. "Hurry up, Jonathan."

It was strange to have him lying naked across my lap, trembling in fear; while Mama had spanked both of us, I'd never done anything like this to my brother, never wanted to really hurt him. I considered stopping there, playing it off as a cruel joke, but Father William's voice, soft and gentle, rang in my mind and I brought the belt down as hard as I could, took sharp, sadistic joy in his pained yelp.

I didn't stop until my belt was wet with blood and Jonathan was bawling like a baby, clutching the comforter in his little fists, almost choking from the force of his sobs. I shoved him off my lap, let him tumble to the floor, and kicked him for good measure before wiping the belt on his jeans and putting it back on. "Get up."

Jonathan made a strangled gurgling noise as I helped him to his feet, stiffened when I pulled him into a hug before melting into my arms. "Chastity," he whimpered, "why-?"

"Father William killed himself," I said softly, alternating between stroking Jonathan's hair and rubbing his back. "He hung himself, back in 2004. Did you know that?"

"No."

"It's your fault. You know *that*, don't you? You murdered his daughter. You murdered a little girl."

"Chastity-"

"You're going to burn in Hell for what you did to her, what you did to that family." Jonathan shuddered convulsively, and I decided to stop for fear that he'd pass out. "But that won't happen until you die. Do you want a bath, baby brother? Let's take a bath together."

Jonathan and I moved into the funeral home when Mr. Kaplan retired. It was my idea, and I insisted on it- Jonathan was creeped out by the idea of living above a morgue. "We're on the second floor, the funeral parlor is on the first floor, and the morgue is in the basement. You never have to go down there- and you really *can't* go down there, you're not licensed."

"You want to live in a house full of corpses," he huffed, crossing his arms.

"Well, no one's saying you have to move in with me, but Granny won't live forever. She's getting older already, I don't want you burdening her."

"She likes having me around!"

"Stay here, then, but I'll be so busy I don't know if-"

"I'll come with you."

"That's what I thought."

"It's a lovely old building," Granny said cautiously, trying to help us carry our things into the funeral home. I kept snatching boxes out of her hands, giving Jonathan lighter boxes when he tried to pick up heavy ones, practically chasing Grampa down to take boxes away from him. "Chastity, please, I'm not some delicate little flower, I think I can help you move a few boxes!"

"You don't have to. Jonathan, put that down, you'll drop it! Here, carry your teddy bears. Grampa, so help me God, you're going to throw your back out if you try to take that, everyone just let me unload everything."

"She's certainly gettin' bossy, now she's in charge of this here operation," Grampa stage-whispered to Jonathan, who looked up at him with wide eyes and stepped away. At twenty-three years old, I was probably way too young to run a funeral home on my own, but Mr. Kaplan'd said he had full confidence in my abilities, and my grandparents were so proud they were telling everyone they met that their granddaughter had her own house and business- although Granny often glossed over exactly what that business was.

"Damn straight," I said under my breath, turning to smile at my funeral home.

TWENTY

I had to kick Jonathan to make him stop squirming in bed our first night in the new room. "I have work tomorrow. If you can't sleep, go lie down in the guest room, but don't-"

"I don't want to," Jonathan said at once, clinging onto me. "I'm sorry, Chastity, I'm just not used to- I mean- isn't it *creepy?* It doesn't bother you at all, being here?"

"Shut the fuck up or you're sleeping in the morgue."

After that first night, Jonathan slept easier, and we soon fell into an easy routine that we both grew to love. He cooked, cleaned, did laundry, and allegedly took care of Citrus, who now "lived" primarily in the living room. The new cemetery was right behind the funeral home, so if neither of us had anything to do we took walks there, until Jonathan was confident enough to go out on his own. "It's just like Granny's backyard, only bigger," I told him when he fretted about being outside without me.

For five months, we were in heaven. I wore suits all the time and felt very stylish when our grandparents came over, while Jonathan wore loose shirts and the sort of flowy pants that looked like skirts at first glance. "Pretty boy," I teased, tugging his long braid.

"I'm just trying to be comfortable."

"Why not go ahead and wear dresses? I know you want to."

"I don't."

"Keep telling yourself that."

The groundskeeper was an old, respectful man who only spoke to me when he absolutely had to. I could see in his eyes that he didn't want to work for a woman barely out of college who'd dragged some mental patient along with her, but he made no complaint. I was satisfied with his work, people praised how pretty the cemetery was, and no one had any issue with him except Jonathan, who was terrified of him from the day they met.

"Chastity! Chastity, there's a man in the cemetery- he's not there to see anyone, he's just stalking around, make him leave," Jonathan cried, running into my office.

"You realize I could have had clients in here."

"But you don't. Please, Chastity, go tell him to get out, I don't want him there!"

"Did he bother you?"

"Yes, I just told-!"

"Did he actually *speak* to you, I mean?"

"Well- no."

"Did he touch you?"

"...no," Jonathan muttered, after a long pause in which he obviously considered lying.

"It's not a crime to wander around the cemetery. If it was, I'd have to kick *you* out, too."

"He's scaring me!"

"Everything scares you. Come sit with me, I'm just going over some paperwork." I read through a letter of final wishes with Jonathan on my lap, sucking his thumb and resting his head against my shoulder. I'd stopped bothering to pull his hand away from his mouth- if it calmed him down, it was fine with me. There were worse habits to have.

The next time Jonathan saw the groundskeeper, we were together. "That man from before is back," he said petulantly, pointing to him.

"Yes, because he works here. You're going to have to get over this."

"I don't *like* him," Jonathan whined, kicking a rock out of the path.

"Well, we can't always like everything. Stop bitching."

Jonathan did not, in fact, stop bitching. He was fixated on the groundskeeper, and after just a few weeks refused to go outside on his own, told me he was bored and demanded I play with him once he'd finished his chores, sat outside my office, and cried if I turned him away. "I'm so sorry," I said to a newly widowed old woman, smiling with clenched teeth as Jonathan sobbed in the hallway. "My brother is… emotionally disturbed."

"I see," she said awkwardly. At least she was temporarily distracted from her monumental grief. "You know, they have very nice hospitals and care homes nowadays. Have you considered anything like that?"

"No. Now, I see your husband wanted daisies instead of lilies…"

Her suggestion stayed with me long after she'd left, though. I slapped Jonathan as soon as she was gone, told him to go sit in our room while I got some work done. "Go play with Citrus, how about that?"

"Okay."

I had no intention of actually sending Jonathan away. Putting him in a mental hospital would, I was convinced, only make him worse. He barely talked to *me* about Mama's boyfriends, and no one had ever believed him before, anyway. Why would a therapist listen when a social worker hadn't? I just needed him to stop bothering me at work.

"Jonathan," I said gently, walking into our room an hour later, "I have an idea."

"You're going to fire the groundskeeper?"

"No, but I hear what you're saying about him. I understand you don't want to be around some strange man you don't know, so I've been doing some research, and I think the best place for you to be is a psychiatric facility. Don't you think so? There'd be lots of nice doctors to help you get over this irrational fear of men, you could have a roommate- a male roommate- and I think they have to give you physical examinations pretty often, so you'd get used to men touching you and stop worrying so much about it. That sounds nice, doesn't it?"

"No!"

"And I think it would be best if you went to a hospital somewhere pretty far away, like Washington, maybe, or California. Maybe even Alaska. I don't want to impede your recovery."

"*No!*" Jonathan shrieked, grabbing my arm. "No, no, you can't make me!"

"No? But don't you want to get better? I mean, if you can't even take a walk in the cemetery because there's a man you don't know outside, I think you need professional help."

"I- I'll stop bothering you," Jonathan said meekly. "I'll stay up here when you're working, I promise. I'm sorry."

"Alright, then. We can table it for now."

"Is Granny still your legal guardian?"

"I would assume so," Jonathan said, shrugging. "Never tried to contest it."

"She's getting on up there. I think I'll talk to her about transferring guardianship."

"I don't need a guardian anymore-"

"Yes, you do. I'll call her tomorrow."

There was something satisfying about getting guardianship of my brother, having legal documentation to prove he was under my control. "I own you," I told him softly as we walked out of the court, grinning uncontrollably.

"All you can do is make medical decisions for me," Jonathan said irritably. He'd gone along with everything, but not without a considerable amount of complaining.

"No, I make decisions for you, period. You can't get married without my say-so; you can't even *vote* without my say-so. You're *mine,* baby brother."

"You have to take care of me," Jonathan said, voice barely above a whisper. "That's part of the deal, too."

"Oh, of course. Of course."

TWENTY-ONE

Lily Faith's friend Savannah died a year after I took over the funeral home. Up to that point, I'd only embalmed the elderly and a few overdose victims, everyone either too old or damaged to catch my interest, but when I had Savannah on a gurney my heart skipped a beat. Lying on her back, she was beautiful, tall, and slender as she'd been in high school; turn her over, and you'd see her skull was caved in. According to her husband, an Adabelle cop, she fell down the stairs and died instantly. The police and hospital agreed that there was no need for a medical examiner to look her over, and her family couldn't afford to pay for a private autopsy, so Savannah Porter's death was an accident.

Aside from the groundskeeper, I was the sole employee of Forge Memorial Funeral Home, recently changed from Kaplan Funeral Home and Crematorium. Jonathan was terrified of the morgue, wouldn't come into the basement if his life depended on it, and the door was always locked anyway. Nobody could interrupt us. I thought it over carefully as I washed the corpse, wondering what Lily Faith was getting herself up to in prison. She still wrote once a month, and I occasionally sent Christmas cards. I doubted anyone would tell her Savannah was dead.

Peggy Lee wanted to be an actress, Missy wanted to live in New York City, and Savannah always said she just wanted to get married. "Nothing else?" I asked her once. "No career plans? Nothing?"

"What's wrong with getting married?" she asked, tearing the crusts of her sandwich. "Don't you got no sense of romance?"

"You could do anything you wanted."

"Cain't afford college. It's either get married or work at Winn-Dixie or a gas station all my life. I'd rather get married, have a few kids, raise me a nice little fam'ly."

"Married the wrong guy, didn't you?" I asked Savannah's corpse, voice echoing in the morgue. She lay still under the harsh lights, perfectly still, young, beautiful, and just starting to go stiff. Her husband wanted her cremated, just wanted an urn full of ash to dump out somewhere, probably wanted it so her family wouldn't have a grave to visit. It didn't matter. Savannah was perfect and I had a way to keep her to myself, *that* mattered.

When it came right down to it, a morgue wasn't all that different from a taxidermy shop, and a dead human was just another mammal. I embalmed Savannah before doing anything else, put her in the freezer, and got to work on building a frame, trying to balance speed with exactness. It had to be perfect. It had to be taxidermy, too; embalming only kept a body fresh for so long, but with taxidermy, I could preserve her forever. I barely considered where I'd put her, told Jonathan I'd be busy in the morgue for a few days and to leave me alone.

"What are you doing down there?" he asked in bed, running his fingers through my hair. "Your hair would be so pretty if you grew it out, you know."

"I'm just busy. Your hair's long enough for both of us."

"Still. It'd look nice."

"Go to sleep, Jonathan."

The frame took a few days, and I laughed when I finished it, clapped my hands like a child. "Now," I breathed, laying Savannah on a gurney, stroking her cold face, "I'll fix up your head, honey. Gonna make you all pretty again, gonna make you perfect. Huh? Yes, you like that." I turned her over as gently as possible, made the initial incision along her spine, and tried to ignore the ugly dent in the back of her skull as I worked her skin off, slow, gentle, careful as a surgeon. I could fix up the back of her skull with fabric and some hair extensions, but everything else had to be exact. No more injuries.

It really was exactly like skinning an animal, not too different from the bobcat Grampa had been so proud of. "Think of it like takin' a sock off," he'd explained, peeling back the pelt, and I repeated his advice quietly until the skin was completely separate. It was always inside-out when you got it off, and I couldn't quite forget she'd been human as I inverted her skin, laid it out to rub salt into every crevice, and finally hung it to dry from the clothesline I'd temporarily rigged up at the far end of the morgue.

My original intention was to just burn Savannah's insides once I had her skinned. I had no use for them, after all, and it would have been morbid to keep her bones lying around- but then I couldn't resist running my fingers over her exposed spine, feeling every ridge, and from there I had to turn her over, push my fingers into the yellow fat of her chest, trace the wet, red contours of her head, what was left of her face. I remembered Missy gushing that Savannah had "such good bone structure" and laughed, pressed my lips against her open mouth.

I'd double and triple checked that the door was locked earlier, so I wasted no time pulling my pants down, tossing everything carelessly aside and climbing onto the gurney, stopping only for a second to make sure it was locked in place. Not for the first time, I wished I was a man, reflected on how much easier this would be if I had a dick, but I made it work. Savannah's raw sinew was slick against my cunt as I rocked myself slowly against her, rolling my hips like a man. I bit my lip to stifle a moan, looked down at the wall of muscle protecting her organs, and experimentally pressed against it, harder, harder, thrusting my hips faster and faster until I accepted it would take more than my hand and grabbed the knife I'd set aside.

I was sweaty and covered in blood by the time I'd finished, barely conscious of the awful smell permeating the room- I'd punctured her intestines by mistake. I was quite literally inside her, kneeling in the torn-open shell of her abdomen, panting through the aftershocks of an orgasm with half her uterus clenched in one fist.

I was about to get up when Jonathan knocked cautiously on the basement door. "Chastity?"

"Goddammit, *what?!*"

"I was just going to ask what you want for dinner," he said, sounding hurt by my annoyance.

"It doesn't-!" I paused, glanced down at the mangled organ I was still holding. "I'll bring you something to cook. Go play outside, okay? I'm going to the store in a minute."

"Can I come with you?"

"No. I'm busy, Jonathan."

"Fine."

I leaned against the fridge and fingered myself as what was left of Savannah burned in the crematory oven, all the undesirable parts disappearing into smoke and ash. I had what I needed- she was going to be eternally perfect, eternally gorgeous. Better than when she was alive, certainly. I remembered dancing with her at prom, the way her boyfriend had glowered at us, the proud set of her jaw when she walked in wearing her mother's dress. She'd grown up in a trailer park, and she always held herself a little apart from the other cheerleaders, projecting an air of aloof confidence. She wouldn't borrow clothes from her friends, I remembered that very distinctly. Savannah Porter didn't need anyone's pity.

"This tastes weird."

"You're the one who cooked it, Jonathan. It's your fault if you don't like it, not mine."

"What is it, anyway?"

"Pork. Shut up and eat your dinner."

Savannah's empty skin looked uncanny laid out next to the frame, but I didn't let it bother me. I liked taxidermy as much as I liked embalming- I wanted to preserve something at the prime of its life, keep it just the way I liked it. Savannah was going to be like my Barbie behind glass, only better (and a brunette).

It wasn't until I had her stuffed and sewn up that I realized the glaringly obvious flaw in my plan: Jonathan was going to lose his mind when he saw Savannah. Getting him to live in a funeral home was hard enough, expecting him to accept a corpse lying in the guest room all the time would be almost impossible, especially if he figured out why I wanted it there. Luckily, he still believed women were incapable of sexual desire, so I doubted he'd connect the dots. I considered just locking the guest room door, but he'd want to know why, probably wouldn't let it go, and besides, I'd need help to get her up there in the first place.

"Jonathan," I began gently, brushing his hair while we watched an old cooking show, "you love me, don't you?"

"Of course I love you," he said warily. "You know that. Why do you ask?"

"I need a favor. It's no big deal, really, but you might not like it, so I'm telling you now because I don't want you freaking out on me. Do you remember my friend Savannah, from high school?"

"No."

"Well, she was really Lily Faith's friend more than mine. Lily Faith killed the cop, remember? Wasn't she nice to do that for us? We love Lily Faith."

"What do you want?"

"Savannah passed away recently. I thought it was awfully sad, her dying so young. I just wanted to keep her around, keep her alive in a way. You can understand that, can't you?"

"I don't-"

"It's just taxidermy, nothing wrong with that. You like taxidermy. I need you to help me carry her up to the guest room, it's too awkward with just one person."

"*What?*"

"It's just taxidermy, it's fine," I repeated, tugging Jonathan's hair warningly when he tried to stand up. "Help me get her into the guest room, then you never have to see her again, okay, baby?"

"That's not- no. Chastity, no, that's- that has to be illegal."

"So is matricide," I said, sugar sweet.

"You're out of your goddamn mind-"

"Help me move her, and I'll fire the groundskeeper. You want him gone, right? Just help me get Savannah upstairs, and I'll fire him tomorrow. You never have to see her again once she's in the guest room."

Jonathan was silent for several minutes, but finally, he nodded yes. "You'll fire him right away?"

"I'll call him as soon as we're done."

Jonathan squeezed his eyes shut as I led him downstairs to the morgue, muttering that it was gross, it was creepy, he didn't want to come down here. "I know, I know, you're doing so well," I said softly, patting his head. "So brave, doing so, so good for me."

When he saw the actual body, he screamed, tried to run back upstairs, but I easily stopped him and trapped him in a tight hug, hushing him. "You're sick," Jonathan choked out, thrashing weakly in my arms, "you're fucked in the head, Chastity, this is-"

"It's just taxidermy," I repeated, squeezing his waist warningly. "Nothing wrong with taxidermy. Help me carry her or you're sleeping in the morgue, do you understand? Jonathan, are you listening? I will lock your ungrateful ass in here all night, I swear to God."

"You're crazy," Jonathan whispered, but he helped me move Savannah just the same, eyes darting around wildly, looking anywhere else but at her. He bolted as soon as we had her in the guest bed, and I had to run after him to make sure he didn't go anywhere- the funeral home was out in the middle of nowhere, he'd just get lost in the woods. Luckily, he was in our bedroom, hiding under the covers with his thumb in his mouth.

"Jonathan," I sighed, arms crossed. He looked like a little boy, tiny and terrified, his pretty face wet with tears- fine lines were starting to show on his face, I'd noticed, the beginnings of wrinkles, but he still seemed so young. "Jonathan, sweetheart, you're overreacting. There's no need for all this hysteria."

"You have a *corpse* in the *guest room.*"

"How many times do I have to tell you it's just taxidermy?"

"She's a person!"

"Priscilla was a person. I don't want to hear anymore whining about the sanctity of life or whatever it is you think you're talking about when you let a little girl burn to death. I preserved a body that was already dead; you murdered a child. Don't think for a *second* you have the moral high ground here. You, of all people, *you* do not tell me what's right and what's wrong."

"That was-"

"Don't you fucking dare say it was a long time ago, you stupid cunt. You're just grossed out by the taxidermy thing, that's fine, you can be grossed out. Do *not* act like you have the right to any kind of moral indignation."

"Fine," Jonathan said softly, bringing his knees to his chest. "Fine. Whatever you say, Chastity. Whatever you say goes."

"Drop the sarcasm while you're at it."

As promised, I called the groundskeeper that night to tell him he was fired. "I really am so sorry," I said, trying to sound as sympathetic as possible.

"I don't understand what I did wrong," he responded, obviously struggling to be civil. "Mr. Kaplan ain't never had no problem with me."

"My brother says you've made inappropriate advances towards him." That wasn't entirely true- Jonathan had never outright lied about the groundskeeper, just insisted he made him uncomfortable, he felt watched, he felt unsafe, he absolutely refused to go outside if the groundskeeper was around. "I'm willing to let this go without pressing charges, I'll even give you a reference for future jobs, but-"

"You got a brother?"

"He's the really petite man with long black hair who plays in the cemetery. I know you know him."

"I thought that was your sister."

"Regardless, you're lucky I'm not pressing charges." I held my breath, hoping the groundskeeper would take this lying down.

"But I didn't do nothin'. I swear, Miss Caldwell, I never touched nobody. Please, I really need the money, I ain't so far from retirement-"

"I'm sorry, sir. I have to take my brother's word over yours. I'll give you a good reference if you need one."

"Nobody's gonna hire an old-"

"I have to go. I'm very sorry."

TWENTY-TWO

"The groundskeeper's gone," I told Jonathan, wrapping my arms around his waist while he made breakfast. "Now you can go outside on your own again- and I'll hire a female groundskeeper next."

"Could I do it?"

"What?"

"I could be the groundskeeper, couldn't I? I like gardening," Jonathan said hopefully.

"Don't be silly. You can't even drive, and part of the job is operating an excavator. Besides, you have such nice skin, you don't want to mess it up working in the sun all the time." I took my brother's small, soft hand, twined our fingers together. "Your hands would get all calloused."

"I'd like to help out more."

"You do enough. You're not ready for a job," I said, pulling away from him.

"When *will* I be ready for a job?"

"When you grow the hell up and stop acting like a child. Stop wetting the bed every night, stop sucking your thumb, stop treating me like your mother, huh? We'll talk then."

"It's not my fault," Jonathan said softly.

"I know, baby, but you're still not ready for any real responsibility. Let me take care of you, alright? Don't worry your pretty little head about anything."

The new groundskeeper was a tough, muscular woman in her fifties who lived with a female "roommate" and gave me a knowing smile when she shook my hand. "My parents owned a funeral home, but I was never very good with sad people," she said with a self-deprecating chuckle. "They put me outside doin' grunt work soon as they could."

"I'm better with the dead than the living," I told her. "When can you start?"

Jonathan liked Dinah, occasionally watched her from a distance while she worked but never actually spoke to her. I appreciated her straightforward, quiet nature; she didn't care about my life, I didn't care about hers. Everything was just fine between the three of us.

"Good kitty," Jonathan murmured, happily scratching behind Citrus's ears. As far as he was concerned, he was spread out on our couch with a cat purring contentedly on his chest, so I gave the dead thing a cursory pat before adjusting my brother and sitting down, resting his head on my lap. "How's your friend?"

"What?"

"Your friend. Isn't she still staying with us?" Jonathan spoke with forced calm, his eyes dreamy and far away. "Savannah. She's sick, she's resting in our guest room."

"Oh." I watched Jonathan stroke Citrus's fur, his hand trembling, and pat his chest. "That's right, she's resting."

"She's just resting," Jonathan said softly, relaxing slightly. I could see the decision to believe it settle in, and his soft red lips twitched into a contented smile. "Resting."

Once he decided Savannah was *just resting*, Jonathan stopped caring about the guest room. He'd been nervous at first, antsy every time he walked by the closed door, but if Savannah was *just resting*, everything was fine. If Citrus didn't eat, that was alright, Jonathan refused to notice; likewise, he didn't think about how Savannah never left her room, didn't wonder what I was doing in there with the door locked.

I'd preserved her as best I could, but it was impossible to taxidermy something female without sewing the vagina and anus shut. All I really did with Savannah after that first day with her insides was sit next to her and masturbate, strip her naked to admire my handiwork before redressing her. I'd put her in a pretty white sundress, patterned with bluebonnets- I vaguely recalled her saying she wanted to live in Texas one day.

I didn't think anything was wrong when the phone rang at 4AM. I got late night calls all the time- I was never really *off the clock*. People didn't die on a 9-5 schedule. "Hello?" I mumbled into the landline, sitting on the edge of our bed to stroke Jonathan's hair. He sighed in his sleep and nuzzled against my hand, and I smiled despite myself.

"Hi, Chastity," Granny said, voice heavy with tears. "I'm sorry, sweetheart, I know it's awful late- or early- I'm sorry. Arnie passed away last night."

"What?" I sat bolt upright, ignoring the way Jonathan whined unconsciously at the sudden loss of contact. "How? He was always so healthy…"

"A stroke. Very fast, in his sleep, very peaceful. I just woke up and he was gone. Smilin', like he was at rest." Granny sobbed, and I shook Jonathan's shoulder violently.

"We're on our way over."

"Oh, no, you don't gotta-"

"I said we're on our way over, Granny. Jonathan, up, now!"

"It's early-"

"Are you at home?"

"Yeah. Yeah, they just came and took him away when I called 911, I didn't know if I should go with them, or-"

"See you in a few minutes." Jonathan was finally awake, and he scowled at me as I hung up. "Grampa's dead."

"Is he really?" My brother sounded more curious than anything.

"Yes. He was old. I know you never liked him, but please, can you just pretend for Granny? You're her favorite, she wants to see you."

"Of course I can."

"Get changed and dressed, hurry up."

"We brought flowers," I said awkwardly, holding out a bouquet of leftover lilies to Granny. The upside of living in a funeral home was that we always had fresh flowers on hand. I'd started encouraging families to leave funerary flowers behind, saying they'd just take up space and they'd surely get more flowers from friends anyway, both because it was true and because Jonathan liked making floral arrangements.

"Oh- lovely. Thank you, darlin'," she mumbled, accepting them with an expression suggesting she'd never seen flowers in her life. I took them away again and went to find a vase while Jonathan burrowed into her arms, whispering something I couldn't hear. Whatever it was, she seemed to appreciate it, and when I came back, they were curled up on the couch with a photo album. "This was the day he proposed to me. I remember it was just a gorgeous day, middle of spring, we went down to the river to swim right after- your grandfather was always an outdoorsman- oh, it was magical. Absolutely magical."

"Sounds like a fairytale," I said, peering over her shoulder.

"It was. I couldn't afford a real nice dress for our wedding, so I had to wear my mama's dress, adjusted it myself, and then here comes the big day- see, here we are together- and I fell flat on my face as we walked outta the church, down that dirt road leads up to it. Tripped over my own damn feet! Arnie fell down, too, tryin' to catch me, and when we got up his suit was all stained- it'd rained the day before, that road was all mud- and my dress had a big ol' tear right in the skirt, here. Oh, Mama never let me live that one down!"

Granny held out an arm for me to snuggle up against her other side, and we sat together on the couch for hours, listening to every last Grampa story she could think of. She wove a tapestry of his life, as if she could keep him alive just a little while longer, and she didn't stop until Jonathan fell asleep on her shoulder. "Lord, but I been babblin', ain't I?" Granny said sheepishly, pushing his hair out of his face.

"No, ma'am. He's just tired."

"I see that," she laughed. "Poor baby. I'm glad you picked up the phone 'stead of your brother, I was scared he'd have one of his fits- he just seems too delicate to handle death."

"Does he?"

It felt strange to embalm my own grandfather, but mostly just because it required seeing him nude. Although Granny had fretted that I'd be traumatized, offered to go somewhere else, I insisted on doing it myself. "One last nice thing," I told her, petting her fluffy white curls, "one last nice thing I can do for him."

"It *is* good to have someone who knows what she's doin'," Granny commented as I walked her through burial options, headstones, caskets, services and last rites. "I had no idea dyin' was so complicated. When I go, just toss me in the ground and get it over with!"

"Not for a long time," Jonathan said nervously. He was sitting on her lap, both of them seated on the other side of my desk, trying to plan a funeral for a man who'd never wanted any sort of fanfare or attention. He was like a cat lately, curling up on her lap every time she sat down; Granny treated him like a living security blanket.

"Well, everyone dies eventually," she reminded him.

"But *you* won't." A slightly hysterical note crept into his voice, and Granny nodded quickly, hushed him.

"How you two like livin' out here? I know I ain't been 'round so much lately." Granny rubbed Jonathan's shoulder, letting him lean against her as we all sat around after the funeral, pretending to eat finger sandwiches.

"It's wonderful. I love my job, and Jonathan loves having so much room to play outside."

"You play in the cemetery?" Granny frowned, and Jonathan just squirmed closer to her, didn't respond.

"It's perfectly safe, Granny."

"It just seems morbid."

"The Victorians had picnics in graveyards, that's why we have them landscaped and made up to look pretty."

"I guess." She sounded doubtful. "Your grampa worked on a dredge boat one time, y'know. Twelve hours a day, seven days a week- I forget why, exactly. He hated it."

"I remember." Grampa loved talking about the various shitty jobs he'd had in his youth.

"And a pig farm, too. Lord, he stunk to high heaven ever' night- that only lasted a few months, and I was on his ass to get a better job the whole time!"

"I'm sorry he's gone."

"Well, I'll see him soon," she murmured, then glanced guiltily at Jonathan to make sure he hadn't overheard.

Granny remained resolutely healthy, though, and I began to joke that she'd outlive us both at the rate she was going. She told me she'd started falling asleep in Grampa's old armchair, but other than that, she was adjusting as best she could to life without her other half. Jonathan was completely unaffected by the old man's death, and I missed him in the impersonal way you miss a dead singer you'd listened to on the radio.

TWENTY-THREE

"How's it goin', Miss Caldwell?" the cashier asked, lazily scanning my purchases. I was fairly confident I'd never told her my last name, but people in Adabelle were starting to know me the same way they'd known Mr. Kaplan, had begun treating me with the slightly fearful respect small-town folks always give undertakers.

"Good."

"That's great. And how are *you,* Jonathan?" She pitched her voice higher to address him, and he scowled, and stepped closer to me.

"He's good, too."

"I don't want to go to the store with you anymore," Jonathan whined once we'd returned to the car, slouching in the passenger seat. "Everyone in town treats me like an idiot."

"You don't talk, Jonathan. It's a small town. All they know is that you don't speak, you live with your sister, you've never had a job- people are going to assume you're mentally challenged."

"You should let me get a job, then."

"Where?"

"The funeral home," he said, as if it were obvious. "I can be your secretary-"

"I don't need a secretary."

"I could garden, then, just around the-"

"Dinah does that."

"You have to let me do *something*."

"You're my housewife," I deadpanned.

"I want a job."

"Well, I'm not giving you one, and you can't go looking somewhere else without my permission. I'm your guardian, remember? I just want what's best for you."

"You say you want me to grow up, but you won't let me do anything on my own," Jonathan muttered petulantly. "Can't even use the stove without you in the room- I know how to use a damn stove."

"You wouldn't last a day without me, baby brother. Why can't you just be grateful I take such good care of you? Most people would love to live such an easy life- all you have to worry about is a few chores here and there, and I do everything else."

"I don't-"

"You're being a brat," I said sharply, hitting the steering wheel and making him jump. "Quit whining about how your life is too easy, you spoiled little asshole. I don't want to hear another word, do you understand?"

"Yes-"

"I *said* not another word!" Jonathan nodded quickly, curled into the fetal position, and started sucking his thumb.

"Take this," I ordered Jonathan, handing him a Valium and a glass of water.

"But I'm not upset-"

"Really? You were throwing a tantrum about getting a job, and all of a sudden, you're not upset?"

"It wasn't a *tantrum*."

"Just take your medicine, sweetheart." Jonathan glared at me but took the Valium just the same, obediently opened his mouth afterwards so I could make sure he'd actually swallowed it. I'd started seeing a psychiatrist recently, claimed to have terrible anxiety, said I was so stressed taking care of my mentally ill brother; the Valium really was helping me, just not in the way my psychiatrist had intended. Jonathan became sleepy and docile once the effects kicked in, infinitely more manageable.

"Happy?" Jonathan muttered, pulling away from me.

"Yes. Good boy." I took his face in my hands again, noticed a bit of stubble he'd missed on the underside of his jaw. "I know you're upset, sweetie, but I really do have your best interests at heart. I just don't think you could handle a job- think about it this way, if you were my secretary, you'd have to talk to strangers every day, male strangers, and they're all grieving. People lash out when they've just lost a loved one, they'd yell at you, threaten you, call you all sorts of nasty things, and you wouldn't like that, would you? No, you'd hate that. I'm only trying to protect you."

"I want to feel more useful," Jonathan insisted, hugging me, and tucking his face into my neck.

"You *are* useful, baby, I promise. You don't have to *earn* my love."

TWENTY-FOUR

The girl showed up a week after Jonathan's thirty-fifth birthday. It was unusually cold, but he'd insisted on going out to play in the cemetery anyway, so I just made him wear a jacket and promise to come back in an hour. I spent the time with Savannah, unbuttoned her dress slowly- I'd been sure to pick one that buttoned up the front- and admired my craftsmanship, ran my fingers over her leathery skin, pressed down on her unnaturally hard breast and briefly rubbed between her legs, over the silk panties I'd bought specifically for her.

"You never wear things like that," Jonathan had commented when he saw me walking upstairs with them, clenched too tight in my slightly sweaty fist.

"They're for you," I said automatically, and he scowled, cradled Citrus to his chest.

I'd kept her legs slightly apart, just in case I ever wanted to change her clothes or pull her underwear down to look at the neat stitchwork- I was proud of it, I'd made her look as pretty as possible- but I rarely did. I just sat back and smiled at her, rubbed her side, and touched myself slowly, occasionally moving forward to stroke her face. Her eyes had been burned along with the rest of the waste, replaced with cheap but perfectly sufficient prosthetics.

"*So* beautiful," I sighed, biting my lip as my pulse picked up, trying not to make a noise- Jonathan could easily come home without my noticing, and the last thing I needed was for him to know what I was doing with Savannah. He firmly, desperately believed she was still alive, but Jonathan was still terrified of sex, still insisted it was all rape, it was all sick and twisted and evil to him.

I buttoned her dress back up as soon as I finished, washed my hands in the guest bathroom and left, locking the door behind me. I always kept the key around my neck, tucked under my shirt. "Jonathan?" I called, walking into the living room- our upstairs apartment was set up with two bedrooms, a kitchen, and a living room, all still decorated to suit Mrs. Kaplan's fantastically feminine taste. Mr. Kaplan told me he liked pink well enough, so he just let his wife do whatever she wanted to the apartment, and we never bothered to change it.

Jonathan was sitting on the floor, trailing his hand through the rose-patterned rug, and playing with a little girl I didn't know, both of them fully invested in the huge, antique dollhouse I'd found at an estate sale. It was a perfect Victorian mansion in miniature and came with articulated porcelain dolls made for the house, molded to exactly the right proportions.

"Who's this?" I asked, smiling stiffly. *How did she get here? Why is there a kid in my house? Don't you realize how this looks?*

"Deedee," he responded unhelpfully. I waited for further information; none was forthcoming. The little girl ignored me completely, continued to move the dolls from room to room, so I cleared my throat and walked over, crouched down to be at her level.

"Deedee? Can you look at me, please? I'm Miss Caldwell- are your parents downstairs?" *Why did my fucking idiot brother bring you up here if they are?* All my questions vanished when the girl turned to face me, frowning. She had brown hair, but her face, her eyes, were exactly like Priscilla's. It was uncanny, seeing my childhood friend's features replicated on this living girl, frowning up at me. If I bleached her hair, they'd be practically identical. "Oh," I breathed, unconsciously reaching to touch her face.

Deedee- no, Priscilla- looked uncomfortable, but sat still as I patted her cheek, smiling twitchily. "Where'd you find her?" I asked Jonathan.

"The cemetery."

"I runned away," Priscilla added, a hard note of defiance in her voice. "My mama's angry all the time, she was always yellin' and then she *hit* me last night, she hit me right in the face, so I *left,* and you cain't make me go back! She said I didn't have to!"

"Her mama has a boyfriend," Jonathan added anxiously, fidgeting with his hair. "I want her to stay with us."

"Where did you run away from?"

"Over there," she said, pointing in what I suspected was a random direction. "We live just through the woods."

I was pretty sure I knew what she was talking about; there was a farmhouse with no farm about a mile down the road, shabby and falling apart. She must have just walked down the road until she got to the cemetery, or else wandered into the woods and got miraculously lucky. I could see a child up and vanishing in the forest.

"I won't make you go back," I promised, running my fingers through the girl's hair. "But this is the wrong color. I'll just fix it, okay? Then you can stay with us."

The new Priscilla was a lot less chipper than the old one, but I was convinced she'd cheer up soon. She liked Jonathan more than me, and I tried not to let it get under my skin- he *was* probably more fun. I looked every inch the undertaker in my all-black suit, raven hair slicked back severely, blank-faced, blue eyes dead and cold, but Jonathan was still a lovely little doll, fae and ethereal, content to be fussed over. He let Priscilla tangle his hair trying to braid it, played whatever games she wanted, and generally let her boss him around as much as I did.

While they occupied themselves in the living room, I called Granny. "Do you still own that old hunting cabin, out in the woods?" I asked, trying not to sound too out of breath.

"Well, we never sold it, at any rate. You takin' a huntin' trip?"

"Thinking about it. Thanks, Granny, I love you. Jonathan says hi."

I stood in the living room doorway, watching them play with the dolls- Priscilla was making up an elaborate story involving a princess in a tower, and Jonathan nodded along, doing exactly as he was told. "What are y'all playing?" I called.

"Rapunzel, kind of," Priscilla responded. She tugged on Jonathan's hair and giggled. "You look like Rapunzel."

"I think he's more like Snow White."

"He?" Priscilla glanced at Jonathan, considered, then shook her head. "She's a girl."

"Alright," I said ignoring the way Jonathan glared at me. "Snow White's a girl. Can I join y'all over there?"

"No. Only room for two," Priscilla replied coldly.

"Can I take Snow White's place, then?"

"No."

"Maybe later?"

"No."

Jonathan was smiling at the exchange, so I made a mental note to have a talk with him later. Priscilla was *my* best friend, not his. He didn't even like her, he'd murdered her last time, but that didn't matter anymore because Priscilla was fine, she was alive, I'd bleach her hair tomorrow. In the meantime, I lurked in the kitchen and listened to them talk.

"My mama used to yell all the time, too," Jonathan said hesitantly. "Does your mama drink a lot, or smoke meth?"

"What's meth?"

"It's a drug, it's these white crystals you-"

"She don't do drugs. My mama ain't no junkie, she's just mean. I guess she drinks, though."

"Whiskey?"

"Wine. Bottle of wine ever' night almost. She's nice when she drinks, so I like her a lot more when it gets late and she's drinkin', it calms her down. She's real nice at night, real funny, but she's just so *mean* all the rest of the time. Ever'thing I do makes her angry!"

"My mama was like that, too."

"She ever hit you?"

"Sure, all the time."

"My mama only hit me once."

"She'll probably do it again."

"You think so?"

"I remember."

"Is that your brother or your sister takes care of you?"

"My sister."

"Are you really a girl?"

"No."

"Well, I want you to be a girl."

"Alright. I can be." They resumed their game for a few minutes, and I'd almost tuned out by the time Jonathan asked, "What do you like to eat? I can cook anything you want. I'm a really good cook." There was an unusual note of pride in his voice.

"Um, grilled cheese, my mama puts mayonnaise on them and it's real, real good."

"Oh. Okay."

Priscilla helped Jonathan cook dinner that night, and I noted how much she adored him with distaste. They'd only known each other a few hours and already she was demanding he carry her around the kitchen while he cooked, wouldn't let him put her down. Jonathan, for his part, obviously loved the attention, happily allowed her to order him about and maintained a cheerful, ever-winding conversation about whatever she wanted the entire time. I glowered at them while we ate. "This tastes like shit, you know," I told Jonathan halfway through dinner, just to watch his face crumple.

"I'll make something else tomorrow night," he said guiltily.

"*I* like it," Priscilla retorted, and I snatched her plate, dumped the contents in the trash. "Hey!"

"It's disgusting. We'll probably all get food poisoning because this idiot can't cook," I snapped, throwing everything else away with it. Jonathan, predictably, started crying, but Priscilla just got up and went to the fridge. "What are you doing?"

"Gettin' food. I'm hungry, and I'm gonna eat dinner."

"You are *not!*" I slammed the door shut in her face, furious and confused- if I told Jonathan he was going to bed hungry, he might whine about it, but he wouldn't do a thing to challenge me. I felt like I'd generally listened to my mama, even if I hated her, so why wasn't Priscilla listening? Children obeyed adults, and anyway, we were best friends. I looked to Jonathan for help, but he just sat there and cried, as always, so I took a deep breath and crouched down, smiled at Priscilla. "Listen. Sweetheart. You can… you can eat something else if you'll let me cook for you, how about that? Help me cook, then you can eat."

"Fine," Priscilla muttered, crossing her little arms firmly.

"Let me carry you."

"If I get to eat," she said reluctantly, and I grinned as I picked her up, bounced her on my hip. She was a cute little thing, exactly like Priscilla, although her clothes weren't as much fun.

"Do you like pink?"

"No. My favorite color's green."

"Well, pretty soon it'll be pink. Don't you like Barbie dolls and all that?"

"I like Monster High dolls."

"What's a Monster High doll?"

"They're monsters who go to high school," Priscilla said, obviously thinking I was a complete idiot.

"I'll buy you some. Are they pink? You had lots of pink dolls when we were younger."

"I never had no pink dolls."

"Yes, you did. Lots of pink Barbies. Look, I'll show you the Barbie your parents bought me."

"My parents don't *know* you. I'm hungry-" Priscilla fell silent as I hurried out of the kitchen, brought her to the living room to look at my Barbie safe behind glass.

"This is Butterfly Princess Barbie. See? We both got one for Christmas, remember, but you took yours out of the box right away. I kept mine in her box, hid her under the truck so Mama couldn't find her, and now she's safe here."

"I never got no butterfly doll. I dunno you, lady."

"You *do!*" Priscilla flinched back when I yelled, and I smiled weakly. "We're best friends. I'll make dinner, okay? Your parents used to cook for us all the time."

"Whatever," she said quietly. She wasn't as chatty as she'd been with Jonathan, who watched us morosely from the kitchen table, but I tried to talk enough to make up for it. I wasn't used to being so verbose. I only made enough for two, pointedly didn't give Jonathan a plate. "Ain't you hungry, Snow White?"

"She fucked up cooking last time, she doesn't get to eat tonight."

"I'm not hungry, Deedee, but thank you," Jonathan said, trying to smile at her.

"Her name is Priscilla," I snapped.

"My name ain't-"

"Your name can be Priscilla," Jonathan interrupted, eyes darting between us. "Just say your name is Priscilla, *please.*"

"My name is Priscilla," Priscilla repeated after a minute's hesitation, scowling. My brother sighed in relief, grinned at her, then jumped when I kicked him under the table.

"Just do everything she tells you," Jonathan whispered. They were at the dollhouse again, and neither of them had noticed me standing a few yards away, dead silent. "Chastity's actually *very* nice, once you get to know her, I promise. She's always been kind to me. But she's used to being in charge, so please, do whatever she wants."

"I wanna go home," Priscilla snapped. "Your sister's crazy."

"No, no, you can't go home! Your mama's not safe, her boyfriend wants to rape you-"

"What's rape?"

"-you need to stay with us, we'll protect you, stay here."

"I bet Mama's lookin' for me," Priscilla said thoughtfully. "I bet she'll be a lot nicer now, 'cause I was always sayin' I'd run away, and now I really done it. Maybe she'll even take them anger management classes she's always goin' on about."

"You're safer here," Jonathan insisted. "Listen, Chastity will take care of us, and I can be your sister, isn't that what you want? What if you go back and she starts hitting you again, and she never lets you out of her sight? You'll wish you'd stayed then, won't you?"

"I'll spend the night, at least. Don't cry, Snow White."

"Our bed's big enough for you to sleep with us," I told Priscilla with forced cheer, trying to find something she could wear as pajamas. The best I could do was an oversized t-shirt previously belonging to Grampa that had somehow ended up buried in the back of our closet.

"Y'all ain't got no guest room?"

"No," I said.

"Savannah's sleeping there," Jonathan said at the same time.

"Who's Savannah?"

"Ignore her, she's retarded," I said quickly. "Snow White, go put a diaper on, we're about to go to sleep."

"*What?*" Priscilla demanded as Jonathan hurried into the bathroom, looking horribly ashamed.

"She still wets the bed. Isn't that gross?"

"No. It's not her fault," Priscilla snapped, glaring at me. "You're a bully."

"I was only teasing," I said, hurt and defensive.

"I don't *like* you." Her jaw was set firmly, and I saw genuine hatred in her eyes, but I ignored it, forced myself to smile.

"Of course you like me, we're best friends. Shut up, we're all going to bed now, alright? Just be quiet."

Priscilla started out in between Jonathan and I, then quickly squirmed over him so he was in the middle, snuggling into his arms. I tried to pull her arm to get her closer to me, but she actually *bit* me, and I was too tired to do anything about it. I fell asleep praying that she'd get over her weird affection for my brother and realize *I* was her best friend, not him. If I bleached her hair, I figured, she'd probably come around a lot faster.

I woke up in the middle of the night to the door creaking open and turned the light on immediately. Priscilla stood frozen in the doorway, looking like she didn't know whether to run or stay, so I stumbled out of bed and grabbed her at once, trying to be gentle- but then she *screamed,* and I had to clamp a hand over her mouth, pick her up so she wouldn't kick so much.

"What's going on?" Jonathan mumbled behind me.

"Hold *still!*" I finally let Priscilla fall to the floor, watched her gasp as the wind was knocked out of her, and knelt next to her head. "Where are you going? You said you wanted to stay with us, didn't you? I just want to be best friends, I know you want to be best friends again, too-"

"You're crazy," Priscilla wheezed. "I ain't never been your best friend, I never seen you 'fore today, and I wanna go *home.*"

"But your mama's mean," Jonathan said nervously, walking up behind me.

"This bitch is mean, too!"

"Don't call me a bitch," I said, offended.

"She'll be nicer," he promised, stepping around me to sit on Priscilla's other side.

"She didn't let you *eat,* and my name is *not* Priscilla! I'm goin' home, right now!"

"You're not," I snapped, grabbing her again. "You're staying with us, and we're going to be your best friends, okay? Well- I'm your best friend. Jonathan's just here. Come *on,* please, you have to remember me, you have to! Remember, we watched Live Aid on Halloween, it was taped-"

"*I don't know you!*"

"Chastity, let her go, you're scaring her," Jonathan whined, holding his arms out like he wanted to take her instead, like he had *any* right, when he took Priscilla away in the first place, he murdered my best friend and now I had her back and the bastard wanted to take her again, he was a murderer and a whore and a-

"Don't tell me what to do," I snarled. "What, you care about protecting kids all of a sudden? You didn't used to give a damn."

"I'm *sorry!*"

"Oh, you're sorry! Did you hear that, Priscilla, he's *sorry* he set your room on fire, sorry he let you die, well, that just fixes everything, doesn't it?!"

"I don't know what the *fuck* you people are talkin' about! Let me go *home!*" Deedee wailed, and I shook her violently, suddenly furious with the stupid little child I'd finally realized was just an imposter, wasn't my Priscilla at all, my Priscilla was long gone, dead at my brother's hand, my brother who sat there weeping and begging me not to hurt this random brat who'd wandered into our cemetery thinking she had it hard because her mama hit her once. Stupid little shit, stupid Jonathan, stupid bitch down the road, I couldn't stand any of them, and I felt like Priscilla had died all over again, left me alone save for my fucking brother, I always had my goddamn brother, dry his tears and pet his hair and-

"You're hurting her!" Jonathan shrieked, and I realized Deedee had gone quiet, my hands were around her neck, squeezing, squeezing, so tight my hands hurt, so tight I couldn't let go at all for another long minute. I finally released her, hands stiff and aching; Deedee collapsed, lifeless, eyes half-open.

"What?" I murmured, picking up her tiny wrist slowly, searching for a pulse. "That's... that can't be right. She's fine."

"Oh, my God. Oh, my God," Jonathan moaned, curling into a ball, and rocking himself back and forth. "Oh, my God."

"Shut up," I said, softer than usual. "This is your fucking fault, bringing some kid over here for no reason. I'll tell the cops you molested her. I'll tell them you killed her. You already murdered one little girl, it's not really a lie at all. Son of a bitch."

"I just wanted to help- she said she'd run away- said her mama hurt her, I wanted- I thought-"

"I don't care what you thought. You keep this between us, do you understand? If you ever think you should go tell the cops anything, remember, *you're* the one who brought her here. *You* kidnapped her."

"I wanted to show her the dollhouse. That's all I wanted."

"Sure, you did. Tell the cops that, Jonathan, they'll think you're a pedophile."

"I'm *not!*" I knew that was probably the worst thing I could have said to him, saw it in the way Jonathan tensed up, gagged, pressed himself further into the wall and sobbed even harder. "I'm not! I'd never, *never-*"

"I don't care. Never tell anyone what happened, do you understand?"

"Yes," Jonathan whimpered.

"That's right. I'll take care of it, so you just sit here and stay quiet."

I carried Deedee down to the morgue, already settled on my course of action. It would certainly be easier to just cremate her, dump the ashes in a river and forget it ever happened, but she still looked so much like Priscilla- more so now that she was still and quiet. All I had to do was bleach her hair and build a frame. There was plenty of space in the guest bedroom, Savannah wouldn't mind the company, and I'd have my best friend back *permanently,* just the way I'd seen her last.

TWENTY-FIVE

I put Priscilla in the fridge- I always felt awkward calling the refrigerated body cabinet a *fridge*, but Mr. Kaplan always called it that, thought it was hilarious- and went back upstairs. Jonathan was still curled against the wall, sucking his thumb, and staring off into the distance. He didn't react when I shook his shoulder, didn't react when I hit him or yanked his hand away from his mouth, so finally I just picked him up and carried him back to bed.

"You're such a crybaby," I sneered, setting him on top of the blankets. "Would it calm you down if I swaddled you, huh? Do you need me to change your diaper? God, you think I'm your damn mother!" Jonathan just stared at the ceiling, gripping our quilt- Granny had done the actual sewing, but he'd embroidered every square, and I wanted to tear it out of his grasp. Why did he have to be so histrionic about every little thing? I ached to feel guilty, I knew I *should* have felt guilty, but when I reached for repentance, there was nothing. "Are you really sorry?" I asked softly, sitting next to my catatonic brother, and combing my fingers through his hair. "Would you do it again?"

Jonathan didn't answer, didn't even look at me, and when I slapped him across the face, he just sobbed weakly.

"You think I'm your mother," I repeated, hot, angry tears welling up in my own eyes, "you think I don't have anything better to do than take care of you? I was supposed to be a ballerina. I wanted to be a ballerina, and Priscilla would have been a mortician- she would have been, if it weren't for *you.* You ruined my life!

"All those times I walked in on you with Mama's boyfriends, I remember. I always had to clean you up, calm you down, you put everything on *me!* I'm still fixing everything for you! You might as well be my child, it's not fair, it's *not fair!* I wanted to be a ballerina!" I was rambling, felt myself crying from a far-off, distant place, so unfamiliar with the feeling it barely registered as real, and I grabbed Jonathan's shoulders, pulled him onto my lap. He didn't resist, just leaned against me, seeking comfort, and I wanted to kill him, too, add him to the growing collection in my guest room- because it was *my* guest room, *my* house, none of this belonged to him, he'd never done a damn thing for me.

Instead, I unbuttoned my shirt and held his head to my breast, pulled his hair warningly when he tried to squirm away. "You think I'm your fucking mother, let me take care of you," I hissed, keeping hold of him with one hand while I shoved my fingers into his mouth, forced him to at least latch onto my nipple even if I couldn't make him go along with it completely.

"You think I'm your mother. You think I'm your *goddamn* mother. I'd have killed you if you really were my son. Fucking bastard, stupid, worthless little *bastard.*" Jonathan trembled in my arms, and my voice fell into a gentle, mocking coo, almost a lullaby. "Everything she did, everything her boyfriends did, you deserved every minute of it."

I woke up alone in bed the next morning, and my heart skipped a beat. I didn't believe Jonathan would ever intentionally tell anyone what had happened, but he very well might have called Granny, asked if he could go stay with her, and if he did that, she'd know something was wrong. Maybe she wouldn't work out exactly what, but she'd be wary of me, she'd want to keep him with her, he might tell her eventually and then we'd both be fucked. I was the only person who could take care of him, no one else would be willing to do it after Granny died. Did he even realize that? "So fucking ungrateful," I muttered, stumbling down the hall in my pajamas.

Thankfully, Jonathan was in the kitchen, reading a book while he waited for something to finish baking. The whole room smelled like cinnamon. "Good morning," he said, smiling nervously.

"You're not supposed to use the oven without me."

"I know how to do it, Chastity. I'm not stupid."

"I'm worried you'll hurt yourself or kill yourself."

"When I kill myself, I'll just take sleeping pills. Sticking my head in the oven sounds too painful."

"Very funny. What are you making?"

"Coffee cake."

"That sounds nice." Jonathan opened his mouth to say something, but visibly reconsidered and kept smiling instead. "What are you reading?"

"*The Gravedigger's Daughter.*"

"Is it good?"

"Yes."

"Well, good. I'm glad." I sat down next to him, patted my lap, and he got up like a well-trained dog, settled in my arms at once. "Did you sleep well?"

"Fine." Jonathan nuzzled at my neck, put his book aside, and murmured, "What are you going to do with the body?" He sounded more aware than he had in days, and I was a little surprised he even remembered what had happened last night.

"What body?"

"God, Chastity, how dumb do you think I am?" Jonathan pulled away from me, glowering, mumbled some excuse about his coffee cake and ran to the oven, acted very invested in looking through the glass door.

"I'll take care of it. Don't worry about the body, okay? I don't want you thinking about that."

"Apparently I'm taking the fall if we get caught, so as a matter of fact I *am* worried-"

"We won't get caught. Why don't you worry about your chores, and I'll worry about Priscilla?"

"Her name was Deedee," Jonathan muttered.

"I don't give a damn what her name was. Don't act like you care, either."

"Sorry."

"No one cares that you're sorry. *Sorry* won't bring Priscilla back to life."

"Do you want coffee cake?" Jonathan's eyes were starting to glaze over, the familiar dreaminess creeping back into his voice, and I could tell he was retreating into himself again, going away to whatever softer, kinder internal world he lived in. "I made coffee cake."

"I'd love some, but Jonathan, remember- if anyone asks, you didn't see a little girl around here. Got it?"

"Uh-huh."

"Tell me you understand."

"I understand, Chastity."

I built the frame in a day, interrupted only briefly to have a meeting with some obnoxious widower who kept trying to show me photos of his newly deceased wife on a cruise she'd taken the year before. It had taken a while to skin Savannah, but I'd got the hang of it with her, so Deedee was a little faster. She was still Deedee until I bleached her hair, I decided, carefully running my knife just under the skin, separating it neatly from the muscle and bone. I threw the rest of her in the incinerator as soon as I had the pelt.

Deedee's skin was still soaking in a mixture of water, table salt and disinfectant when her mother walked into my office. I mistook her for a customer at first, more than used to weeping women wandering in uninvited, and was just gearing up for my usual spiel about calling ahead when she handed me a flyer. "Sorry to bother you," she mumbled, rubbing at her bloodshot eyes, a stack of more crumpled flyers clutched to her chest, "but my daughter been missin' two days now. Cops ain't no help."

I looked at Deedee's photo, reflected that her face had looked awfully different after I peeled it off her skull, and politely said, "I'm so sorry to hear that, ma'am. I'll be sure to keep an eye out."

"We live just down the road, 'bout a mile that way. Didja see anything on Tuesday? She's real social, but she ain't too friendly, if that makes sense. I mean, she wants to talk to ever'body, but, Lord, the girl's got a mouth on her."

"No, sorry. I'm pretty busy here."

"You got people comin' in and outta the graveyard, right? Maybe one of 'em saw somethin'?"

"I couldn't tell you. I don't really pay attention to who visits the graveyard."

"But they'd be in the parkin' lot out front, right? You noticed any unusual cars on Tuesday?"

"No, ma'am."

"You got security cameras anywhere?"

"No, ma'am, I'm sorry."

"Well, you should," the woman muttered, fidgeting with the corner of a flyer, and tearing it. "My phone number's on there, look. Eden Lewis, right there, and my email and home address, ever'thing. So's you can find me. It's that big gray house, right down there, if you go out your driveway and take a left."

"I appreciate that. I'll certainly let you know if-"

"Does anyone else live here?"

"My brother, but he's mentally handicapped. He won't be able to tell you anything."

"Can I talk to him anyway? Please? He *can* talk, cain't he?"

"Well… he has trouble with strangers…"

"Please," Eden begged, her eyes brimming with tears. "Listen, maybe I shouldn't tell you this, but I- I ain't been the best- I hit her, not long before she disappeared. Runned off. I didn't mean to, honest, I was- I get so mad- I been wantin' to take some anger management classes, some therapy, I don't wanna hurt my girl. She's only six years old, she turns seven next month, she's a real good girl. I'm scared she thinks I don't love her."

"Let me ask him," I said, gesturing for her to take a seat.

"Thank you," Eden mumbled, biting her lip so hard she'd probably draw blood.

Jonathan was in the living room, petting Citrus and staring at the dollhouse, a scarily blank expression on his face. "Deedee's mama wants to talk to you," I said, and he jumped, set Citrus down on the carpet.

"I didn't do anything wrong," he whined, squirming closer to the dollhouse. "I just wanted to play with her, I didn't do *anything wrong!*"

"Like I told you before, Jonathan, that won't hold up in court. Nobody can tell how she died anymore, so it's my word against yours, which means you'd better keep your fucking mouth shut. Go down there, let her ask you some questions, and act like you never met Deedee in your life, got it? Don't say a fucking word, just let me do the talking. You never talk to strangers, anyway, shut up and let me handle it."

I led him downstairs by the hand, sat him next to Eden, and stood with my hand on his shoulder. "Tell this nice lady where you were on Tuesday, Jonathan." He stayed quiet, exactly as I'd instructed, kicked his heel anxiously against the leg of his chair. "Jonathan? Can you speak up for me, please? I told you he's scared of strangers," I reminded Eden apologetically, offering a weak half-smile.

"Oh. Well, um, Jonathan, dear, lemme show you a picture of my daughter, okay? She's a sweet little girl named Deedee, and maybe you seen her on Tuesday?" Eden handed him the flyer, and Jonathan inhaled sharply when he saw Deedee's photo, pushed it away immediately. "Do you recognize her?" He shook his head, turned to cling tighter to me.

"I'm so sorry, ma'am," I said, patting my brother's back. "He was just in our living room all day Tuesday; he wouldn't have seen her. Is it alright if we continue this conversation alone? I think Jonathan's a little overwhelmed."

"Sure," Eden sighed, slumping back in her seat.

"Go upstairs, sweetheart," I instructed my brother. He didn't need to be told twice, and I sat down across from Eden as soon as he was gone. "I really am sorry, Mrs. Lewis."

"Call me Eden, please. I ain't married."

"Of course. I hope you find your daughter soon, and if I see anything, I'll let you know right away."

"I appreciate that. What's your name, now?"

"Chastity Caldwell."

"That's a real purty name. Well, I'll… I'll go."

"Eden." She turned to face me, and I saw the awful pleading in her eyes, the dread, the certainty without proof that something horrible had happened to her daughter, the crushing knowledge that it was, in some way, her fault, and I said, "I'm sure Deedee wants to come home."

"I didn't like her," Jonathan commented over dinner that night.

"Who, Eden?"

"Yeah. It's her fault Deedee ran away in the first place; she shouldn't be going around pretending to miss her."

"I'm sure she really does miss her. You can love your child and still be a bad mother."

"Mama used to love me," he said thoughtfully. "Before Daddy came back, when we lived with her parents. You know she was fourteen when she had me, right?"

"Yes."

"Her parents didn't want her to drop out of school, so they raised me the first few years. They didn't want her around Daddy either, but once she was eighteen, they got back together. He was already living out in the trailer, I'm not sure how he knew the landlord, but she moved in with him right away. She was just drinking at first, she tried to stay away from meth, but Daddy kept pushing her, and then she got addicted pretty fast once she tried it."

"And you were eight, when…?"

"It was Daddy's idea. He promised me it would only happen once." Jonathan chewed his lip. "He told me to be a good boy for his nice friend."

"Did he ever touch you?"

"Our father? Not really."

"What's that supposed to mean?"

"He helped me clean up afterwards, said I was too young to do a good job. Never did anything else."

"Why'd he leave, anyway? I don't remember."

"I don't know. He just up and left one day."

"He's probably dead by now."

"Almost certainly." After a minute, Jonathan quietly added, "Mama really did love me, I think. She never loved you, but before she went crazy, I remember she used to hold me on her lap in the evenings, once her homework was done."

"Are you sure it wasn't her mother?"

"I guess it could have been. I just liked to think it was her, especially at first, with her boyfriends. Maybe I imagined it."

"You must have."

Jonathan shrugged, went to put his plate in the sink. "Doesn't matter anyway. Even if she did love me, it's not enough. I'll never feel sorry about *her*." He scrubbed the plate calmly. "I didn't mean to kill your friend, and I'm sorry I did, but I'll never care about Mama."

I decided it would be too much work to bleach Deedee's hair, so once I had her stuffed, I shaved it all off instead, bought a little blonde wig and sewed it to her scalp. I took some of my old clothes from Granny's house, pretended Priscilla was just borrowing some of my things, and finally ordered little pink cowboy boots online. It was a risk, but one I was willing to take- the cops in Adabelle didn't give a fuck about the missing children of alcoholic single mothers.

Finally, Priscilla was complete, and she was perfect. I put her in a sitting position, set her on a chair in the guest room and talked to her every day, covered her eyes and ears when I spent time with Savannah, and generally adored her. I'd stitched her mouth into a small smile, lips pulled back just slightly to show her teeth- Priscilla had always been grinning- and played Queen for her. Jonathan was as affectionate as ever; I honestly couldn't tell if he was pretending nothing had happened, or if he'd genuinely forgotten. I made an effort to be gentler with him.

"How's your anxiety?" my psychiatrist asked. He kept glancing at the clock behind me.

"Better."

"Do you think the medication is helping?"

"Yes, definitely."

"What about…" He squinted at his notes. "You mentioned feeling frustrated with your brother, is that still a problem for you?"

"Not as much. No."

"Are you depressed at all?"

"I killed a little girl."

"What was that?"

"I said I feel fine."

TWENTY-SIX

I was studying photos of a middle-aged alcoholic when Officer Thompson knocked on my office door. "Please come in," I said distractedly, setting them aside. He'd died in a car crash, and since his family inexplicably insisted on an open casket funeral, I had to reconstruct his face. "I'm sorry, I don't believe I had any appointments today- did you call?"

"I'm actually not here about a funeral," the visitor said, smiling politely. "I'm Officer Thompson, I just gotta ask you a few questions. A little girl named Deedee Lewis went missin' nearby a week ago, you heard anything 'bout that?"

"Her mother came over here with flyers, asked if I'd seen her."

"Had you?"

"No."

"Well, is it possible for me to have a conversation with your brother?"

"I'd like to know why. He's mentally handicapped, so I don't want to stress him out for no reason. I'm sure you understand."

"Oh, sure, sure. I got me a cousin like that. Ain't no big deal, really, it's just that Mrs. Lewis wants him brung in for questioning, says he was out in the graveyard the day her girl disappeared. Accordin' to her, you said he was inside all day, but she talked to a lady in the grocery store who says she came to the graveyard to pay respects and saw him talkin' to a kid. We all sorta took that with a grain of salt, though- Mrs. Lewis drinks too much, and she heard it from a lady drinks even more'n she does. Between you and me, I think it's just a desperate mother pointin' fingers and the town gossip wantin' to be at the center of things, so I'll just talk to him here, if that's alright."

"That should be fine," I said calmly. "Is it alright if I stay? Jonathan's very skittish, so I'm afraid you won't get much out of him either way, but he might have a panic attack if I leave him alone with a stranger." *Especially a cop.*

"No problem."

I smacked Jonathan on the thigh when I got upstairs. "What the fuck's wrong with you? You didn't bother to see if anybody was around before bringing some kid inside our house?"

"What are you *talking* about?" Jonathan stepped away from me, wincing.

"Someone saw you talking to Deedee."

"I didn't notice- oh. I guess there was a woman out there, but she was sort of far away, I wasn't paying attention."

"And you brought a kid into our house with her *watching?*"

"I think she was gone by the time we went inside."

"You didn't make sure?!"

"I wasn't trying to do anything bad! I didn't think I had anything to hide."

"Goddammit," I muttered, pinching the bridge of my nose. "Okay, Jonathan. Okay. Well, there's a cop here to talk to you about it, but lucky for you- lucky for *us*- he thinks the bitch is lying. So just sit quietly, don't tell him shit, let me do all the talking, alright?"

"Alright," he said, barely above a whisper. His hands were already trembling.

Jonathan grabbed my arm and froze when he saw Officer Thompson, whimpering. I remembered how often Mama's cop boyfriend had shown up in uniform, and tried unsuccessfully to soothe my brother, urging him forward. If he was a cat, his fur would be standing on end, I reflected with more than a little amusement. "Sorry, sir, he's not… I don't think he'll sit down."

"That's fine. So, Jonathan, do you know a girl named Deedee? She has brown hair, brown eyes, she's about this tall, does that sound familiar?" Jonathan just trembled in my arms, gave no indication of even hearing, let alone understanding, Officer Thompson's question. "Have you ever talked to a little girl in the graveyard?"

"Can you try to answer his questions, sweetie?" Officer Thompson stepped closer, laid a hand on my brother's shoulder, and Jonathan cried out in terror, clung to me even tighter. I heard liquid trickling to the floor a moment later, looked down to see he'd lost control of his bladder, and sighed in genuine irritation. "My apologies, Officer, he's…"

"No, no, it's my fault," Officer Thompson said, moving back with blatant disgust. "Thanks for your time, at any rate. I'll talk to Mrs. Lewis. Y'all have a good day, now."

"I hope you know you're the one mopping my floor," I told Jonathan as soon as the cop was out of earshot.

Eden showed up unannounced the next afternoon. "I need to talk to your brother," she demanded, and I smiled, stood to greet her.

"Eden, I understand you're upset, but-"

"No, you don't understand! You couldn't possibly understand, you don't got children! My baby is *gone,* and nobody gives a damn, nobody's helpin' me find her! Cassie told me she seen your brother talkin' to her the day she went missin', and *you,* you lied to me, you said he was inside all day, I need to see him!"

"Eden, please, have a seat. I didn't mean to lie- I really do think Jonathan was inside."

"So, Cassie's lyin', is that it?"

"Maybe Cassie saw someone else talking to her."

"No, Cassie said she thought it was a woman, she didn't realize it was your brother 'till I told her what he looked like, and she said it was him- long black hair, real pale, wearin' loose, modest clothes. That's why she didn't go up to them, she didn't really see who it was, just saw a woman talkin' to a kid and figured it was a mother and daughter. Lemme talk to your brother."

"Jonathan is mentally handicapped and emotionally unstable," I said firmly. "I'm sorry, but I won't let you upset him because of something your friend *thinks* she saw."

"Officer Thompson said he was real nervous, like he was hidin' somethin'."

"He was raped by a cop when he was a child, that's why he was fucking nervous," I snapped, losing my patience with this pathetic, whiny woman trying to blame someone else for her own shitty parenting. "I realize you're looking for your daughter, but you are wasting your time trying to harass an innocent, disabled man when you could be organizing a search party, encouraging the cops to investigate *actual* leads. If you come here again, I'm going to file a restraining order- this whole situation is causing my brother undue distress."

"My baby could be dead," Eden sobbed, and for a wild second I wanted to take her upstairs, show her exactly what had happened to the baby she didn't care about until she lost her.

"I'm sure Deedee is just fine, ma'am, but you're failing her by wasting time with us. I have to ask you to leave the premises."

"She's out of her mind," I told Priscilla after Eden was gone, fidgeting with my CD player. "She has *no* proof, none whatsoever, and here she is bothering us for no real reason. That cop said Cassie's a drunk, and I believe him- but of course Eden's a drunk, too. Just like Mama. A bottle of wine every night, Deedee said." I sat back and smiled at her, the opening notes of "39" washing over us. "We used to dance to this song, remember that? It was one of my favorites."

I wondered if the cops would actually follow through on Eden's leads. How hard was it to get a warrant to search someone's home? You needed probable cause, and while a strange man talking to a child right before she disappeared next to his house definitely qualified, the police didn't believe Cassie or Eden. They wouldn't get a warrant just to ease her paranoia, would they?

I looked from Savannah to Priscilla, chewing my lip in consideration; it was technically true that Jonathan had kidnapped Deedee, and they couldn't prove which one of us had killed her, but no one who'd met him would believe he was responsible for my macabre taxidermy. Granny would testify that he'd never set foot in Grampa's taxidermy shop, while I practically lived there, and besides, *I* was the mortician. I couldn't blame everything on him, and I didn't want to- as often as I threatened him with it, I didn't really want him in prison.

I doubted they'd actually search my house, but just in case, I decided I needed to move Savannah and Priscilla, just for a little while. Mr. Kaplan's hearse had come with the funeral home, and no one would question me taking it out of town for repairs- *hearses need special maintenance,* I heard myself saying, if anyone even asked. Nobody in Adabelle really cared what Jonathan and I did. We were accepted as eccentric, creepy, but ultimately harmless local fixtures, the same as Mr. Kaplan had been.

"Jonathan," I called, stepping out of the guest room, "help me put something in the hearse, will you? We're going for a drive."

"Don't you like Loretta Lynn?" I asked, turning the radio up. Jonathan was leaning his head against the window, thumb in his mouth, eyes half-lidded. He nodded slightly, obviously not listening. "What's wrong? I'm sorry if you're uncomfortable in the hearse, but we won't be in here very long, okay? We're going to this old cabin Grampa owned-you can drive right up to it, so we don't have to carry them very far."

"Taking our friends on a trip," Jonathan whispered, muffled. There was drool on his chin, but I decided not to comment.

"Exactly right, baby brother. We're taking our friends Savannah and Priscilla on a trip, that's all."

"Just taking a trip." Jonathan occasionally mumbled to himself throughout the rest of the drive, and I had to tell him to get out of the car several times when we got to the cabin. It was rundown, almost completely exposed to the elements-I couldn't leave them there for too long.

"We're going to clean the living room when we get home, okay? Everything Deedee touched; we're cleaning very thoroughly."

"I'm good at cleaning."

"Yes, you are. My helpful boy."

"You can't put bleach on their clothes," Jonathan said, trying to take the dolls away from me. "They're antique."

"Deedee was playing with them; I need to get rid of any fingerprints. Do you want to be arrested?"

"Shut up! Stop it! All you ever do is say I'm going to jail! I didn't hurt her, *you did!* And- and I don't know what you did with her, but I don't know how to use a crematorium,

I don't know- Granny will believe me." He was sobbing by the time he finished, curled into a ball with his face buried in his knees, and I sighed.

"Jonathan, listen. I'll *never* tell anyone what you did, I'm just trying to get through to you that you'll go to prison if we get caught. You understand that, don't you? You understand that even if you didn't kill Deedee, the last thing anyone saw was a grown man talking to a six-year-old girl, and then she went missing. If they find her DNA anywhere in here, that's enough to convict you, so you need to help me clean this house, okay?"

"I didn't kill her," Jonathan muttered as he scrubbed the floor of the dollhouse with a sponge.

"You killed Priscilla."

"When I was a *child*."

"You were seventeen! *She* was a child, you son of a bitch!" I tugged his hair sharply, backhanded him across the face and reached for my belt, but withdrew my hand when he hugged me tightly, sobbing a nearly incoherent apology and whimpering *no no no no*. Whether he thought I was threatening to spank him again or implying something worse, I don't know. "I don't want to hear excuses for setting a little girl on fire."

"I didn't-"

"*Jonathan.*"

My brother fell silent, curling closer to me and tucking his head under my chin. He smelled sweet, like honey and lemon- it was a perfume I'd bought him, after he told me my cologne was nice. I only wore cologne because Granny had worried the smell of death would start clinging to my clothes and hair, "what with you bein' around… *bodies*… so often." While I always came up from the morgue smelling faintly of embalming fluid, that was more of a sharp, aggressively clean chemical smell, and the only time I actually smelled bad was immediately after fucking Savannah's flayed corpse.

"I just don't want you to ruin her clothes," Jonathan muttered after a minute of silence.

"Hiding the evidence is a little more important than your doll's clothes, you get that, right?"

"If her clothes are covered in bleach stains, that looks like you tried to get rid of blood or something," he pointed out, and I had to admit he was right. Ultimately, I let Jonathan wash their clothes gently in the sink, while I violently scrubbed the porcelain with bleach. By the time I was satisfied everything was clean, our whole apartment reeked, so I opened every window and decided to wait 24 hours before inviting the cops over to have a look around.

"I want to help ease your mind, that's all," I said, trying to sound both sympathetic and put-upon as I led the cops and Eden upstairs. I'd sent Jonathan to the cemetery in an attempt to keep him from freaking out or saying anything stupid, and my guests seemed quietly relieved he wasn't there. "Have a look around, officers. Eden, can I offer you some tea?"

"Sure," she said, eyes darting everywhere like she expected Deedee to just be sitting in the living room. I poured us both a tall glass of the sweet tea I'd made earlier that morning and sat down across from her. "Thanks for, um, humorin' me. You're awful nice, Miss Caldwell, and I don't mean to stress you out none, I'm… I miss my daughter, that's all."

"Well, like I said, my brother couldn't hurt a fly. I just wanted to set your mind at ease."

"How long have you been a funeral director?"

"About two years, now."

"You're very young."

"I had a childhood friend who wanted to be a mortician, but she passed away before she got the chance."

"Ah." Eden nodded, stirred the ice in her glass with a fingertip. "Seems like I never seen a young funeral director before."

"Most people go into this career later in life, I guess."

"I'm real sorry 'bout your friend."

"Thank you."

We sat in awkward silence until the cops returned, both of them looking like they wanted to punt Eden across the room for wasting their time. "Well, there ain't nothin' here," Officer Thompson said shortly. "We really are *so* sorry to keep botherin' you, Miss Caldwell."

"No trouble at all. I hope this helped, Eden?"

"Could we search the graveyard, too?" she asked weakly.

"You're more'n welcome to do that on your own time, assumin' Miss Caldwell don't take out a restraining order," Officer Thompson snapped. "We got things to do, Mrs. Lewis."

"I... I understand. Of course." Eden nodded at me, and I should have just nodded back, reached to shake her hand, said some vague, comforting nonsense, but instead I met her eyes and smiled, just for a second, a quick, uncontrollable, triumphant smile. It was gone in a flash, but Eden had noticed, and I saw her eyes harden. "Are you sure-?"

"Mrs. Lewis. *Leave.*"

"That went well," I told Jonathan as we brought Savannah and Priscilla back in the hearse.

"How much maintenance can this thing possibly need? People will ask questions."

"It's the middle of the night, the odds of someone seeing us twice-"

"What kind of auto shop does car repairs at 2AM?"

"No one would give it that much thought. Can't you just be happy everything's over? Eden's off my ass, the cops think she's crazy, we're in the clear."

"In the clear," Jonathan muttered scornfully, curling closer to the window, and slipping his thumb between his lips.

"You know, your teeth will get crooked if you keep doing that."

TWENTY-SEVEN

I saw Eden a few months later, buying four bottles of cheap wine at Winn-Dixie. "Have you found your daughter yet?"

"No," she said, barely looking at me. Either her hair had been dyed when I first met her, or it had just gone gray very, very fast. Her clothes were obviously unwashed, she hadn't bathed in at least a week, and she'd lost weight she couldn't afford to lose.

"I'm terribly sorry."

"Are you? I wonder," Eden muttered, running her finger obsessively over the zipper on her wallet. "I told you I hit her before she ran away, didn't I?"

"Yes."

"But I didn't tell your brother."

"Uh, no, I don't think so."

"I didn't. I know I didn't, but when I seen him in the graveyard two weeks ago, I tried to talk to him. He walked away at first, said somethin' about not talkin' to strangers, but I followed him, I kept askin', and he said- *maybe you shouldn't have hit her, then.* That's what he said to me, *maybe you shouldn't have hit her.*"

"I must have told him about it. I'm sorry, I tell him pretty much everything-"

"Y'all acted like he couldn't talk; first time I met him."

"Selective mutism."

"She would've told him if she met him in the graveyard. That child-"

"Listen, Eden, I don't really remember every conversation I have with my brother, but I must have told him about it at some point."

"I'd do *anything*," Eden said hoarsely, grabbing my arm with a claw-like hand. "Please, Chastity, I would do anything, anything in the world, to have my girl back. I was a bad mother, I know that, I didn't mean to be- you know, my daddy was awful to me, and when I was a little girl I always promised myself I'd be better, I wouldn't get so angry, and then I... I never wanted to yell at her like that. I *love* her. You can't understand how much I love my daughter."

"I wish I could help you," I said, shaking her off.

Jonathan yelped like a puppy when I punched him in the face, fell to his knees with his hands over his nose. "Chastity!"

"You fucking *spoke to her?!*"

"Who-?"

"Eden! Eden fucking Lewis, you told her about Deedee, you practically admitted you met her!"

"Oh- I- I wasn't-"

"You weren't *thinking?* Yeah, I know! I know you weren't fucking thinking, you goddamn retarded little whore!" I pulled him up by his hair, ignoring the way he shrieked, pleaded for me not to hurt him, and dragged him downstairs, through the funeral parlor. Jonathan wailed when he realized where we were going, tried to get away, shoved at me ineffectively but couldn't really fight back, always the weaker sibling, always submissive.

"Chastity, I'm sorry, I'm sorry, I'll never talk to her again-"

"Every problem we have, it's always because you're too stupid to think anything through!"

"Chastity-"

"SHUT UP!"

I dragged Jonathan into the morgue, kneed him in the groin to make him stop flailing around so much, and pulled open a drawer in the fridge while he hyperventilated. I was so furious I'd forgotten that drawer was occupied by the late Mr. Joseph Nelson, so I slammed it shut and opened another, empty drawer, picked Jonathan up and set him on the cold metal slab, noticing that he'd gone into one of his little catatonic states again.

"Jonathan," I said sharply, slapping him across the face. He blinked, tried to focus on me, reached out for me with pathetic desperation for forgiveness.

"I'm sorry," he said hoarsely.

"Lie down."

"Huh?" Jonathan shook his head, trying to wake himself up, remembered where we were and cried out; I shoved him backwards before he could get away, forced him to lie flat and closed the drawer. He started screaming at once, banging on the metal walls and wailing like a dying animal, obviously thrashing around in there.

"Jonathan, baby, these drawers are airtight," I called, yelling to be heard. "You'll suffocate if you don't calm down." He either didn't hear me or was too panicked to care, so I opened the drawer after a minute, let him cling onto me. "You're cold."

"I'll never do it again, I'll never do it again, I'll never do it again, I'll never-"

"I know you won't, sweetheart. I believe you. But just to make sure you remember, you can stay down here tonight, okay?"

"No-!"

"Yes, you'll stay here with Mr. Nelson. He's right in that drawer if you get lonely. Sleep on a gurney or on the floor, I don't care, and think about what you did. If anyone believed Eden, what you said to her would be evidence against you. Don't you realize that?" Jonathan made a choked sort of moaning noise, clung to me like he a drowning man, and I had to pry him off to go upstairs. He didn't move, just stayed curled against the fridge, rocking himself slowly back and forth.

I briefly panicked when I walked into the morgue the next morning and didn't see Jonathan, but he was just sleeping in a corner further away from the fridge, shivering in a puddle of urine. "Clean that up, then go take a shower," I ordered after shaking him awake. Jonathan complied without a word, moving like a zombie.

"How was your night?" I asked once he was clean and dry.

"I want to live with Granny," Jonathan responded.

"Don't be silly, she's too old. She'll die soon."

"Will you stuff her like an animal, too? Like Deedee?"

"I might. Listen, Jonathan, I don't *want* to scare you like that. I want us to get along, and we usually do, right? You make me punish you when you do stupid things like tell Eden you met her daughter."

"I didn't-"

"You said something you could only have heard from Deedee, or at least, something she *thinks* you could only have heard from Deedee. If the cops ask, I told you. Eden was already suspicious of us, and now she's even more suspicious, because you talked to her after I specifically, *very clearly,* told you not to."

"I said I was sorry."

"I wanted to make sure you really were."

"Don't *ever* treat me like that again," Jonathan whispered. "I'll kill you if you do."

"If you ever do anything that stupid in the future, I'll kill you first."

Despite his little threat, Jonathan had forgiven me by afternoon, and that night in bed he was his usual snuggly self.

TWENTY-EIGHT

For two years, Eden left us alone. I occasionally saw her at Winn-Dixie, but she never came back to the cemetery, and the cops never bothered us about Deedee again. We settled back into our usual lives, and Jonathan forgot anything had happened at all, spent his time cooing over Citrus, playing outside, and reading endlessly. I started ordering him books online, since he'd read almost everything the tiny Briar County library had to offer. Granny took up jogging, Savannah and Priscilla remained in perfect, pristine condition, and Peggy Lee Watson moved back to Adabelle.

"Hey, Chastity!" she shrieked gleefully, barging into my office.

"Is my phone number not showing up online? Why does no one ever call ahead?"

"Good to see you, too! So New Orleans didn't work out." Peggy Lee flopped down across from me, beaming. "Thought I'd have a better chance there than LA."

"You wanted to be an actress, right?"

"Yep! Turns out I suck at it, but I tried for a while, got in a few commercials. I was the lead in an organic dog food commercial," she said with a sort of self-deprecating bravado, tossing her hair dramatically. "And then the company went bankrupt. I'm such a bad actress, I drove a whole company out of business! Actually, the CEO was arrested for bestiality."

"So, you moved back here."

"Yeah, I'm renting a mobile home down where Savannah used to live. I heard she'd passed; I didn't know what to think- I couldn't afford to come back for her funeral. Missy says her husband killed her." Missy never did end up moving to New York City, but she had briefly left Adabelle to attend college, then came back to take care of her aging father and eventually became an elementary school teacher.

"Everyone knows he killed her, but he's one of five cops in Adabelle. The other four weren't willing to investigate their friend."

"God," Peggy Lee muttered, twisting a strand of hair around her fist. "She was so smart, too."

"It's nice to see you again."

"Oh, thanks. How's your brother?"

"Jonathan's doing alright."

"He live with you?"

"Yes."

"They got those programs for disabled people over in Statesboro. Maybe if y'all moved-"

"He's not disabled, he's mentally ill. I like having him around anyway."

"That's good, then. You wanna go out for dinner sometime this week, catch up a little?"

"I'm busy, but thank you for the offer."

"Next week, then?"

"I'll still be busy." Peggy Lee's face fell, and I tried to smile at her. "Sorry. I don't like to leave Jonathan alone for too long."

"He can come, too."

"He can't handle restaurants."

"Y'all could come over to my place?"

"Are you lonely, Peggy Lee?"

"I just miss y'all," she said, grinning. "Been talkin' to Missy, but we don't got nothin' in common no more. She says I act like a damn Cajun."

"Has she ever actually met a Cajun?"

"Well, my wife's Cajun, but I think that's the first time she ever-"

"Your *wife?*"

"Oh, yeah," Peggy Lee giggled. "I gotta introduce y'all sometime. She's my *roommate* if anybody asks, okay?"

"Of course."

"You got yourself a roommate yet, Chastity? We all knew how you was back in high school."

"Not exactly."

"I guess it's hard to meet women here, huh? I met Bastien at Cafe Lafitte in Exile- you been to New Orleans?"

"No."

"Well, Cafe Lafitte's the oldest gay bar in the country, down on Bourbon Street. They're all obsessed with Jean Lafitte down there, got at least four bars named after him, and one of 'em's his old blacksmith shop. He was a pirate or somethin', I think. You gotta go to Bourbon Street if you ever end up in New Orleans."

"I don't drink."

"Go anyway. Are you *sure* you cain't come over for dinner? Bastien's a real good cook, and I provide the entertainment."

"Bastien's an unusual name."

"Well, her real name's Bernadette, but she goes by Bastien."

"Bernadette's pretty unusual, too."

"Like I said, she's Cajun. Y'all comin' for dinner or not?"

"We can't. Sorry."

"It's alright," Peggy Lee sighed.

"My groundskeeper, Dinah, has a 'roommate'. See if the four of y'all can't get together sometime."

"Guess who I saw today?"

"Who?"

"Peggy Lee Watson, from high school."

"I don't remember her."

"She was friends with Lily Faith. She married a woman."

"That doesn't make any sense," Jonathan said, frowning as he peeled potatoes. "Women don't want to get married."

"How do you know what women want?"

"The only reason anyone gets married is-"

"Yeah, yeah, I know. All men are rapists and sex is evil and marriage is slavery, I'm familiar."

"I just don't understand what two women would want from each other."

"They're in love."

"In love," Jonathan scoffed. "You can't love anyone you're not related to."

"Romantic love and platonic love are different things."

"Yeah, and one of them's fictional."

"Maybe they just wanted to get married so men would leave them alone, how about that?"

"Oh! That makes sense."

"Forge Memorial Funeral Home, how can I help you?" I asked smoothly, picking up the phone a week after Peggy Lee had dropped by unannounced.

"Forge Memorial?" I thought I recognized the voice on the other end but wasn't sure where from.

"Yes, ma'am."

"This is Chastity Caldwell, isn't it?"

"Um, yes, ma'am. To whom am I currently speaking?"

"Apple Forge."

"Apple," I said, feeling my heart beat faster. "How… good to hear from you. I thought you'd moved away."

"I did. I still live in Gatlinburg, I'm just visiting Adabelle for a week. I'd love to see you sometime."

"Oh, of course. Of- of course, yes. I have a funeral tomorrow, but I'm free the day after, or tonight. She's ready. For her funeral, I mean, the body, the body is ready, so I don't need to do anything else with… the body is embalmed. I'm free tonight, is what I'm saying. So sorry."

"That's alright," Apple laughed. "I'm free tonight, too. Is that cute little diner still open, the one on Main? What was it called?"

"Susie's Kitchen. Yeah, it's still open."

"Perfect! I'll see you there at seven, then?"

"Yes. Fine. Good. Uh, yes. Yes, can I bring Jonathan?"

"Jonathan? Sure. How's he doin'?"

"Still weird. I'm his legal guardian, now, so he lives with me."

"I hope he's recovered from what happened to him."

"Not really. What about you? Have you…?"

"Oh, you'll see at dinner," Apple said, laughing bitterly. "I'm not married, I'll tell you that much. And I don't date. Mama gets upset when she sees me- I guess I should tell you now, since Jonathan's probably too fragile to hear it, huh?"

"No. No, he's fine. He should know."

"I don't want to," Jonathan whimpered, curled up in the car.

"Too damn bad. Get your ass out here or I'm telling her what you did."

I led my brother into Susie's Kitchen with a hand between his shoulder blades, briefly froze when I saw Apple. I hadn't seen her in decades, but I couldn't have mistaken her for anyone else- her skin was mottled in some places, shiny and red in others, twisted, melted, hideous. She waved us over, and for a second, I wondered how she knew it was us before remembering Jonathan was sucking his thumb and trying to hide his face in my shoulder.

"Apple, how good to see you," I said, practically shoving Jonathan into the vinyl booth. "How long has it been?"

"Twenty years, give or take. Can I get a coffee?" she asked the waitress, ignoring her blatant staring.

"Just water for us," I added.

"Comin' right up," the waitress mumbled, already scurrying away.

"Wow, twenty years," I murmured. Jonathan was clinging to my side, breathing heavily and trembling, but I ignored him for the time being.

"You look healthy, Chastity. I hope life's treated you well?"

"Yes. I guess it has."

"Good. That's very good. I've been… alright, I guess. I mean, I've been *great,* in a way- the worst thing that'll ever happen to me already did. Maybe it's better to get it out of the way early, huh?"

"Should I tell you I'm sorry?"

"Huh?"

"All I ever do is tell people 'I'm sorry for your loss, my condolences,' that sort of thing. And it's true, I *am* sorry, but sometimes I wonder if it's just offensive, you know? Because I can't possibly understand how they must feel. I certainly don't understand what it was like for you, and I'm sure you've heard a million 'I'm sorry's, so I don't want you to think I'm just another insincere asshole who's secretly glad it didn't happen to them."

"I guess you shouldn't, then," Apple said after a brief pause, smiling. "You were such a quiet kid. I don't think I've ever heard you talk that much."

"I'm still pretty quiet."

"Well, Priscilla was also just really loud." Apple didn't notice the way my breath hitched, the way I dug my nails into Jonathan's thigh. "It's funny, I think about her so much it doesn't even hurt anymore, but sometimes I'll see some little thing that reminds me and just start crying out of the blue. I walked past a toy store the other day, and they had this big display in the window, this huge plush unicorn. And I just remembered y'all's birthday- d'you remember? She wished for all these things, ended it with wanting a unicorn. I just started crying in the middle of the mall, stood there looking at this stupid unicorn and crying like a baby."

"I changed the name of the funeral home," I said softly. "I really only became a mortician because Priscilla didn't get the chance to. Maybe she would've changed her mind if she'd grown up, but I don't know, so…"

"I figured it was named after her. That's nice, Chastity. That really is very sweet."

"You said something about your mother, on the phone?"

"Oh, yeah." Apple thanked the waitress as she set our drinks down, picked up a spoon to stir her coffee. "I don't know if you heard, but my father ended his life eleven years ago. My parents got a divorce not long after the fire, and he went back to Louisiana- he grew up there. Quit the priesthood. We stayed in touch, he wanted to see me, but he was so… sad. That sounds stupid, it's such an understatement, but it's true. He was *so* unhappy, and he never said it, but I knew I made it worse, seeing me, my scars. I stopped visiting as much, and then he- you know- he killed himself. And Mama sort of went crazy when she heard the news."

"My God, Apple, that's…"

"She's been in a nursing home for a few years now. I think she's pretty happy there." Apple tapped her spoon against her cup. "She thinks Priscilla's still alive, so I don't visit her that often. She remembers the fire every time she sees my scars." Noticing the expression on my face, Apple laughed weakly. "Sorry, Chastity! I swear, I'm not as depressed as I sound. You have to move on, y'know? Priscilla and Daddy are in Heaven, I know that for a fact. Life goes on."

"I'm… glad you're able to see it that way."

"I have to. So, enough about me, how have y'all been?"

"Good. I love my job. What brings you back to Adabelle?"

"I'm kind of an amateur journalist," Apple said, shrugging. "I keep an eye on the news here- I always thought it was ridiculous, the way they didn't investigate y'all's mother after Jonathan was hospitalized. I've noticed a few other things, reading between the lines in local papers- they're all online now, it's great- and I'm here 'cause I saw a little girl vanished without a trace two years ago and they never even put together a search party."

"Are you?" I kept my voice perfectly even, but Jonathan tensed in my arms.

"Yeah. I write for a true crime blog sometimes, it's got a pretty wide reach, so I thought if I came down here and actually looked around a little, I might be able to draw more attention to the case, maybe help find the poor kid."

"That's really admirable," I managed. "You said you're an *amateur* journalist? What do you do for a living, then?"

"I'm an Episcopal priest, believe it or not."

"Really!"

"What's an Episcopal?" the waitress chimed in, blushing when we both turned to look at her. "Sorry. Just never heard that before."

"No problem," Apple laughed. "We're basically Catholics with a hippie mindset, if that makes sense."

"I can't believe you're a priest," I said once the waitress was gone.

"I know, right? Last thing anyone expected from me," she laughed. "I feel sort of like a cult leader, just 'cause my name's so ridiculous, people call me 'Mother Apple'. I don't know *what* Mama was thinking with that one."

"Well, I hope it makes you happy."

"It certainly does."

"What are the odds, huh?" I asked as we drove home. "Can you *please* take your thumb out of your mouth? I'll buy you a fucking pacifier if you don't knock that shit off."

"We're going to prison," Jonathan said.

"We are not going to prison. She said herself she's just an amateur journalist, and anyway, the cops already searched our house. Eden doesn't even glare at me when she sees me anymore."

"We're going to *prison.*"

Jonathan laid on the living room rug as soon as we got home, petting Citrus listlessly for almost an hour. I went to the guest room, sat across from Priscilla and just stared at her, occasionally reaching out to pat her knee. "I loved you," I told her quietly, honestly. "I could've loved Lily Faith, I think, if you hadn't died. I don't know. My daddy was born rotten, everyone swears it, so maybe I would always have turned out like this, but I don't know. I did love you."

When I came back to the living room, Jonathan was still on the rug. "Don't fall asleep there," I warned him.

"Citrus is dead," he said quietly.

"What?"

"Citrus is dead. Savannah is dead."

"Citrus isn't dead, sweetie, she's your pet. You take such good care of-"

"She's dead. This is a dead cat, and those people in the guest room are dead, too."

"Aren't you tired, Jonathan? Why don't we get ready to go to sleep?"

"They're all *dead.*"

"Priscilla's dead," I snapped, fed up with his glassy-eyed insanity. "You murdered a child, you disfigured her sister, her father killed himself because of you, and her mother lost her mind. You completely destroyed that family, so don't talk to me about dead things, Jonathan. Shut up and go get ready for bed."

"I know what I did," Jonathan whispered, getting slowly to his feet, "and I know what you're doing, too."

"*Go to bed.*"

We woke up tangled together as usual, but when I told my brother good morning, he just stared blankly at me. "What's wrong with you?"

"I want to live with Granny," Jonathan said dully.

"You're not allowed to suddenly act all morally superior when you-"

"I know I killed Priscilla, I know, I know, I *know,* but how am I supposed to make up for it if I'm pretending there's not a-"

"Who's gonna believe you, huh? I'll burn the bodies, and then what? You go crying to Granny that I'm so mean to you, tell her I've got some kind of fucking human taxidermy in my house, you have no proof, and everyone already thinks you're crazy- she'll just have you institutionalized. And I'm your *sister,* Jonathan, we're family! Are you seriously going to betray your own sister like that?"

"I'm scared of you," Jonathan sobbed, and I got out of bed, pulled his nightgown up around his hips.

"Scared of me? I'm your guardian, *sweetheart*, I'm your caretaker. Look at yourself, you fucking freak, you're almost forty years old and you're lying here in a wet diaper, crying that you're *scared*. No one else is gonna put up with this, can't you get that through your head? Stop *crying!*"

"Leave me alone," he whimpered, tugging his nightgown back down, pulling the blankets over himself. I sighed and sat on the edge of the bed, stroked his hair back to kiss his cheek.

"Jonathan, please. You're being ridiculous. I love you more than anyone else in the world, you know that. Don't you know that? Haven't I always taken care of you, made sure you're safe?"

"I think you need help. Maybe if you told a therapist why you did it-"

"Do you love me, Jonathan?"

"Of course I-"

"Then forget about Deedee. Citrus is your pet, Savannah is sleeping, and you never met Deedee, okay? It's been two years since that whole thing happened, why do you care now?"

"I ruined Apple's life. I never- I never saw- I didn't want to-"

"And you'll ruin *my* life if you don't let this go. Is that what you want?"

"I don't want to be a bad person."

"Well, it would be bad to betray your only sister. Wouldn't that be very, very bad? After everything I've done for you?" Jonathan nodded hesitantly. "That's right. Be my sweet boy and forget about this."

TWENTY-NINE

Jonathan apparently took my advice to heart and had happily resumed playing with Citrus by afternoon. I left them in the living room when I went down to my office, didn't spare a thought for anything outside of work until Apple showed up with a bottle of hard cider that evening. "I think it's funny," she said, holding the bottle out sheepishly. "Because I'm named…"

"I got the joke."

"It's my go-to gift. Can I come in?"

"Sure. Nobody ever calls ahead anyway."

"Sorry, I don't know your cell number, and I figured it was too late to call your work phone, so I decided to just pop by."

"I don't have a cell phone."

"Ah. Well, that's probably smart, you really don't need one. Drives you crazy. Oh, this place is so beautiful! Is that stained glass?"

"Yes. It's a secular funeral home, but we try to have a sort of church vibe, if that makes sense." I led her upstairs, where Jonathan was lying flat on the rug with Citrus and gestured vaguely around the living room. "The previous owner liked pink."

"Priscilla would have loved it," Apple said, smiling sadly. "Why is your brother on the floor?"

"Sometimes he's a trip hazard. Here, let me get some glasses. Should I put ice in this?"

"You can if you want, but I don't want any in mine. Jonathan, how are you?" When I returned with cider for myself and Apple, she took her glass with a smile, still trying to get Jonathan off the floor. "Does he want any-?"

"He doesn't drink."

"I want to," Jonathan said suddenly. I was shocked that he'd actually spoken in front of a stranger, but I just smiled, set my glass down on the table and crouched to pat his chest.

"You can't drink, sweetie, you're not… it's not good for you."

"Whatever you say." There was a hard, unfamiliar glint in Jonathan's sky-blue eyes, and I considered sending him to our room but decided not to make a scene in front of Apple.

"So, Mother Apple," I said, taking a seat next to her, "what's it like to be a priest? I didn't know women could get ordained."

"Depends on which denomination you are. Catholics don't ordain women, but with Protestant sects, it varies. The Episcopal church is pretty progressive."

"I'm glad you've found something you're passionate about."

"Me, too." Apple sipped her cider, grinning a little as she did. "Sorry, it's a dumb joke. I just think the apple cider thing is really funny."

"Hilarious."

"So, I have to admit, I had a couple reasons for coming over tonight. Remember how I told you about that girl who went missing a couple years back?"

"Yes."

"I kind of wanted to see if you knew anything about it. I spoke to her mother- her name's Eden- and she said Deedee might have been in your cemetery before she disappeared."

"Eden spoke to us two years ago," I said, polite but firm, trying not to sound as annoyed as I felt. "Neither of us saw anything."

"I understand."

"What got you into this blog thing?"

"I've just noticed that a lot of mainstream newspapers are really biased when it comes to things like murders, kidnappings, all that. Lots of them have some kind of agenda, and even if that agenda is just 'this case makes for a better story,' it really hurts victims. To be completely honest, I got a little obsessed with Deedee- I followed the case as it was happening, but there was only one report in the newspaper, ever. Eden kept talking about it on Facebook, though. She looked a lot like Priscilla, I think that's why I… shit, that sounds creepy, doesn't it? I'm sorry."

"Not creepy at all," I reassured her. Apple tossed the rest of her cider back.

"Anyway, yeah, that's why I'm here. I kept hoping they'd find her, that's why I waited so long. My friend owns this blog, so I asked if I could run on down and check things out, but it probably won't make much difference. I just feel so bad for Eden."

"That's terrible," Jonathan said suddenly. "I murdered your sister."

Everything froze. I gripped my glass so tight I hurt my hand, and Apple slowly looked up at him, her forehead creasing. She was missing an eyebrow, I noticed, fixating oddly on that tiny detail of her ruined face to distract myself from the painful pounding of my heart.

"What did you say?" Apple whispered. She tilted her head, tried to smile like he was joking, glanced at me for help before locking eyes with Jonathan again.

"I murdered your sister. I set your house on fire, on Halloween. I did it because I was jealous." While Jonathan's voice trembled with anxiety, his face was oddly emotionless. "You never locked your doors, no one did, so I just walked in. Neither of you woke up, but I started the fire in your bedroom. I watched you sleeping for a minute, I remember that. I threw gasoline on the carpet, set it on fire, and ran away. I didn't… I didn't think it would spread so fast. I wanted her dead, but I didn't want to kill her."

"He's crazy," I said weakly.

"I'm not. I burned your house down, Apple, I killed your sister- and Deedee is dead in our guest room." I wanted to punch my brother in the face, but that would only have confirmed my guilt, so I sat still, listened to him talk faster and faster. "I just wanted to talk to her, show her my dollhouse, she said her mama hit her, had a boyfriend- I was never a whore, or I never meant to be, it was Mama's boyfriends- I brought her in here, and Chastity thought she looked like Priscilla, wanted to keep her, Chastity strangled her. Chastity strangled her, and I didn't stop her, and she's in our guest room with Savannah, stuffed like an animal. Taxidermy. *Just taxidermy,* she said, go look, go *look*, you'll see."

Silence descended on the room, broken only by Jonathan's pained hyperventilation, and when I turned to Apple her fists were clenched in her lap. "Jonathan's crazy," I repeated.

"Then show me your guest room," she said hoarsely.

"I- I can't. I can't do that, I'm sorry." My mind was racing- was it possible to convince her my brother was insane, get her back to her hotel room long enough to move the bodies back to Grampa's hunting cabin? No, she had a cell phone, she'd call the police in the car, but would they listen? Surely, they had to at least check on something so extreme, didn't they? "Jonathan's just confused; he doesn't know what he's-"

"Listen to me," Jonathan choked out, staring at Apple. "I'm telling you the truth. I'm *sorry*."

"I have to go," Apple whispered, her face twisting into something inhuman, hatred etched into every line, every scar. "Whatever happened, God will forgive you both, but I can't. Let me leave, and we'll get this all sorted out later."

"No!" I cried, jumping to my feet as she stood up. "No, he's lying, he's a fucking lunatic, listen, Apple, I'm a good person, I didn't kill her, I-!"

"Get out of my way!"

Apple was taller than me, but she was skinny, it must have been hard to put on weight with such extensive scarring. I grabbed her by the shoulders and shoved her down, practically collapsed on top of her, hit her head against the hard edge of the coffee table while she screamed, tried to push me off, but I was stronger, I was angrier, I *wasn't going to fucking jail*. Jonathan didn't move, just rocked himself and sobbed so hard he barely sounded human, and I didn't stand up until Apple was unconscious.

"Stay here," I told him, voice cold and dead. I took my shirt off, wrapped it around Apple's bleeding head, and dragged her downstairs by the shoulders. She was still breathing when I threw her in the coffin, started to twitch just as I slammed the lid closed, and I thought I heard her scream before I closed the cremation chamber door.

"She's dead," I told Jonathan dully. He was shivering on the floor, staring at the spot where Apple had been sitting. "Good job. You've killed every member of that family except Beatrice, do you want to go find her in Gatlinburg and finish the job?"

"I didn't kill Apple."

"If you hadn't told her what I did, she would've walked out that door alive. It's your fault, you stupid whore. Priscilla was your fault, Mama was your fault, Father William was your fault, Deedee was your fault, Apple was your fault- it's always your fucking fault, Jonathan. You are a selfish, whiny, pathetic, *worthless* piece of shit, and all you've ever done is fuck over everyone around you. I'd trade your life for Priscilla's in a heartbeat. If you'd never been born, everything would be *perfect*. God, I wish you were never fucking born."

I didn't really mean everything I said. I loved my brother, I did, but he'd almost gotten us both arrested. It was my job to think things through, my job to punish him when he didn't. Like training a dog, he'd never learn if I didn't teach him. "Why'd you tell her that, anyway?"

"Confession," Jonathan mumbled. "She's a priest."

"That's not why. Why'd you *really* do it?"

"I just… felt bad."

"What, exactly, did you think you'd accomplish there?"

"I don't know. I felt bad. I don't know."

"No, of course you didn't fucking know. You don't know anything. You thought she'd just be okay with that? You thought she'd fly into a rage and kill you, and you'd somehow be absolved? Newsflash, Jonathan, *nothing* can absolve you. You murdered a child, you drove her parents crazy, and right when her sister figured her own life out- you killed her, too. She's burning alive, or she was. Dead by now. Isn't that a horrible way to die, Jonathan? That's how Priscilla died. Apple burned to death the same way her baby sister did, and it's *all- your- fault.*

"What? Don't you have anything to say? Are you just gonna sit there and feel sorry for yourself? She's still in the oven, I'll take you down right now to apologize. I'll give you her ashes when it's done, I'll let you put her bone fragments through the cremulator. Would you like that?"

"No," Jonathan whispered.

"No? You don't want to help me pour her ashes over Priscilla's grave?" Priscilla was buried in our cemetery; I'd never been to her grave, couldn't handle seeing her name carved in granite, a little lamb or angel and a verse about going home to God, as if she'd died gently in her sleep, as if she hadn't died in agony in the ICU, scared out of her mind, praying for anything, anything to make it stop hurting.

Jonathan didn't answer, so I grabbed his bicep and pulled him to his feet. "Get ready for bed. I have to wait until the oven's done, then I'll come join you."

Jonathan was asleep when I returned, curled up in the fetal position with his thumb in his mouth, and I sighed, stopped to kiss his soft, pale cheek before slowly undressing and crawling into bed. I didn't bother with pajamas, just laid down in my underwear. Apple's car was still in my parking lot, and I figured I'd just leave it there for a few days before reporting it. There was a hiking trail not too far down the road, people had used my parking lot for that before- it wasn't unrealistic that she could have just gotten lost in the woods.

I really had liked Apple when I was younger. She was a mean, temperamental teenager, but she'd had her moments of unexpected civility, Priscilla had loved her. I might have had a little crush on her- I remembered thinking she was pretty. *I'm not married, I'll tell you that much.* Had she ever tried to date, or had she just assumed her scars would drive any potential suitors away? How common, I wondered, were female priests in the Episcopal church? Would it be surprising to see any woman, let alone one with such a severe deformity, behind the pulpit?

I dreamt that I was walking through a dead and dying orchard, barren trees casting twisted shadows along the overgrown, barely visible path, the grey sky above me choked with vultures and crows, and one dove flitting between them all, never still long enough for me to be sure I'd seen it. I remembered Priscilla giggling that doves were really just glorified pigeons, once, and stopped trying to catch sight of the little white bird, kept walking the winding path, the trees growing closer and closer together until they blocked out all light, until I couldn't see the birds at all.

I walked until I came upon a sort of clearing, a circle of trees whose branches intertwined and formed a roof above me, and saw Lily Faith standing dead center, holding a shiny red apple in her palm. She wore her stolen jean jacket over a bright orange prison jumpsuit and smiled when she saw me, the cold, wolfish leer I'd only seen a few times.

"Chastity," she called, and her voice was Priscilla's voice layered over Jonathan's layered over Apple's, her own voice layered over Grampa's layered over Granny's, echoing in the dim clearing. Thin, weak light pierced the roof of branches, just enough to illuminate her, light up her blonde hair like a halo. "*Remember me as you pass by.*"

"What?"

"*As you are now, so once was I.*"

"Lily Faith, what-?"

"*As I am now, so you must be.*" Lily Faith stepped closer, holding the apple out, everyone's voices ringing out of her mouth so loud I wanted to cover my ears, everyone I'd ever loved or thought I loved or tried to love screaming deafeningly, "*PREPARE THYSELF TO FOLLOW ME.*"

I woke in a cold sweat, gasping for breath, and instinctively reached out to my brother, but he was gone. I sat up slowly, the dream already fading from my mind, got out of bed to find Jonathan. I doubted he was in the bathroom, but I checked anyway, and unsurprisingly found it empty. He'd never wandered off in the middle of the night before, so I had no idea what he'd be doing, called his name softly as I walked down the hallway. He wasn't in the kitchen or the living room, either. "Jonathan!" I yelled, starting to panic- had he gone outside? Surely, he'd be creeped out by the cemetery at night. The guest room door was still locked, and I had the only key, so I ran downstairs, checked my office, the viewing room, every inch of the funeral parlor before I finally noticed the basement door was open.

I'd locked it when I came back up, yes, but he knew I left the key on a bowl right inside our living room, he'd seen me toss it there a thousand times. Jonathan was terrified of the morgue, especially after I locked him in it overnight, I never thought I'd have to worry about him going down there on his own.

"Jonathan," I called, walking slowly down the stairs. The morgue door was open, too, and the lights were on. "Jonathan, sweetie, what are you doing? Don't you know what time it is? It's late, honey, let's go back to bed. Jonathan? Are you in here?" I stepped inside, shivered at the chill- I usually wore a sweater when I worked in the morgue- and looked around, still calling my brother's name. It took me a minute to process what I saw, but once I did, I screamed loud enough to wake the dead.

Jonathan was crumpled on the floor, a bottle of formaldehyde shattered next to him, vomit staining his nightgown and caught in his hair, his blue eyes wide open, empty as a doll's eyes. He looked like a porcelain doll, my brother, still pretty and delicate and feminine after all these years, my beautiful brother dead on the morgue floor.

"*Jonathan!*" I shook his shoulder violently, gagging on the smell, vomit and feces and formaldehyde, and drifting from the crematorium, the faint, lingering odor of burnt flesh, overpoweringly human and chemical, everything too *much.* "Jonathan, baby, no, *no,* come on, sweetheart, wake up, wake up, no, you can't..."

I pressed on his stomach, forced my fingers down his throat, briefly attempted CPR, but I already knew it was pointless. When Mr. Kaplan hired me, I'd joked that the embalming fluid was so colorful, the glass bottles so weirdly romantic, that I was tempted to drink the stuff, and he'd laughed, told me drinking even an ounce would lead to a swift, painful death- convulsions, first, then corrosive gastrointestinal injury and finally respiratory failure.

Rigor mortis hadn't set in, so he couldn't have been dead long, but I didn't call an ambulance. I checked my brother's pulse again, as if something would have changed, then picked him up and laid him on a gurney. If I didn't look into his eyes, I could pretend he was any other body- wipe the vomit off his face, undress him, wash him in a disinfectant solution, massage his limbs, wash his hair, everything except embalming. I closed his eyes and put him in the fridge, tried not to think about how he screamed the last time I forced him in there, stopped to rest my head against the cold metal.

"I'm right here, Jonathan. I know it's dark, but I'm right here, okay? I'll let you out in a little bit. I just need to build a frame."

THIRTY

I didn't sleep, didn't eat, didn't take calls until the frame was built. I wanted him lying down, resting next to Savannah, peaceful and content. I took a Valium and forced myself to nap on the couch before skinning him- I couldn't risk making a mistake. When I opened the drawer, part of me expected Jonathan to sit up and ask why I looked so sad, why I'd made him sleep in the morgue again, but he just laid there, stiff, and bloodless, cold to the touch.

Skinning him was easy once I'd made the initial cut down his back. Neither the empty skin nor the red mass of muscle and organs left behind looked like my brother, wouldn't look like my brother until I stuffed it and put it over the frame, so I had no problem tanning the flesh, incinerating the waste. I had to pause and take a breath every few minutes as I sewed him back together, stop and rest constantly when I half-carried, half-dragged him up to the guest room, but finally, finally I laid my brother next to Savannah, pulled the covers up to his neck.

And there he was, skin white as snow, lips red as blood, hair black as ebony, in a bed rather than a glass coffin but on display nonetheless, Snow White with his heart torn out, Snow White in his glass coffin. When we were children, when Mama was the witch, I fancied myself a knight in shining armor, waiting to rescue Snow White- ready, yes, but waiting until I was bigger, older, and stronger, until I could kill her boyfriends and run away to a lighthouse by the sea, keep Jonathan safe forever. I hadn't wanted him safe like this, gone somewhere far beyond my reach, a pretty doll for me to pet and fawn over and talk to like a crazy person, like he'd talked to Citrus.

"I didn't mean- I didn't want to hurt you," I mumbled, stroking his leathery cheek. He always had such soft skin, I couldn't replicate it, couldn't really make him look convincing. "I'm sorry I was mean, Jonathan. I shouldn't have said… it wasn't your fault. I'm sorry, Jonathan. I'm really sorry." I heard my own voice as I said it, *no one gives a damn that you're sorry! Sorry won't bring him back!*

So, I sat in my guest room, alone with the only people I could love, Savannah and Priscilla, watching me watch Jonathan, praying for him to move, to speak to me, to be with me. Before I grew up, before he drove me crazy with his neediness, I loved him completely, and still I loved him, pieces of him. The piece of Jonathan that devoured 600-page books in a day, the piece of him that held his arms out to be hugged, the piece of him that danced through the headstones to imaginary music- *Jonathan dances with the dead,* I told Priscilla once, *I look out the window and watch him dancing with the dead and the damned.*

I watched the sun rise through the guest room window, wondered how long I'd spent preparing my brother's body to be skinned and stuffed and mounted, and got to my feet with painful delicacy, stood over Snow White. He could have been sleeping, if you didn't look too closely, if you saw him in low light. I leaned over Jonathan's body and pressed my lips gently to his, wishing I really was a prince or a knight or whatever I had to be to bring him back. I straightened up slowly, watched him for any sign of life, as if I hadn't cut him apart myself, as if I hadn't driven him to it, and finally I left him lying there, went to the living room and set Citrus on my lap.

When I was a little girl, my greatest desire was to burn the world down around us, run far away from our rotting gingerbread house and bring Jonathan somewhere safe, somewhere beyond the monsters' reach. I never meant to become the witch in the woods.

"Why don't Mama's boyfriends want me?" I'd asked him when I was a little girl, barely six years old, watching him shave his legs in the shower.

"Because I asked her to let me do it as long as I could," Jonathan answered, flinching as he nicked his ankle.

"Why? I know you hate it."

"I love you more, though, and it's my job to protect you."

"Why?"

"Because I'm your big brother. Stop laughing!"

"You're so little, though," I teased.

"I'm bigger than you!"

"Bet I'll be taller when I grow up."

"Maybe. I'll still be older, though, so I'll always protect you."

"When we grow up, *I'm* gonna protect *you.*"

"Well, we'll see. We'll just see about that."

Iphigenia Strangeworth

About the Author

Iphigenia Strangeworth was born and raised in Houston, Texas, where she began writing horror stories as soon as she found out what death was. She now splits her time between Texas and Virginia and, when she's not writing, can be found reading, sewing, baking, embroidering, and being a little weird about her doll collection. She enjoys hyper-violent horror and sparkly pink unicorns in equal measure. Like most authors, she is semi-nocturnal and might scurry away if you encounter her in the dead of night; ask her about Monster High and give her a cookie to gain her trust. Should you find yourself without a cookie, she'll take a fun fact about spotted hyenas in a pinch.

You can find her online at:
iphigeniastrangeworth@tumblr.com, where she reblogs a great deal of *My Hero Academia* fanart, or, occasionally, in small-town antique stores, cooing over the most haunted porcelain dolls she can find.

Iphigenia Strangeworth

OTHER HELLBOUND BOOKS

The RED Trilogy

Evil takes on many forms -– something Rachael Daniels, an innocent care worker, is about to find out... personally.

Something is roaming the streets of the city where she lives, something monstrous with a taste for sweet, red, human blood.

Something that can be anything it wants to be.

Soon, Rachael learns the hard way that not even the friendliest faces can be trusted.

As she makes her way across that city one night on an errand of mercy, she quickly discovers the terrifying creature will definitely have no such consideration for her…

Together in one book for the very first time ever, *The RED Trilogy* is a modern, urban reworking of a classic fairy tale, which puts the horror spin on an old favorite.

Blood RED picks up straight away after the events of *RED*, the first installment, while *Deep RED* throws you into a nightmarish future scenario. If you dare to open these pages, you'll face a terrifying journey into the unknown – courtesy of award winning and #1 bestselling author, Paul Kane (the sellout *Hooded Man, Monsters, Sherlock Holmes and the Servants of Hell*).

The Horror Zine's Book of Monsters

With an introduction by Shirley Jackson Award-winner Gemma Files, this oustanding anthology of all things monstrous includes spine-chilling stories from Bentley Little, Simon Clark, Elizabeth Massie, Tim Waggoner, Sumiko Saulson, plus some of the best emerging horror writers working today.

"This anthology gives us a chilling glimpse at the dark and dangerous things prowling in the minds of some of today's best horror writers." – JG Faherty, author of *Ragman* and *Songs in the Key of Death*

"Throughout the pages are creepy tales by up-and-comers who you may have read, plus writers brand new to a horror reader's discerning eye. Embark on a journey to the realm where monsters—familiar or unique—dwell. Highly recommended to horror aficionados obsessed with eldritch fiction—this one's for you!" – Nancy Kilpatrick, author of *Thrones of Blood Series* and *the Darker Passions series*

The Toilet Zone: Number Two
"Restroom reading at its most terrifying!"

Imagine, if you will, you're traveling through the unknown, hellbound, with no roadmap or stars to guide you. The light fades as you descend into a shadow realm where supernatural terrors make their lair and evil lurks at every turn. Here, dead things don't always stay dead, for this is a world where things that shouldn't be… *are*, and things that should be are not.

In this world, it takes between 2,500 and 4,000 reading words to pay a visit to the smallest, but terrifyingly necessary, room, and stories are written precisely to chill the bones as you wait for nature to make its call.

You open up the book, and one of the 32 tales skulking within its hellish pages chooses you…

It's too late to turn back now. You are about to set foot into another dimension, so best watch out for that signpost up ahead...You've just crossed over into... The Toilet Zone

TENEBRION

"The Devil's in the detail."
Amateur filmmakers inadvertently invoke a demon when they break into an abandoned school to perform and film an authentic Black Mass for their entry into a short movie competition. Dave Priestley and his crew film in Watsonville elementary school – the site of a horrific tragedy nine years before. Tenebrion – the malevolent demon of darkness – makes preparations of its own within the dark recesses of Hell. The demon requires a specific set of circumstances and sacrifices to rend a fissure between the worlds and set free its brethren; it has manipulated humans for centuries to put things into place, and the moviemakers are the unfortunate, final pieces of its nefarious puzzle.

Priestley, ever the stickler for authenticity and detail, accidentally sets free the denizen of Hell. And while Priestley and his skeptical friends attempt to return Tenebrion to the pit of Hades, it hunts them all down – one by one – for inclusion in its hellish gateway.

The Horror Writer
"The most definitive guide into the trials and tribulations of being a horror writer since Stephen King's 'On Writing.'"

We have assembled some of the very best in the business from whom you can learn so much about the craft of horror writing: Bram Stoker Award© winners, bestselling authors, a President of the Horror Writers' Association, and myriad contemporary horror authors of distinction.

The Horror Writer covers how to connect with your market and carve out a sustainable niche in the independent horror genre, how to tackle the writer's ever-lurking nemesis of productivity, writing good horror stories with powerful, effective scenes, realistic, flowing dialogue and relatable characters without resorting to clichéd jump scares and well-worn gimmicks. Also covered is the delicate subject of handling rejection with good grace, and how to use those inevitable "not quite the right fit for us at this time" letters as an opportunity to hone your craft.

Plus... perceptive interviews to provide an intimate peek into the psyche of the horror author and the challenges they work through to bring their nefarious ideas to the page.

And, as if that – and so much more – was not enough, we have for your delectation Ramsey Campbell's beautifully insightful analysis of the tales of HP Lovecraft.

Featuring:

Ramsey Campbell, John Palisano, Chad Lutzke, Lisa Morton, Kenneth W. Cain, Kevin J. Kennedy, Monique Snyman, Scott Nicholson, Lucy A. Snyder, Richard Thomas, Gene O'Neill, Jess Landry, Luke Walker, Stephanie M. Wytovich, Marie O'Regan, Armand Rosamilia, Kevin Lucia, Ben Eads, Kelli Owen, Jasper Bark, and Bret McCormick.

And interviews with: Steve Rasnic Tem, Stephen Graham Jones, David Owain Hughes, Tim Waggoner, and Mort Castle.

**A HellBound Books LLC
Publication**

www.hellboundbooks.com